MATEHUB:
Legend

MARIE REYNARD

MATEHUB: LEGEND

AN ELEMENTAL BONDS NOVEL

MATEHUB
BOOK ONE

MARIE REYNARD

PLACE GARDEN
PUBLISHING

Standard Cover by Moor Books Design

Alternative Cover by Deranged Doctor Design

Illustrations by GetCovers

Additional stock imagery from DepositPhotos

Beta read by Amy Pittel (Amy Pittel Author Services) and Megan Dischinger (Blue Beta Reading)

Edited by Kate Wood (Kate Wood Proofreading)

Standard Cover ISBN: 978-1-958002-07-0

Alternative Cover ISBN: 978-1-958002-08-7

First Edition

Published by Peace Garden Publishing, LLC

 Formatted with Vellum

CONTENT WARNINGS

This book contains scenes of role-played nonconsensual sex and one instance of a character having a panic attack.

MATEHUB: LEGEND

The contract was simple: three months, seven scenes, zero feelings. Following it was not.

Richard Knotz is a legend in the world of supernatural adult entertainment, and he knows it. While most paranormal adult actors shy away from the temporary bonds needed to perform knotting scenes, he's made them his brand. Bonding a human could never threaten to tear his empire to the ground, no matter how tempting that human smells.

Hunter Savage thinks Richard Knotz is a smug son of a wolf, but when he's offered a contract to work with him, the payout is too lucrative to say no. Three months bonded to Richard could make his entire career. He just doesn't expect to find a soft side under Richard's prickly exterior, or for the apartment they're forced to share to start feeling like home.

The bonding contract is easy and painless as long as they remember one cardinal rule: don't get attached. Their employer has no use for unprofessional fools who let feelings jeopardize profits. But in between filming scorching scenes with ridiculous scenarios, they discover they're more compatible than either could have imagined.

As their limited time together winds down, they face a choice—risk their careers for the unexpected connection they've found, or lose their bond forever.

MateHub: Legend is a high heat, arranged bonding, forced proximity, dislike-to-love M/M paranormal romance featuring an arrogant wolf shifter who thinks a little too highly of various parts of his anatomy, the feisty human who finally takes him down a few notches, nosy fans, meddling friends, knotting, and a contract that is destined to fail.

This stand-alone novel is set in the Elemental Bonds universe and guarantees a HEA for its main couple. It does not contain mpreg or cheating.

ONE

Richard Knotz walked through the upscale corporate apartment he'd been living in, checking he hadn't missed anything in his bedroom or bathroom. He already knew he hadn't—packing up and leaving this place was part of the ritual for him—but there was another reason he was keeping himself occupied.

As he made a circuit through the spacious kitchen, he felt Blaze's blue eyes on him. A twisting nausea roiled in the back of Richard's mind, but it had nothing to do with how he was feeling. He ignored it. Less than an hour to freedom. Sixty minutes until his head would be entirely his own again.

Blaze hadn't even started packing, as if that'd stave off the inevitable. As if another temporarily bonded couple wasn't scheduled to take their place in a few hours. They'd be in this apartment for three months, as Richard and Blaze had been, and then Richard would be back.

But not with Blaze.

Just once, he wanted to make it through the bond-severing day without needless emotional complications. Apparently, he wasn't that lucky. So he made another pass through his bathroom. His gaze trailed over the marble countertops, deep tub, and separate glass-enclosed shower.

Yep, he had his toothbrush. No toiletries left in the vanity.

The bedroom, with its king-size bed dressed in soft gray Egyptian cotton linens, was equally devoid of personal belongings, and the dirty clothes hamper in the walk-in closet stood empty.

Unable to think of anything else to check for a third time, he admitted defeat and headed to the living room. The goddamn mage better show up soon, or this was going to get uncomfortable.

More uncomfortable.

Blaze searched his face, a touch of sadness written in the lines of his full lips, and Richard suppressed a sigh.

He'd figured an incubus would be able to keep their shit together better than this. Sex was their whole thing, and he'd been so careful not to send any mixed signals. Plus, their scents weren't remotely compatible, which was why Blaze had been perfect for this arrangement—smoking hot, amazing in bed, and totally wrong for Richard.

Three months bonded to someone so they could film knotting scenes shouldn't engender feelings of true love, but somehow, it always did. The endorphins released by the mind-blowing orgasms eclipsed every shred of logic and reason his co-stars possessed.

It was the one downside to the bonding contracts he did for MateHub. He was the site's top star, his scenes drawing in a ridiculous number of views considering only the paranormal community—and a few select humans— could access the site at all. It had magical protections to keep the uninitiated out. If you knew, you knew. And the people who knew couldn't get enough of his knot.

The money was great; the sex was even better. But every time he did one of these contracts, it ended like this.

Best to get it over with.

"So, what's the first thing you plan to do with your freedom?"

"Freedom?" Blaze asked, his brow furrowing.

Richard nodded. "Now that you won't have an unnecessary presence in your head."

Blaze's frown deepened. "I hadn't thought... Actually, I wanted to talk to you about that. These last few months, they've been good, right?"

Only years of practice kept Richard from groaning. "Yeah, man, it's been great."

"I think you might have ruined me for sex with anyone else," Blaze said, trying to force a laugh.

Richard chuckled as well, but there was no humor in it. "You're going to have a hard time finding work if that's the case. But you can tell your agent to contact mine and see if we can do another scene together."

He wouldn't have offered if he hadn't been damn certain Daniel would run interference for him.

"I don't know. After the last three months, I'm not sure I can imagine having sex with you without that knot of yours."

Damn it. There was hope in his eyes. Why did they always have hope? What did he ever do to make them believe there was hope?

"Maybe our agents can line something up the next time I'm on a bonding contract."

"What do you mean?"

Richard shrugged. "You kept me way busier than most,

but I always manage to squeeze in a few scenes between the main ones. No point in letting my knot go to waste on days we aren't filming."

While he might need to be bonded to do it, once he was, his knot didn't care who was wrapped around it. It wasn't like this was a true bond; it was a business transaction and nothing more.

"Wait... Those days you had to go into the office?"

"What did you think I was doing? Paperwork? You must have felt me get off through the bond. So yeah, have your agent reach out to mine and let him know you're interested in doing a scene when I've got a bond."

"But... It was so faint. Your presence in my mind has always been impossible to read. I assumed you were by yourself. How could you... With someone else? I can't even think about touching anyone but you." Blaze's eyes were getting watery, and Richard held back another groan.

Every. Damn. Time. Wasn't there a single person in this industry who could keep things professional?

"The contract wasn't exclusive," he said, making Blaze flinch.

The apartment intercom buzzed, and Richard nearly sighed in relief. About fucking time. He got up and hit the button to let the company mage in.

Blaze was watching him with increasing desperation.

It only took a few seconds to get from the building door to the elevator, then another thirty or so to ride up to the fourth floor. One minute more, and the mage should be there.

"I heard..." Blaze said, a tremor in his voice. "I heard wolf shifters can't bond the same person twice?"

Richard refused to wince. "You heard right."

Was the elevator running slow today, or was the damn mage dragging his feet?

"What if we... I mean, maybe we shouldn't sever the bond just yet?"

Richard didn't bother responding to that. It took effort not to tap his foot in impatience.

Blaze tried again. "We could, I don't know, go for some coffee? See where this goes?"

Oh, thank god. That was the chime announcing the elevator's arrival on their floor. The sound of footsteps coming closer was the best thing he'd ever heard.

"I'm not thirsty," Richard said, opening the door before there was even a knock.

He repressed the urge to hug Tristan when he saw him in the hall. Instead, he gave him a pointed look. Tristan had severed the majority of his previous bonds; he knew what that look meant. He shot Richard a glare, then swept into the apartment.

"Alright, I'm going to set up this room. Before the ritual, I need you two apart so your energy doesn't interfere with my work. Why don't you go to your bedrooms? I'll call you when I'm ready."

It was a bullshit excuse, but Richard wasn't complaining. He retreated to his bedroom and tossed himself down on the bed, pulling out his phone and sending a quick message to his agent.

RICHARD

Never book me with this guy again.

It didn't take long for his agent to respond.

DANIEL

Aw, did he catch feelings?

RICHARD

He asked me out. For coffee.

DANIEL

Oh no. Poor bastard committed a cardinal sin.

Thinking you have feelings.

RICHARD

Just because I can keep work WORK doesn't mean I don't have feelings.

DANIEL

No, the fact that you don't have feelings means you don't have feelings. But I'll put him on the list. With everyone else.

At the rate you're going, you'll blacklist the entire industry by the end of next year.

He ignored that comment. They had more important things to discuss.

RICHARD

Any luck on the new contract?

DANIEL

I've got a meeting with his agent tomorrow to negotiate the details. We'll get this settled well before your three months of mandatory recovery are up.

Richard snorted at his phone.

RICHARD

I still can't believe MateHub makes me do this shit. Haven't I proven by now I can handle these contracts and don't need to 'recover'?

> But that doesn't matter. Just get the deal done. Whatever he wants, it's fine.

DANIEL

On it.

"I'm all set up," Tristan called out.

Not a moment too soon. The ball of emotions in Richard's head was oppressive, intruding on his every thought. He needed it out *now*.

Blaze tried to stop him, his expression pleading, but Richard brushed past him.

In the living room, Tristan had drawn a circle on the hardwood floor. Candles burned at each compass point.

When MateHub had been looking for an apartment to rent for its temporarily bonded stars, this one's main appeal had been having enough space to do the severing rituals right there. It meant they didn't have to return to the studios to do them.

There was no need for Tristan to tell him where to go; Richard already knew. He shucked off his shirt, tossed it on the couch, then took his place, kneeling in the circle.

Blaze dragged his feet but came to kneel beside him. He turned to Richard, opening his mouth to speak.

Before he could say a word, Tristan clapped his hands together, his dark brown eyes cool and professional. "Okay, let's get started. I need quiet to work."

Richard could have kissed the mage, but it'd probably get him a fireball to the face.

The ritual was a simple one, involving minimal setup—just the circle and the candles. The only requirements were that it was done on a new moon and both of the bonded pair were present. From what he understood, it didn't even take that much magic.

Tristan leaned down and placed a hand firmly over Richard's heart, then did the same to Blaze.

Richard closed his eyes and breathed in, his nose itching as the scent of Tristan's magic filled the room, abrasive even after all the times he'd done this.

Dull pain stabbed through Richard's chest, making him clench his teeth as a blade of magic sliced into the bond.

He exhaled, forcing himself to relax. A couple minutes of discomfort, and this would be over.

Beside him, Blaze hissed as Tristan started on his side of the bond.

Every person who entered into a bonding contract was warned repeatedly about what to expect from this ritual. They also got told it'd be easier for them if they remained unattached to their temporary mate. From the spike of pain that lanced through their dimming bond, Blaze hadn't listened.

They never did.

Richard breathed through the muted burn and steadied himself. The next part would be the worst, but it was always fleeting. And once it was finished, he'd be a free wolf, his mind no longer chained to another.

When the final cut came, it was with a blinding flash of pain—there and gone so fast, he scarcely had a chance to acknowledge it.

Blaze moaned, sharp and shallow, so different from the noises Richard had wrung out of him during their time together.

The magic that had been swirling around them settled, though the lingering stench of it still made Richard's nose twitch.

He took in a deep lungful of air and sighed it out.

Fucking finally. Freedom. He felt lighter than he had in months, no longer carrying that extra presence with him.

Opening his eyes, he found Blaze slumped forward, bracing himself on one shaking arm while his other hand grasped his chest. His porcelain skin was now a ghostly white.

Richard stood and saluted Tristan. "Thanks, man. I'll see you after the next one." He grabbed his shirt, pulled it on, and turned to leave.

"How the fuck have you done this twelve times?" Blaze asked, voice strained.

"Eh." Richard tossed his packed leather bag over his shoulder. "You get used to it. Nice working with you. It was fun."

Without looking back, he left the apartment and hit the elevator call button. The doors had barely shut behind him when his phone vibrated with a message.

TRISTAN

If you leave me with one of your sobbing exes another goddamn time, I'm charging your unfeeling ass double.

RICHARD

Not my ex. If he caught feelings, that's on him, not me.

TRISTAN

Right. Because what kind of pathetic loser catches feelings from three months of highly intense sex?

RICHARD

The contract specifically warns against developing feelings.

TRISTAN

Well, if that's what the contract says.

Asshole.

The elevator chimed as it opened, and Richard saun-tered through the lobby, slipping his phone into his pocket.

Not his fault if people couldn't follow the rules. Only an idiot would develop feelings for someone when the rela-tionship was transactional.

Stepping out into the LA air, he was greeted by the distant hum of traffic and the warm glow of the mid-morning sun. He inhaled the earthy scent of the bougainvillea and the faint floral fragrance of the birds-of-paradise planted around the apartment building. It all washed over him, relaxing him further, and he grinned to himself as he strolled to the parking lot, fit his custom bag into the frunk of his matte red Ferrari SF90 Stradale, and got in.

He checked his reflection in the rearview mirror, tilting his neck and pulling down his collar. The mating bite there had already begun to fade—a softening silver against his tan skin. It'd be gone completely by this time next week, as if the bond had never happened.

Just the way he liked it.

Why MateHub insisted his temporary mates bite him, he'd never understand. They claimed the fans liked it, but Richard couldn't see the appeal, and it certainly wasn't necessary for the scenes they were filming. Whatever. If the fans liked it, he'd do it.

He pressed the button to start his car, the hybrid engine a quiet whir as he pulled out of the lot.

His wolf yawned and stretched, subdued by the new moon and unconcerned about what they'd just been through. The first time he'd done a transactional bond, it hadn't liked the idea. But as soon as it'd realized it was a temporary thing—that Richard had no intention of staying mated to a shifter who'd smelled all wrong—it'd given the wolfy equivalent of a shrug and let it happen. Twelve bonds later, it was indifferent to the whole ordeal.

Sure, it thought he was foolish. It didn't understand why he'd mate someone whose scent clashed with theirs, why he'd want to knot someone who'd never truly be their own, who they'd never belong to in return. But then, his wolf would never understand how lucrative bonding contracts were. The fans loved knotting videos, and Richard's were the best in the industry.

It was a short drive to his real apartment. Stepping inside, he dropped his bag by the door and inhaled deeply, enjoying the scent of his own space. Even if he hadn't been there for three months, it still smelled like his, and his alone, not a temporary accommodation overrun by the odor of someone else.

Though, his scent wasn't the only one in the air.

He snorted. He should have known he wouldn't be coming home to an empty apartment.

"When are you going to stop letting yourself into my place without my permission?" he asked.

His older sister, Charlotte, walked around the corner, her arms crossed over her chest, an unimpressed look on her face. "Good to see you too. I brought groceries. You're welcome."

He rolled his eyes. "You're early. You should have sent a message. I might have been bringing someone home."

"Not even you work that fast." She scoffed, then gave him a once-over. "You okay?"

"Why wouldn't I be?"

"Yeah. Why would you be messed up by a mage using magic to reach into your chest and cut out part of you?"

"It's not like I was particularly attached to that part."

"I don't get you. If anyone tried to sever the bond between me and Sofia, I'd rip their fucking throat out. Slowly. Savoring every second." She cocked an eyebrow at him. "Did this one catch feelings too?"

He scowled.

"Aw, how horrible for you. That must have been really rough," she said, her words dripping with mock sympathy as she walked over and hugged him. "You reek of magic, but it's nice that incubus's scent is fading. Never have been a fan of that weird, drugged scent they have. I mean, if you have to do this, must you pick people who smell vile on you?"

The sheer absurdity of that question made him laugh. "Why would they need to smell good on me? Besides, now I get to knock the incubus square off my bingo card. I'm getting so close to blackout."

Finding someone whose scent mixed well with his was missing the point. And frankly, it was a little dangerous. He didn't want to be bonded to someone he was actually compatible with. His fans didn't care about sentimental shit like that; it wasn't like they could smell how their scents combined. Their primary concern was the visuals. And for all his inability to separate emotion and pleasure, Blaze, with his stunning looks and sophisticated vibe, was as hot as his name. His black hair and toned, slender build had been a perfect contrast to Richard's golden brown locks and more muscled physique.

Char shook her head. "Only you would want to knot your way through the entire paranormal community. At this point, is there any supernatural creature you haven't fucked?"

He grinned at her. "Funny you should mention that."

"Don't tell me next on your list is a vampire," she said with a groan.

"Ugh, no. I'll get there eventually. But my next contract..." He paused, letting the anticipation build.

"If you're waiting for me to ask, you're going to be waiting a long time. I'm just not that invested in your dick."

"Must you always ruin my fun?"

"Obviously, yes."

"Fine. I'm telling you anyway. The contract Daniel's lining up for me is with a human."

A look of genuine surprise crossed her face. The number of humans who knew about them was kept as low as they could manage, mainly confined to the handful mated into their community. Which meant humans working in supernatural adult entertainment were exceedingly rare. He almost couldn't believe they'd found one willing to be bonded.

The papers weren't signed yet, and Richard hoped he wasn't jinxing it by telling his sister. But man, this would be profitable if they made it work.

"Well, at least humans have subtle scents when they aren't doused in perfumes and colognes. I might even be able to stand having lunch with you while you're bonded to him. But," she said, jabbing a finger at him, "make sure you go see Mom during your mandatory time off. I'm sick of covering for you. 'Oh, he's been so busy at work. Last I heard, he was getting absolutely slammed.'"

"Hey now. At work, I do all the slamming," he said, and she punched him.

"That falls squarely under the category of more detail than I want to know."

He swiped at her, but she easily dodged the attack.

"Alright. Lunch," she said, walking into the kitchen. "You can tell me all about how badly you broke this one's heart."

"I don't break people's hearts. That's their own doing."

"Sure. Keep telling yourself that."

Shaking his head, he washed his hands and grabbed a knife to chop up the vegetables.

It didn't matter what she thought. The important thing was that he was free, and he had every intention of enjoying the next three months to the fullest.

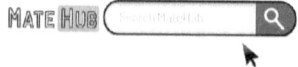

SPECULATION: *Who's Next?*

MagicalHWood:
This is going to make me sound horrible, but I'm so glad the contract with Blaze is over. He's gorgeous, but he was getting annoyingly clingy, and you could tell Richard wasn't into him.

KnottyWolf69:
Same, man. Richard was as smoking hot as ever, but Blaze was way too invested. Poor dude.

MagicalHWood:
They all get that look during their final few scenes with him. Can't blame them though. I'd happily and shamelessly beg for his knot if given the chance.

tindrwolf:
It must be fucking good with how desperate they are for it.

BramStroker:
Who do you think is next? Maybe another wolf? It's been a while since he's bonded one of his own.

MagicalHWood:
I still say he found our KNOTZ bingo card. His last three bonding contracts and most of his side scenes have knocked off squares.

KnottyWolf69:
So what do we have left? Vampire, fae, shark shifter, mage?

MagicalHWood:
I volunteer as sacrificial mage. He can Richard me down any fucking day of the week.

saerys69:
I don't think fae is gonna happen. Are there even any currently working in the industry?

BramStroker:
GOD PLEASE VAMPIRE. Can you imagine XXXavier Sinclair feeding off Richard while Richard has him knotted? Fuck, I'd give my fangs to see that.

saerys69:
That would be insanely hot.

HuntMeDown:
He should bond Hunter Savage.

KnottyWolf69:
snort

MagicalHWood:
Yeah, right. Get back to your own board, fanboy. No human could keep up with Richard.

HuntMeDown:
Sure. Keep telling yourselves that. I'll be back with

an 'I told you so' when Hunter has Richard on his knees, begging for more.

KnottyWolf69:
You're delusional. Richard is the one who makes his partners moan for Dick, not the other way around.

tindrwolf:
Seriously. That knot of his is too much for a human to handle.

MagicalHWood:
Now, who wants to place bets on who it'll actually be?

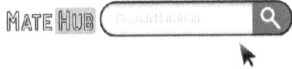

TWO

H unter Savage paused his game as a key turned in the lock and his roommate let himself into their cramped apartment. He'd laugh at the wobbly way Chance drifted into their living room, but he'd been in that state himself on more than a few occasions.

Chance slithered to the floor next to him, his head flopping back onto the seat of their secondhand couch, his muscular body melting against the well-worn furniture. As he rolled his head to the side to smile smugly at Hunter, his tawny hair fell into his eyes, but lifting his hand to brush it away seemed like too much effort for him at the moment.

"Good scene?" Hunter asked.

"It was with an incubus *and* a succubus. I don't think I'll be able to come again for another month." Chance sounded as languid and thoroughly fucked as he looked.

Hunter shook his head. "So, tomorrow?"

"Probably. But damn, that was a thorough deboning. You know those videos of an octopus squeezing through some tiny hole? That's me. I'm that octopus. Zero bones."

"I realize there's a joke in there about you squeezing into tiny holes, but I'm going to pass it up because I need to ask... Are octopus shifters a thing?"

"Hoping MateHub's up for shooting some tentacle porn?"

"No. Well. Probably no? But also, are they a thing?"

Chance made a noncommittal noise. "You could ask them to book you with a kraken."

"Oh, fuck off. I still haven't forgiven you for convincing me unicorn shifters were real."

"Every time you find out another type of supernatural creature exists, your first reaction is always, 'Oooh, can I fuck one?' So you'll forgive me for not giving you an exhaustive list."

"It is not! I've had that reaction three times, max. And in my defense, your dicks are rocking some serious game-altering upgrades. Like shark shifters? Come on. Who wouldn't want to give a dude with a double dick a try? And fae shouldn't count either. They're so pretty in human form."

"Sure, when they aren't being unbelievable bastards."

"Those two things aren't mutually exclusive."

"Fair point."

"Speaking of pretty, unbelievable bastards. I signed the contract today."

"Ugh. Did it have to be a wolf?" Chance whined. "You're going to reek like dog."

Hunter rolled his eyes at his over-dramatic friend. He'd heard rants about canine shifters often enough over the last two years that he'd known Chance would never approve. Go figure a mountain lion shifter would have issues with a wolf shifter. Cats and dogs, no matter the form.

"It'll only be for three months. You can handle it for that long. And I won't even be here. They're making me stay in this super fancy apartment near the MateHub head-quarters."

"Oh no. Poor you. Being forced to live in luxury. How will you survive?"

"You know I'd rather be here. Even if your dirty laundry seems to be organizing itself to stage a coup any day now. But they're acting as if I won't be able to get three feet from his dick without having a breakdown or some shit. For real. When I said they could cut that part from the contract, my agent and his exchanged a glance, shook their heads, then told me I'll want to be close to him after we're bonded." Hunter snorted. "Yeah, right."

"I don't know. I've heard rumors about the guys he's had bonding contracts with. A few dropped out of the industry after he was done with them."

Hunter's eyebrows rose. "You've gotta be kidding me."

"I'm serious," Chance said. "Bonding contracts can fuck you up. There's a reason Richard is a legend. The only other person who's done anywhere close to as many is Duke Moorhead, and he's on maybe his fifth or sixth. Everyone else does it once, then never again."

Hunter gave him a skeptical look. "It can't be that big of a deal. I've been bitten before."

"You were fed on, not bonded. There's a world of differ-ence between the two."

A frisson of nerves ran through Hunter, but he shoved it down. "Maybe that's what it's like for you supernatural types, but not for humans. None of the scenes I've done with vamps or incubi have been anything like how you and some of the other guys describe them. I mean, yeah, it feels good. But I heard a bear shifter say coming while a vampire feeds on you is the best orgasm you'll ever have. Please. I've given myself better orgasms."

Surely being bonded couldn't be that different. Besides, his fans had been vocal about wanting to see him get knotted.

"You really want to do this?" There was a thread of concern in Chance's voice.

"What's the worst that could happen? I realize my roommate isn't entirely human, find out he's actually a fucking mountain lion *and* a secret porn star, somehow let him talk me into doing 'just a scene or two,' then end up with a werewolf knotting my—oh, wait."

"You like it." Chance nudged him.

"Hence letting the werewolf knot my ass. But honestly, the money is insane. And my agent says if I do this, my career is guaranteed to blow up."

Chance smirked. "Gonna make it *expand*?"

"Oh, shut up. Not like that. Though... yeah, I guess, literally like that."

"Are you nervous?"

"The filming itself sounds completely different. They do everything in one take with as many cameras as possible once the sex starts. No stopping to get other angles or anything, which makes sense. Can't exactly do a take two for those kinds of scenes. At least not without waiting a good while. Plus the fans say they like the more natural feel of it. So, a bit nervous, yeah. I'd hate to fuck things up when there's no redo."

"You know that's not what I meant."

Hunter shrugged. "I've been watching his videos, trying to figure out what to expect. I think it'll be fine. And I... I may have also purchased his, uh, merchandise."

Chance cackled. "Really?"

"I was curious."

But what kind of jackass thought so highly of their dick they had it made into an extremely lifelike magical dildo, complete with an inflatable knot and the ability to ejaculate?

Though, he had gotten that offer to have his asshole made into a Fleshlight with magical heating and clenching power, and the money had been enough to make him consider it, so maybe he shouldn't judge.

"How was it? I've always been a little curious too. But there's no way in hell I'm doing a scene with Richard Knotz. Or any canine, for that matter. Definitely never getting bonded to one."

"Eh. It was decent." Hunter would not be admitting that one of those 'I've given myself better' orgasms had happened while riding Richard's... merchandise. No one ever needed to know that. "Whatever the mages do to those toys, they're realistic. *Really* realistic. Borderline uncanny valley—retractable foreskin and everything. But as long as it doesn't get bigger than that, it'll be okay."

"How big?"

"You want to hear how it felt when I made it all the way to level-ten inflation?"

Chance paused, considering, then made a face. "Ugh, no. I'd rather not know that amount of detail about what your ass can handle."

"The feeling's mutual," Hunter said with a snort.

They settled into silence for a moment before Chance spoke again. "Just please don't fall for him? I know he's the biggest star on MateHub, but you can do so much better."

"It's just a contract," Hunter said, laughing. "We aren't going to be dating. And like I said, I've been watching his videos. He's hot, alright, but I don't see why people are so obsessed with him. I mean, he clearly knows what he's doing and how to make his co-stars come hard. I saw a few pass out from pleasure, and they weren't faking it for the camera. But there's something about him that pisses me off. He seems so arrogant. If he's that smug twenty-four-seven, I might kill him before the three months are over. If I do, do you think they'll dock my pay?"

"Do I think MateHub will cut your compensation if you kill their biggest star? Yeah, probably."

Hunter huffed. "Fine. I'll play nice."

"When do you start?"

"In a little over a month. Apparently, they always schedule the bonding scenes on the new moon because he'll be gentler. Then the second scene, they want to film when he's at his wolfiest, so that'll be two weeks later on the full moon."

"He better be gentle with you," Chance said darkly.

Hunter scoffed. "He better not be. That's definitely not what I'm signing up for. But I got a concession during the negotiations that I'm looking forward to."

Chance cocked an eyebrow at him. "What'd you get?"

"Are octopus shifters a thing?"

Chance shrugged.

"Then I guess you'll have to wait and find out with everyone else."

"You're no fun. Fine. Just, seriously, don't fall for that asshole."

"Zero risk of that happening. Now, grab a controller. I doubt said asshole is a gamer, and if I have to be stuck in an apartment for three months with someone who doesn't play, I want to be absolutely sick of games before then."

Chance groaned. "What part of 'deboned' did you not understand? I can't play video games while I'm an invertebrate. You're going to kick my ass."

"Perfect," Hunter said, grinning. "My favorite kind of games."

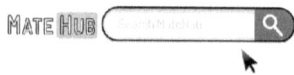

THREE

R ichard sat in his agent's office and skimmed through the contract. Sunlight streamed through the large windows, casting the rich wood and plush leather furnishings in an amber glow.

He recognized the standard boilerplate language they'd hammered out years ago. After a dozen similar agreements, he knew what to expect. However, this one held a few noticeable changes.

"Seven scenes? We normally do twice that."

Daniel glanced up from where he'd been typing on a sleek black laptop and leaned back in his chair before answering. "He's human. We don't know how he'll react to the bond, or how long it'll take him to recover from the scenes."

Richard snorted. "He won't be the first human in history to take a knot. He'll be fine."

"First to take yours," Daniel muttered. "You're not particularly known for being gentle. Remember he doesn't heal like a shifter."

"Oh, fuck off. I'm not going to hurt him. I make damn sure all my co-stars feel good."

It was Daniel's turn to snort. "Uh-huh. Right up until the scene ends."

That jab didn't deserve a response, so he ignored it. "I suppose this just gives us more time to fit in scenes with other people."

"I already have a few I'm negotiating in the back half."

"Considering how open this schedule is, there's more than enough room to do a few in the first half too."

"You know I can't do that," Daniel said, shooting him an unimpressed look, and Richard scoffed.

MateHub had too many regulations in place for these things. Knotting scenes were their biggest moneymaker, and they tried to have at least one temporarily bonded couple at any given time so they could consistently release new ones. But they were so paranoid they'd lose stars over them, the rules were never-ending.

The performers shouldn't be compatible because there was a risk they'd end up with a true bond.

Three months max—longer than that and more permanent attachments might form—followed by the mandatory three months of rest and counseling to ensure the actors recovered fully after the bond was severed.

Living together while bonded to prevent feelings of withdrawal or rejection, but no sex between scenes because that'd deepen the connection.

No additional co-stars or scenes outside the bond until they were certain there would be no adverse effects, which meant waiting at least a month before they were allowed.

But most of all, nothing that would affect MateHub's bottom line. Nothing that would lead to the transactional bond developing into something more, something closer to a true bond. Because if their actors caught feelings, they might not want to work with anyone else, and MateHub had no interest in porn stars who'd only film with their mates.

As if that'd happen to Richard. Doing knotting scenes and keeping it professional was what he'd been born to do.

They should know by now that he was fine without their excessively cautious bullshit. He'd pioneered these damn bonding contracts, after all.

Whatever. They could be as careful as they liked as long as it didn't hurt his paycheck. If anything, this was better for him. A pared-down filming schedule and significantly more money? He couldn't complain about that.

The same could not be said for the list of scenes they had planned though.

"A domestic scene? Again? Those are so boring. Why do they always want that shit?"

"Fuck if I know," Daniel said. "Your fans are apparently under the impression your prickly ass is capable of genuine happiness and love. Mass delusion, I'd say. Or maybe they secretly like to watch you suffer."

"My fans love me."

"They love parts of you."

Richard didn't roll his eyes, but he wanted to. "Can't we just add another scene where I hunt him down and fuck him in the forest? Those are fun, and the fans eat them up."

"There's already one of those. We have it scheduled on the full moon and everything."

"There's usually two."

"What part of 'limited schedule' are you not understanding? We only have him for seven scenes, so they need to be as different as possible."

Fine. If his fans got off to him playing house before

slow-boning his dearly beloved mate, he'd give them that lame shit.

He was reaching for the pen when his gaze caught on the description of the scene before the domestic one. As he read through the basic outline, his eyebrows rose steadily higher.

"Are you fucking kidding me with scene five?"

"You said 'anything,' and that's what he wanted." Daniel's dark eyes studied him.

"No one wants to see that."

"Oh, believe me, there are tons of people waiting to see the big bad wolf get fucked. The fact that it'll be some weak human doing it will just make it that much better."

Richard scowled at him.

"What? Don't think you can handle it?" Daniel's expression was sly enough to make any fox shifter proud.

"Fuck you," Richard said, grabbing the pen and aggressively signing the contract.

Daniel clapped his hands, giving a wide, sharp smile. "Excellent. I'll prepare the press release. Lucky number thirteen."

Despite himself, Richard grinned back. "After this, find me a vampire."

There were so few wolf shifter/vampire scenes out there, and none with knotting. He didn't love the idea of letting a vampire feed off him, especially not multiple times, but he bet he'd get a decent contract out of that too. Maybe not as lucrative as bonding a human, but fair compensation for having a grave-like stench hanging around him for three months.

Plus, his sister would hate it. Meeting her for lunch with that scent all over him would be incredibly entertaining. Who could ask for a better reason than that?

Daniel chuckled. "I knew it was a horrible idea to show you that bingo card."

"It's the only good thing you've ever done," Richard said, standing to leave.

"Do you want me to talk the higher-ups into letting you do a few scenes during the remainder of your mandatory recovery or not?"

"Have I told you you're the best agent ever lately? Because you are."

Daniel huffed. "I'll contact you when I've got something lined up."

Richard saluted as he turned to head out of the office, but Daniel called after him.

"When should I schedule the pre-bonding meeting between you and the human?"

"Unnecessary," Richard said over his shoulder as he walked through the door.

No way in hell was he compatible with a human.

There was a little over a month left of his leave. He'd enjoy life, film a scene or two on the side—though his fans were never as satisfied when he wasn't knotting his co-stars, and he had to admit, he missed his knot when it was gone. It was such a shame he needed to be bonded to experience it.

But he'd deal with MateHub's ridiculous regulations, and then he'd be back at it. Everyone called him a legend for a reason; he'd make sure he continued to be worthy of that title, filling up his bingo card along the way.

29

Once home, he tossed his keys on the kitchen counter and slipped off his shoes.

He grabbed his laptop and sprawled out on his couch, pulling up his MateHub watch history and clicking on a video he'd seen more than a few times over the last couple of months.

Not needing to see the setup—the broke human begging his bear shifter landlord for an extension on his rent—he skipped ahead. MateHub might be the premier adult site for the supernatural community, but damn if it didn't like its cheesy porn scenarios. *My pack alpha got stuck in a window, and I had to fuck him out of it! The fae made my sex doll come to life, and now it won't stop riding my dick! A pride of feline shifters captured me and made me the lions' share!*

The MateHub writers were truly doing god's work. Absolutely devoted to their craft. How else would they create such cinematic masterpieces as *Mages Gone Wild! The Sex Ritual You'll Have to See to Believe!*

He'd seen it; he still didn't believe it.

The most replayed marker on the progress bar made the part he was looking for easy to find, as if he didn't have the timestamp memorized. It was after the obligatory blow job, when Kodiak Timber bent Hunter Savage over a table to "collect his rent."

The first time Richard had watched it, he'd been curious about the new human people kept mentioning. He'd wanted to size him up, to see if it'd be worthwhile to work with him.

It hadn't been hard to figure out why the fans kept raving about him. His thick, dark curls would be perfect to grab, to use to yank his head to the side and give Richard full access to his neck. And since he was human, any marks

Richard left there would linger long after they'd fade on a shifter.

Hunter had the kind of body most shifters came by naturally, but for him, it spoke of hours in the gym. Richard could appreciate that dedication, especially when it meant he'd be strong and flexible enough, Richard would be able to bend him into whatever position he desired, and his ass could handle one hell of a pounding. But he didn't just lie there and take it. His hips met each thrust, his back arching as he got closer to coming.

He might be a newbie, but he knew how to work a camera, how to give the viewer a good show.

Except, while Hunter was clearly enjoying himself, it was equally obvious he wasn't getting what he needed. It was written in the shifting of his hips, his face more focused than euphoric, as he corrected Kodiak's careless angle, not hitting his prostate right.

Richard had figured this scene must be a fluke, but the more scenes he'd watched, the more he was certain. No one was making Hunter come as hard as he needed to. Sure, they got him off, but he was doing the bulk of the work.

It made Richard grind his teeth at the absolute incompetence of the people he'd worked with for years. He'd thought they were better than this. Couldn't they see what Hunter needed? What his body was begging for? There was no excuse for that kind of sloppy behavior from a top. And with someone so new to the industry.

He, at least, held himself to a higher standard. He'd give Hunter exactly what he needed until he was loose-limbed and glassy-eyed. Until he couldn't remember his own name and the only words he'd be able to get out were 'please' and 'more' and 'Richard.' He'd pin Hunter down, sink his teeth into him, knot him, make him come so hard he'd white out and see stars. Bring him to heights of pleasure he'd never known, satisfy him in a way he'd never experienced. And he'd do all that while putting on the best show MateHub fans could ask for.

He squeezed himself through his pants. He'd never been able to get off to Hunter's scenes, not with these travesties of tops failing to do their jobs properly, but the idea of showing Hunter what a true MateHub star was capable of... Now *that* he could get off to.

Knowing he'd soon get to do precisely that added fuel to the fantasy. He'd fuck Hunter better than every single co-star he'd had before.

Sure, living with a human for three months would annoy the shit out of him, but he'd put up with it. He always did.

On screen, he could swear Hunter was repressing an eye roll as Kodiak's thrusts grew erratic far sooner than he should have been coming.

Hunter played up his breathy moans as he arched his back and quickly jerked himself off before Kodiak could finish.

Richard shook his head. It was a sad day when an amateur human was making seasoned professional shifters look bad in their scenes.

He was going to make sure that stopped with him. He'd blow this newbie's goddamn mind and get paid an insane amount to do it.

Richard entered the elevator in MateHub's headquarters and hit the button for the studio on the sixth floor. He leaned against the wall as the elevator started to climb.

This mandatory recovery period had been entirely too long. He'd try to get Daniel to negotiate a shorter break next time. There'd been no need for him to wait months for this contract.

He breathed in, catching a trace of... *something*. The usual stale air smelled a little fuller, a little brighter, but he couldn't put his finger on what it was. The scent was too faint.

With effort, he prodded his wolf forward. It was content to lie dormant on bonding days. Between the new moon dampening their energy and his wolf's general lack of interest in his co-stars, it couldn't be bothered to make an appearance.

With his wolf as close to the surface as he could coax it, he inhaled deeply again, using his enhanced senses to the extent they were currently capable of.

The scent was still faint, but it sprang into clearer focus. Something subtle and clean, soft yet hard. Something he couldn't place but that had him taking in another lungful of air to get more of it.

His wolf stirred, more alert than it'd ever been on a new moon. He expected it to fade to the background as he released it, but it lingered, waiting, feeling for all the world like it was poised to ambush its prey.

Interesting. Richard had never thought of forcing his wolf to the surface for these scenes. He'd let it do whatever it wanted, and frequently, what it wanted was to have nothing to do with their transactional bonds.

He rolled his shoulders and ran his tongue over his canines, finding them tingling and ready to drop, then grinned. Scenes were better when his wolf was near the surface. It made the sensations that much more visceral— every instinct sharper, every touch more pleasurable.

Today was going to be fun.

The elevator chimed and let him out on the sixth floor, and he auto-piloted to the studio.

It was set up for the scene. A massive bed dominated the space, well-lit and surrounded by half a dozen cameras. Beyond that was the love seat where they'd sit for the pre-bonding interview, placed so the bed loomed in the back of the shot as they were asked trite questions about the contract and whatever else MateHub thought their fans wanted to hear. Not that Richard ever gave much of an answer.

He nodded to the director, Brandt, who returned the gesture before leaning down to adjust a camera. Next to him, his new assistant director, Everett, listened attentively as he explained the framing of the shot. The MateHub rumor mill claimed the little snow leopard shifter was fresh out of film school and had been hooked up with the job by a family contact. His petite frame was dwarfed by Brandt's size—massive even by grizzly standards. The only thing larger was the amount of big teddy bear energy Brandt exuded.

Richard headed to his dressing room. Inside, he checked himself out in the vanity and was greeted by a voracious, predatory leer. His wolf really was closer to the surface than normal, and it showed.

Oh, his fans were going to love this shit. He'd seen several of them talking about how they wished MateHub would let him bond someone on a full moon. Unfortunately, that would never happen, but this might be a decent substitute. There was no denying how wolfish his reflection looked, no mistaking him for anything remotely human.

He should have thought of this ages ago.

Still grinning to himself, he stripped and stood naked, enjoying the cool air brushing against his skin. He rolled his shoulders again. His wolf wasn't even close to its full strength; this wasn't how he felt on a full moon, but he could work with it. Work with the banked fire inside him, the seductive desire to shift, to run, to hunt.

His dick hung heavy, and he reached down to give it a quick squeeze. The base of it was already tender in anticipation of exactly what they were about to get up to.

Reluctantly, he pulled on the black silk robe they'd left for him and loosely tied it. They never wanted them to do the pre-bonding interviews naked. A shame, honestly. Richard knew how much his fans enjoyed seeing him in all his glory, and the fine silk felt heavy and oppressive on his skin.

But it didn't matter. He wouldn't be wearing it for long.

Nearly whistling to himself, he stalked out of the dressing room and over to the love seat, casually sitting on it, not bothering to fix the robe when it fell open, exposing most of his chest, one side falling over his leg, leaving it bare, the other side a breath away from not covering him at all. The way the silk draped over his dick left little to the imagination, and he spread his legs so the camera would capture the excellent view.

"You alright there?" Brandt asked from next to the lone camera they used for the interview.

Richard smirked at him. "Why wouldn't I be? Finally get to use this thing how it's meant to be used again." He gave himself another squeeze.

Everett's pale cheeks colored slightly, and if he was flustered by something that tame, he was in for an eye-opening experience.

Brandt shot Richard a look. "I don't know. You almost seemed happy for a moment. Nearly didn't recognize you."

Before Richard could respond, the love seat dipped, and he turned his head to find Hunter settling against the cushions, an easy smile on his lips.

"Hey, man," Hunter said, holding out his hand. "I'm looking forward to working with you."

A whisper of his scent floated toward Richard with his words, and Richard froze as the realization hit him.

That soft, delicate scent from the elevator, so subtle it demanded he inhale more of it.

The reason he'd forced his wolf out of its slumber.

The reason his wolf had stayed present.

It was Hunter.

Hunter's scent was making Richard want to haul him forward, to sit him in his lap instead of on the cushion. To bury his nose in his neck and breathe him in.

He didn't, but it was tempting.

Instead, he shook Hunter's hand.

His scent didn't matter; the fans didn't care about that.

He dropped his hand and gave Hunter a once-over. MateHub had given him a white silk robe to wear. They did enjoy their wedding imagery during these bonding scenes. They'd probably want some fated mates bullshit if they thought Richard would go along with it, but they had to settle with putting the not-so-virginal bottom in pure white to contrast with Richard's black.

Hunter was as hot as he always was in his scenes—his grin mischievous, his eyes sharp—and Richard knew the tanned body under that robe was going to be a blast to play with over the next few months. He had a list of places to touch and things to do that would make Hunter squirm and every intention of exploiting that list to the fullest.

He was already imagining stripping that robe off him, exposing his sculpted muscles, stretching him open, sliding inside.

"Alright, you two," Brandt said, pulling Richard out of his spiraling fantasies. "Get closer for the interview."

Hunter didn't hesitate, just slid across the short distance between them.

All Richard could do was watch, his pulse kicking up a notch as Hunter tucked himself against his side like he'd been there before.

Fuck, his scent was intoxicating—somehow heady despite its subtlety.

Richard hadn't realized a human could smell this good.

Hunter's hand fluttered down, coming to rest on Richard's exposed thigh, that light touch alone scorching against his skin.

His wolf rumbled its approval, agreeing with Richard completely. Today was going to be *fun*.

Richard repressed the shiver that thought caused and tried to ignore how Hunter's scent was twisting itself around him, so soft and alluring.

Teasing him.

Impossible to ignore.

What the fuck had he gotten himself into?

"Okay," Brandt said. "Let's get this scene started."

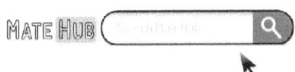

BREAKING NEWS: *Richard Knotz to Bond Hunter Savage*

HuntMeDown:
DickHunt is happening, baby!

MagicalHWood:
DickHunt? No. We aren't calling them that.

KnottyWolf69:
Yeah, that's vetoed.

HuntMeDown:
Whatever we call them, it doesn't matter. You just better get yourselves ready to swallow my big fat I told you so.

MagicalHWood:
Yeah, right. Some twunky human is not getting the best of Richard Knotz.

HuntMeDown:
We'll see what you have to say in a few months.

KnottyWolf69:
In your dreams.

forgetmeknot:
I don't know, guys. Hunter's new, but have you seen his scenes? They're fucking hot.

BramStroker:

I have to agree. MateHub always has him play this scared little human whenever he's with a vamp, but fuck, by the end of the scene, it's like the vamps are the ones under thrall. Seriously. Look up "A Vampire Bit Me, so I Sucked Him Dry." The vamp topping him all but begs Hunter to let him come, and then when Hunter tells him to, he does so perfectly on cue. He even says thank you. It's. So. Hot. I wish they'd let Hunter top one of these days. I bet he'd make his bottoms come as hard as Richard does.

MagicalHWood:

Shit. I think they're getting to Bram. This requires an intervention! Let's spam him with Richard GIFs until he returns to his senses.

BramStroker:

Oh no! Not the Richard GIFs! What a horrible punishment! That'll definitely show me.

forgetmeknot:

I may also need punishing while we're at it.

KnottyWolf69:

Same. Bring on the Richard pics. Anyone got some of that squad of privates being inspected and drilled by Sergeant Knotz?

MagicalHWood:

Do you even need to ask?

CHAPTER

FOUR

R ichard Knotz was a smug jackass, but he was a hot smug jackass; Hunter had to give him that. His videos didn't begin to do him justice. Hunter's fingers itched to mess up his perfectly styled golden brown hair, and the lighting in the studio made his pale green eyes sparkle in an annoyingly attractive way. He also might as well not have even been wearing his robe with how it hung open, revealing a tan expanse of hard muscle.

As with every pre-scene interview Hunter had watched, Richard didn't bother contributing more than a word or two, leaving Hunter to carry the bulk of the conversation. His economical answers weren't doing any favors to Hunter's resolution to not kill his co-star before he received his full compensation.

"Have you watched any of each other's scenes?" Brandt asked.

Richard shrugged, the motion jostling Hunter against his side. "A few."

He didn't elaborate, and Hunter forced his expression to remain pleasant.

"And you, Hunter?"

"I mean, who hasn't watched one of Richard's scenes? I may have done a fair amount of... research, in preparation for this."

Brandt chuckled. The deep timbre of his laughter filled the room, his dark complexion radiant with an infectious smile. "Research. Is that what the kids these days are calling it?"

"It was very thorough," Hunter said, the corner of his mouth quirking up.

"Any favorites?"

Hunter's grin grew downright sinful. "Let's just say I'll never be able to run through a forest again without getting hard."

Beside him, there was a rumble from Richard—so low, Hunter doubted the mics had picked it up. But it vibrated through the press of their bodies, resonating in his core. Apparently, he wasn't alone in looking forward to that particular scene.

"Why don't we have you two kiss for the first time?" Brandt said.

Hunter turned toward Richard, then froze, his breath catching.

He'd seen Richard in dozens of scenes, from these bonding scenes to cheesy domestic scenes to ones with a darker edge. The Richard in those videos was not the one sitting next to him on the love seat. Even in his wolf form, pretending to chase down his prey in the woods, he'd still seemed human, seemed in control.

There was nothing human about this rapacious creature staring at him.

The air around Hunter thickened with a primal tension that had his instincts screaming for him to run, to fight, to surrender himself to anything and everything this untamed version of Richard wanted to do to him.

Richard's eyes were bright and flashing with his wolf, burning with wild things Hunter couldn't name, his expression predatory, his hands too greedy to be gentle as one wrapped around Hunter's waist to gather him closer and the other wound into his hair.

His grip verged on painful as he tilted Hunter's head, drawing a soft gasp from him that had the beast within Richard showing his teeth in a feral approximation of a smile. He swooped in and ran his nose along Hunter's neck.

A growl resounded in Richard's chest as he scraped sharp canines over Hunter's throat. "You're going to smell so fucking perfect when you're mine," he said, and Hunter's eyes threatened to roll back into his head.

This was not how Richard had acted when he'd been told to kiss his other co-stars during these interviews. Those kisses had been perfunctory, an item to be checked off before they moved on to the good stuff. But this? This seemed like something Richard was reveling in.

"You want that, don't you? You want to be mine. I can smell it on you, smell how ready you are for me to fuck you. Claim you. *Knot you.*"

The words were punctuated by the graze of teeth, and Hunter's hands desperately attempted to find something to hold on to, anything to hold on to. They ended up fisted in Richard's robe, trying to pull him closer, though little space was left between them.

Well, this was fucking unfair. Hunter hadn't been prepared for this. Not even remotely. He hadn't expected Richard to tug his robe aside and suck hard on the juncture of his neck right where he'd be biting him, hadn't thought anything Richard could do to him before they made it to the bed would leave him panting, his dick hardening, the silk against it frustratingly not enough.

Richard brought his lips tantalizingly close to Hunter's. "I'm going to make you feel so good. Fuck you and make you mine. Stretch you wide open on my knot so the whole world knows who you belong to, and you're going to love every second of it."

Unfair *and* uncalled for. Since when had Richard Knotz started talking like that? He rarely talked at all. There was even an interview where he'd said he preferred not to talk so people could enjoy the various noises he wrung out of his co-stars. It was probably the longest answer he'd ever given.

But Hunter couldn't retain that thought when Richard was leaning in, brushing his lips against Hunter's in the most maddening tease, hot breath ghosting over his skin. How could he say shit like that, then barely kiss him? Hunter moved to deepen it, but Richard used his grip on Hunter's hair to hold him back from what he wanted. Hunter made a small, embarrassing noise of frustration.

"Tell me how much you want it," Richard said, a murmur against his lips.

Hunter nearly gave a growl of his own. Fuck this self-satisfied son of a wolf. He wasn't begging. "Kiss me," he demanded.

To his surprise, Richard complied. He brought their mouths together, hand tight in Hunter's hair, keeping his head tilted, slipping his tongue into Hunter's mouth and owning him with it. The kiss was all-consuming and raw, filled with the desire to claim, to brand every inch of him as Richard's until Hunter couldn't breathe, until he wasn't sure he wanted to breathe, not if it meant stopping this, stopping the insistent way Richard was pushing him against the arm of the love seat, about to pin him down—

A loud clap sounded, startling Hunter and causing him to wrench his mouth away from Richard's. Richard grumbled a dark protest but let him go.

Hunter looked around the room, wide-eyed, and found Brandt staring back, his eyebrows at his hairline, while Everett was a charming shade of pink.

"Well," Brandt said, face as shocked as Hunter felt. "I had other questions, but, uh... I think we can skip those? Yeah, let's skip those. Why don't... why don't you two make your way to the bed before you get too carried away, and we'll get started."

Before Hunter could think about getting up, Richard stood, then grabbed him, tossing him over his shoulder like he weighed nothing and stalking toward the bed.

This was not how this scene was supposed to go. There'd been an outline. A plan. Some vague choreography of which acts they'd do in what order. But he couldn't remember it and couldn't be bothered to care. However things went from here, he knew they'd be good.

He blinked at Brandt, who was shouting orders and waving his hands frantically. There was a mad rush as everyone scrambled to get from where they'd been waiting out of frame to their assigned positions.

Hunter enjoyed watching the chaos for all of three seconds before he was unceremoniously dumped on the white silk sheets of the king-sized bed. Then all he saw was Richard looming over him, ripping off his robe to stand there naked and glorious, his cock leaking precome that Hunter desperately needed to taste.

Richard preened under his gaze. He took himself in hand, gathering the beads of precome on his tip before giving himself a few strokes, putting on a show. Not for the cameras, not for anyone else. Just for Hunter.

The sight had Hunter scooting to the edge of the bed, about to slide off it, but then Richard's hand was back in his hair, keeping him from falling to his knees. Hunter glared up at him, annoyed at being denied. Him giving Richard a blow job had definitely been part of the plan; he remembered that.

"Uh-uh. Not this time. This time is all about you," Richard said, his voice rough.

Hunter was pretty damn sure whether or not he got to suck Richard's dick was all about him too, and he was going to say as much, but he was stopped short when Richard shoved him back onto his elbows and dropped between his legs, his hands tearing Hunter's robe open.

There was another scramble as the cameramen moved closer, trying to get a good angle, but Hunter didn't care about that either, not when Richard was spreading his legs farther apart, farther than needed, leaving Hunter exposed in all the best ways.

Richard bent forward and breathed in, eyelids fluttering shut as he inhaled. Another of those low rumbles rolled through him like thunder.

When he opened his eyes, they were glowing amber, and the sheer hunger in them had Hunter shivering.

But the bastard didn't even touch his cock. Instead, he lifted one of Hunter's legs and rasped his stubble along his inner thigh, nuzzling into him, nipping at him when he squirmed. Hunter's thighs had always been more ticklish than he liked to admit.

Richard dragged down to Hunter's knee, rubbing his nose along the underside, making Hunter's leg twitch. He paused to leer up at Hunter, then repeated the motion as Hunter bit off a curse, his toes curling.

How the fuck did this self-centered asshole know how sensitive he was there? It had to be a coincidence. A lucky guess.

Richard's smirk said otherwise.

As if reading his thoughts, Richard grabbed his hand, bringing Hunter's wrist to his lips and sucking on the delicate flesh there.

Hunter tried not to squirm again.

Okay, that one was explainable. Richard must have watched a scene where a vampire had fed from his wrist. Hunter always came extra hard when they did that.

But Richard wasn't finished proving his point. He climbed onto the bed, and Hunter let him strip him of his robe, then arrange him to his liking. He wound a hand into Hunter's hair, tugging until his neck was arched and bared.

God, he liked that, didn't he? Liked controlling Hunter's head. Whenever they got around to Hunter blowing him, that'd be fun. But Hunter couldn't focus on that either because Richard was nuzzling his ear.

"And here," he said, so quiet there was no way it'd been caught by the mics. He sucked at the spot right behind Hunter's ear, the one that always left him writhing and cursing. Richard chuckled wickedly against his skin. "I know exactly what you like, exactly how to make you feel better than you ever have before. Make you come harder. Make you beg for my knot."

Hunter scoffed at the arrogance in his tone. "Never gonna happen."

Richard drew back to look down at him, cocky air firmly in place, but it wasn't the usual smugness that irritated Hunter whenever he saw it in Richard's scenes. No, this was something different, something wilder. Something deeply sure of itself and ridiculously hot because of that confidence.

Slowly lowering himself, Richard kept his body away from Hunter's, not allowing him any friction or contact. His core strength would have been impressive if it weren't pissing Hunter off. He wanted that friction, that contact, more than he would have thought possible.

"Ask nicely," the bastard said, his lips quirking with wicked delight at Hunter's defiance.

Glaring up at him, Hunter snorted. "You wish."

Richard's eyes flared amber, and he dropped low enough that his dick was a hot, hard line against Hunter's hip.

It took every scrap of Hunter's willpower not to reach out and yank him closer. Not to wrap his legs around Richard and demand they get this shit started properly. But he kept his hands splayed out, grasping at the sheets, refusing to give in to the temptation to touch Richard.

The one logical corner of his brain that was still functioning tried to remind him that this was a performance. It wasn't real. Even if Richard was playing it differently, this was just number thirteen for him. There were crew members surrounding them, watching them, filming them, ensuring the lighting was right so the fans would be able to see everything in crystal-clear detail.

Hunter always tried to keep the cameras in mind. Tried to remember angles and what would look best. What the fans wanted.

But at that moment, it was impossible to focus on anything except Richard's lips hovering over his. The heat of him sank into Hunter's body; the smoky scent of him filled his lungs.

Richard's expectations hung in the air between them, his haughty belief that Hunter would break and beg to be claimed.

They'd be there all night if he was waiting for that.

Fuck him. And fuck the cameras. They'd get what they'd get.

Hunter surged up to kiss him. Richard's tongue slid into his mouth and devoured him. His lips were soft against Hunter's, and damn, he tasted delicious.

The kiss seemed to break Richard's resolve to tease Hunter senseless. He pressed down, bringing skin against skin, their hips slotting together, cocks grinding against each other.

Hunter gasped into the kiss, heart racing. The glide of Richard's dick against his was divine. It was all Hunter could do to stop himself from clutching Richard to him, suddenly starved for him.

Richard grinned against his mouth like he could sense that desperation, and he eased his movements to an unhurried drag, drawing out the pleasure until Hunter had to choke off a whimper.

"Ask for it," Richard said. He pulled back and looked at Hunter. "Beg for my knot, and I might give it to you."

Hunter huffed. "Fuck you."

"Uh-uh. That's not how this is going to go."

His grin growing almost indulgent, Richard lowered his head again, sucking on Hunter's neck, leaving another mark before inhaling Hunter's scent like it was oxygen.

Hunter's hands didn't release their hold on the sheets, but they flexed, fighting the instinct to grab Richard's muscular ass so he could rut against him.

Richard inhaled once more, then let loose a throaty

groan, and Hunter quivered at how that pleased, possessive sound pulsed through him.

"Ask me to give you everything," Richard all but purred in his ear, the quietest of whispers.

Hunter swallowed hard, but Richard pulled away, sitting back on his heels between his legs. His hands hooked behind Hunter's knees, fingers tickling enough to make Hunter jerk, before slowly but firmly spreading his legs open as far as they would go, then bending them toward Hunter until his ass was off the bed.

He sat there and stared, his breath accelerated and shallow, his eyes feasting on Hunter.

Hunter'd had cameras all up in his business, filming every part of him in obscene close-up. None of that had left him feeling half as exposed as he did under Richard's ravenous gaze.

A gush of precome leaked out onto his stomach, and he tried to calm himself, to remind himself again that this was a scene. Nothing more than a show.

But the scenes he'd watched hadn't prepared him for this—the intensity of it, how Richard's intoxicating lust stroked over his body, touching him more than the shifter himself was at that moment.

"When you're ready to beg," Richard said, "I'll give you my bite and my knot. But until then..."

The 'fuck you' on Hunter's lips died as Richard leaned down, his tongue finding Hunter's asshole.

Hunter jolted and choked off a cry, his legs trying to close around Richard's head, but Richard's strong hands kept them spread as he circled Hunter's hole with his tongue.

This wasn't fair. None of his research had indicated

Richard was a tease. Sure, he might engage in some occasional orgasm denial, but he never seemed to have the patience for foreplay, never turned his co-stars into mindless messes *before* he started fucking them. He seemed to enjoy getting them to beg after he was buried balls deep in their ass.

Hunter was already stretched; he'd prepped himself before the scene. And that morning, he might have gone a round with a certain magically enhanced dildo he'd become rather fond of over the last month—another thing he wasn't going to admit to anyone. He'd wanted to be good and prepared for this, for taking the real Richard's knot.

But all his efforts just made it easier for Richard to lick into him. Hunter's head fell back, and he struggled to breathe as Richard lapped at his rim, making his ass clench, before pressing the tip of his tongue into Hunter again, teasing the ring of muscle.

That wasn't for the cameras either—his head was in the way; the move was too subtle. It was Richard tasting him, savoring him, trying to drive Hunter out of his mind.

Hunter balled his hands into fists, digging his nails into his palms to prevent himself from grabbing for Richard, from wrapping fingers in his hair and demanding that, if he wanted to make a meal out of him, he should do it properly.

He groaned, unable to stop himself from shaking with need. Richard paused to press a smirk against his inner thigh. It should have been infuriating, but then he was swooping back in, not teasing this time, his tongue fucking into Hunter's hole, and Hunter was too busy trying not to ride his face to be annoyed.

Oh, fuck. Fuck yes. That was exactly what he wanted.

His hips rolled, pushing his ass against Richard's mouth with more force than he'd meant to, but if the guttural noise Richard let out was any indication, he liked it; it spurred him on. He delved deeper inside, thrusting his tongue in over and over, and Hunter's vision blurred, his body quivering as he took Richard's rhythm.

Richard let go of one of his thighs, and then a finger was working into him alongside his tongue, teasing Hunter's rim, making him buck. Richard didn't give him time to adjust, just added another finger, then another. Hunter clenched tight on his hand, and Richard growled against Hunter's ass, the vibrations shooting straight to his dick.

That felt deliriously good, his body eager for the sensations buzzing through him, every nerve ending alight and firing off signals of pleasure.

Fuck, he needed Richard to—

Suddenly, the fingers and tongue were gone.

He tore his eyes away from the ceiling, where he'd been staring in an unfocused haze, and found Richard sitting back, running his hand across his wet, reddened lips.

He cocked an eyebrow at Hunter, a clear 'Well?' written in its arch.

Panting, Hunter glared at him, but it only made Richard more smug.

"Fuck off," Hunter forced out, his voice rough with desire. "I'm not begging."

For some reason, that answer seemed to delight Richard. His eyes took on a devilish gleam. Challenge accepted. Hunter's breath stuttered as he wondered what he'd gotten himself into.

Richard leaned in and snapped his teeth closed over the sensitive flesh of Hunter's inner thigh. Hunter yelped, hips jerking upward, his legs closing convulsively before they were forced open by the viselike grip of Richard's fingers. The piercing bite of teeth was replaced by kisses, then Richard licked over the mark he'd left.

Hunter's eyelids fell shut, only to fly open again when Richard moved up and lapped at a drop of precome. His mouth closed around the head of Hunter's dick, sucking gently, tongue swirling.

A needy groan ripped out of him as Richard took him fully into his mouth, impossibly slow at first, eyes on Hunter the entire time, reading him far too easily. The bastard probably enjoyed watching Hunter reel as pleasure swept over him.

How anyone could manage such an arrogant expression with a dick down their throat, Hunter didn't know, but Richard did, and fuck, he looked gorgeous while doing it.

Hunter had never seen Richard give anyone a blow job. He got them in virtually every scene he was in, but apparently, once a person became a legend, they got worshiped, they didn't do the worshiping.

Which was a shame because damn did Richard know what he was doing.

He bobbed up and down, building to a steady rhythm that had Hunter gasping, his hands moving against his will from their grip on the sheets to fist in Richard's hair. His hips would not stop undulating, chasing the warmth of Richard's mouth.

Richard was emitting a carnal rumble that Hunter felt in his balls more than he heard, the sound more wolf than man as Richard's hot, wet mouth enveloped him. He sucked Hunter's cock like it was his life's purpose, not just his job.

If he kept this up, Hunter wasn't going to last until the actual fucking and knotting.

The thought of Richard knotting him hit him hard, and Hunter groaned, long and desperate.

Richard pulled off him with a final wet pop, flicking his

tongue against the slit and feathering a quick kiss over the head before looking up at Hunter, his eyebrow raised.

"Fuck you." Hunter panted, breathless. "Just fuck me already."

Richard chuckled, a dangerous, devious sound full of unholy promises that sent a thrill racing through Hunter. "That's close enough. This time."

Hunter was unsure how to respond to that, but he didn't have to. Richard hauled him none-too-gently up to the pillows. The sheets slid against his body, a silken counterpoint to the rough handling.

Richard reached under a pillow and fished out the lube the crew had hidden there. He popped the top, not breaking eye contact with Hunter as he drizzled lube into his hand and coated his cock with it, rolling his foreskin over the engorged pink head a few times for Hunter to watch.

Then his hand forced Hunter's thighs wide again, his well-lubed fingers skating along the crease of his ass, grazing over his hole in a teasing brush before he pushed three inside.

Richard's fingers were thick and strong, twisting and spreading and working him open even though Hunter was more than ready.

He didn't seem to care what Hunter was ready for, just kept thrusting his fingers into him, aiming right for his prostate, the onslaught causing a pleasant burn that had Hunter's hips bucking, his body arching off the bed as he bit his lip to keep from cursing the jackass out, to keep from begging for his dick the way Richard wanted him to.

"You know," Richard said, voice infuriatingly smug, "I've fucked virgins with less prep than this."

"Oh, fuck you." Hunter was not the one holding up this show.

"I'm starting to think those are the only words you know, little human. Let's see if we can teach you 'oh god' and 'please' next."

Hunter scoffed. "Oh, god. *Please.*" The sarcasm was heavy and unmistakable in his voice.

Richard laughed, that fucking smirk taking on a fiendish edge, his clean hand coming up to thread through Hunter's hair, the other wandering over his chest.

Hunter's eyes closed as Richard's lips found his, the kiss heated but too brief for his liking. He couldn't complain though, not when Richard broke away to line himself up. Hunter shivered in anticipation.

Richard hummed. "You sure you don't want to beg for it?"

He didn't wait for Hunter's inevitable 'fuck you,' just kissed him again, deep and thorough, ravaging his mouth as the slick, blunt head of his cock sank into him, slow and steady, spearing him open.

This was different too. In every bonding video he'd seen, Richard had taken his co-stars from behind. No kissing as he bonded them, the position ideal for showing off their expressions as his knot stretched them wider and wider.

Richard didn't seem to give a shit about that now. His tongue fucked into Hunter's mouth as relentlessly as his cock slid into his ass.

Knot or no knot, he was thick in his own right, and the stretch was sublime as he buried himself in Hunter's body like it was his home, like he was entitled to fill him fuller than he'd ever been.

Richard pressed forward, not stopping until his balls rested against Hunter's ass. Hunter's head tipped back, his body shuddering as he dug his heels into the mattress.

No dick should feel this satisfying; like it was made for him, made to fill him so completely and thoroughly full.

Hunter's breath came in short, sharp gasps, and Richard pushed himself up onto his forearms. Hunter expected a taunting expression, another invitation to beg. Instead, there was a soft look on Richard's face, a quiet smile on his lips—still hungry, but such a contrast from every other time Hunter had seen him, all brash and conceited, well aware of how hot he was, how many people wanted him.

This Richard was worlds apart and infinitely more attractive. He stared, eyes locked on Hunter as he eased out, then pressed back in, his pace agonizingly slow. He did it again and again and again, each movement deliberate and controlled, aim dead-on and merciless.

His gaze never left Hunter's face, seeing every emotion, every sensation play out, that soft smile gaining a cocksure edge as he found the perfect angle to make Hunter writhe with need, to make his vision go white.

Hunter's hands gripped Richard's back, his knees locking around his waist, his whole body trembling as the blazing pleasure inside him intensified, taking him to the brink of insanity.

He felt that rumble in Richard's chest again as he put his forehead against Hunter's, their noses bumping. The rigid length in Hunter's ass continued its leisurely drag as Richard inhaled his scent.

His mouth trailed over to Hunter's ear. "Ready for me?" he asked, and for once, his tone was devoid of arrogance.

"Fuck yes," Hunter breathed out.

Richard pulled almost all the way out, then rammed back in. Not gentle. Not even close. Hard, hot, and demanding. Exactly what Hunter wanted. The snap of Richard's hips pounded into his ass, pinning him against the bed.

Richard's exhales danced over his neck, quick and impatient as he held Hunter there, as he fucked him open, deep and insistent. His growl built to a near snarl.

Sharp teeth scraped against his skin, and Hunter whimpered—actually fucking whimpered—with how much he wanted what was about to happen. He'd be embarrassed by that, but he was too consumed by needing Richard's teeth to sink into him, needing Richard to claim him, to make him so thoroughly his that he branded himself on Hunter's goddamn soul.

Richard's hand worked into Hunter's hair again, yanking his head to the side, giving him complete access to his neck.

"*Yes*," Hunter hissed. "Do it."

Richard's teeth closed around the juncture of his neck, and Hunter moaned, low and shameless, only to have that cry hitch in his throat as Richard bit down carefully, savoring it to the fullest.

Hunter's head snapped back, a shudder racing up his spine. He gave a long, helpless whine.

Even the pain was heavenly, and it became his entire world—a bitter-sweet bliss as Richard's canines punctured his skin.

Something bloomed inside him, something new and exquisite, and his world spun as he realized what it was.

It was Richard, now a feverish ball of sensation in his mind, an insatiable need that matched his own, a torrent of instincts that weren't his, yet somehow were, at the same time.

Richard's pleasure washed over him, washed through him—the tight heat of Hunter's ass around him, the demanding throb of his knot expanding, the need to be tied together, to fill Hunter with his come, to let everyone know who he belonged to.

The moan that escaped Hunter's throat was high and broken, a keening wail.

He fixated on Richard's shoulder, his jaw aching with the sudden urge to sink his teeth into the muscle there, to leave a mark of his own, to stake his claim in return.

All he could feel was Richard. His fangs piercing deep, hands greedy and grasping, his cock thick and hard, driving into him, every thrust stretching him further. All he could smell was Richard, some intoxicating mix of smoke and wood and sex on his skin. All he could hear was the sound of their fucking, their harsh pants, the slick noises of Richard pumping in and out of him, the slap of his heavy balls against his ass.

Richard broke away from his neck, but not before dragging kisses along the now-tender skin. Hunter bit off a curse, squirming on his dick, and fuck if Richard didn't love how that felt. The perfection of it cascaded through him, then crashed into Hunter, making him squirm that much more.

He braced himself over Hunter, staring at him, eyes devouring him.

There was no arrogance in his gaze, only hunger and something that made Hunter feel foolishly like he was the most beautiful thing Richard had ever seen.

Richard watched as Hunter gasped and took his expanding knot, each withdrawal catching more on Hunter's rim, each thrust needing more force to plunge back in, drawing little hoarse, punched-out noises from Hunter that drove Richard to take him harder.

In Hunter's mind, Richard's presence smoldered with

satisfaction, half-physical—Hunter around his knot, their scents mixing and filling his lungs—and half something more primal, something deeper that Hunter couldn't understand. Couldn't even try to work out when he was this close to coming and didn't have a hand on himself. He never came like this, but he knew Richard was going to make him do just that. The thought of it alone had him shaking, and still Richard stared, watching him come undone, like there was nothing else he'd rather see. Richard's eyes were alight, a constant amber glow filling them, so focused, so intent.

Hunter couldn't look away either, his world narrowing down to Richard and the need to come—both his and Richard's.

He was so close. *Richard* was so close. He needed to knot Hunter, and he needed to do it *now*.

Hunter had no idea whether that was his thought or Richard's, but it didn't matter.

Richard ran a hand over his skin as if trying to memorize his body, his claws out, scraping hard enough to leave trails in their wake.

"I've been waiting to do this. Waiting to show you exactly how good I can make you feel." His hips snapped into Hunter, hitting his prostate each time, his knot expanding to the point he could scarcely get it back in. "Waiting to knot you. To make you mine."

Hunter clenched down, locking them together, earning an animalistic growl from Richard that had every muscle in Hunter's body straining for release. The euphoria echoing between them swelled with Richard's knot until Hunter was almost unbearably full, too full to even breathe.

Movement limited, Richard ground into him, his knot a relentless pressure that had Hunter clinging to him as Richard demanded his release, not saying it, but demanding all the same. Demanding Hunter come on his cock.

"You're mine," Richard rumbled in Hunter's ear. His claws dug into Hunter's skin, borderline painful if not for the thundering orgasm about to explode through Hunter.

Tension built in Hunter's balls, and Richard's teeth grazed along his neck, gentle this time, settling over the bite mark, coaxing a strangled noise from him that rose into a breathy scream as Richard bit him harder.

Richard's pleasure shimmered through their bond. There was no separating the two of them, no knowing where his body ended and Richard's began. He was on fire, blazing from the inside out.

It was too much. He'd been too close for too long. He couldn't take it anymore. Richard's knot was stretching him open, caught on his rim, his hot cock buried as deep as it'd go, grinding into him until Hunter nearly sobbed with it, his eyes screwed shut.

He tried to cry out, but it twisted into a soul-racking howl. He came, spilling between them, the warmth of his release making Richard's teeth clamp down on the fresh bite mark as he followed, pumping spurt after spurt of come into Hunter, a feral snarl on his lips.

The world dissolved into white noise and unimaginable bliss as he floated with Richard, tied together, their ecstasy reverberating between them.

Hunter didn't think he'd ever be able to move again, didn't think he'd ever be the same.

His eyelids fluttered against the bright lights of the room, his breath nothing but rough gasps, his body racked with the aftershocks that coursed through him.

The sound coming out of Richard was a pleased purr as he nosed at Hunter's neck, then nipped at his ear.

Off to the side, a shutter clicked, and Hunter jumped, the reality of the situation crashing in around him.

He blinked up at the ceiling, suddenly aware of the cameras surrounding them, how many people were in the room with them, how they'd all seen *that*.

No matter how tenderly Richard was holding him, how he was still moving in him, the motion lingering in a way that tested Hunter's sanity, it wasn't real. It was a scene. It was for their contract.

Their temporary contract.

Richard rumbled another low, "Mine," in his ear, and that seemed like a headfuck now that the moment was over. Now that Hunter's body was cooling and he remembered why they were there. That an hour ago, he hadn't even met Richard.

No wonder people got messed up by this. By this jackass saying shit that made them think it was more than it was. MateHub must cut these bits out of the scenes. Maybe dubbed over them. He couldn't blame people for thinking Richard meant what he said when that warm ball of pleasure was in their mind, so smug and satisfied and content—emotions that weren't their own, but felt like they could be.

Well, that shit would not be convincing Hunter. He would not be falling for this asshole's mind games.

Richard sucked on his bite mark, and Hunter arched up, gasping despite himself, only one thought in his head.

What the fuck had he signed up for?

FIVE

Fuck, Hunter smelled good covered in Richard's scent. Just as perfect as Richard had known he would. It was an intoxicating combination, better than any thrall a vampire could hope to produce, better than any incubus's lure.

This was what he'd been missing every time he'd done one of these scenes—this scent surrounding him, this man under him.

The warm ball of pleasure in his mind chilled, growing spiky and cold, and Richard pulled back, needing to see Hunter's face.

Before he could, a sharp blow struck his leg. Richard snarled, turning, his knot tugging where he and Hunter were connected, making them both groan.

He blinked away the stars of ecstasy that swam through his vision, then looked over to see what had hit him.

The main cameraman, Rhys, stood there, an eyebrow cocked. He wiggled the camera he was holding, then made an impatient gesture with his free hand, from Richard to Hunter, then back with a jerk.

Oh, right. He had a job to do.

This was the shot everyone was waiting for.

Although his knot hadn't fully deflated, it'd gone down enough that he'd be able to pull out.

He leaned back so Rhys could get in close, then withdrew slowly, his half-full knot catching on Hunter's rim, stretching him wide.

Hunter gave a breathy moan as Richard's knot popped out of him with an audible squelch. A gush of come followed.

Shot or not, at the sight of that, Richard couldn't stop himself from diving in, every instinct in his body demanding he bring his mouth to Hunter's hole and lick him clean.

Hunter cursed, his fingers weaving into Richard's hair as he writhed on his tongue. He tasted as good as he smelled, and Richard wanted to flip him over, get his ass in the air, and eat him out until his jaw ached. Until Hunter finally did beg to be fucked.

He gripped Hunter's hips, about to do that, when Hunter yanked on his hair. Richard glanced up at him, at his lust-blown eyes, the heightened color in his cheeks, how thoroughly fucked he appeared.

"Let me taste you," Hunter gasped out.

Something was off about how he said it, something not as desperate as Richard needed him to be, but he couldn't say no to a request like that. He slipped fingers into Hunter's stretched hole alongside his tongue, twisting them, stroking them across Hunter's over-sensitized prostate, earning him a few more filthy curses, then he gathered up a load of his come and held his hand out.

Hunter didn't hesitate, just leaned forward and sucked his fingers into his mouth, his eyes jumping to the side for a second. He gave an almost imperceptible nod, but then his gaze was locking on Richard's as his tongue stripped away every trace of his release.

God, that was hot. If Hunter kept that up, Richard would be ready to go a second round in no time.

There was another strike to his leg, making him growl again. The next time someone did that, they'd be leaving this studio horizontally. In a bag.

But Hunter shook his head. "Let them see," he said, his voice wrecked.

It took effort, but Richard moved away so Hunter could spread his legs and let Rhys zoom in on his used hole, still leaking come. Hunter slid a hand down, toying with his entrance before skating his fingers up through the mess on his abs. Rhys panned up his come-splattered chest to his satisfied face.

Richard swelled with pride, knowing the world would now get to see how well he'd fucked his mate, how he'd marked him, how no one could satisfy Hunter but him.

He wanted to do it again, to have Hunter on his dick, moaning his name so no one would forget who Hunter belonged to. Who Richard belonged to. His cock throbbed at the idea.

Yeah. He'd do that. Push Rhys out of the way. Sink into Hunter's heat.

"Cut," Brandt called out, chuckling uncomfortably, his voice strangled. "Well, that's not how we normally do things, but that's a wrap."

Richard's wolf retreated, smug and satisfied, its job done, leaving Richard to deal with the aftermath.

The haze he'd been in lifted, and he looked around, remembering where he was. Brandt's eyebrows seemed to have permanently relocated to his hairline, while Everett's expression could only be described as thunderstruck arousal.

Most of the crew smelled turned on, and it made Richard want to cover Hunter's body with his own, to growl at them until they got the hell out of there and left them alone.

He blinked again. He wanted to *what*?

No. He didn't want to do anything of the sort.

Hunter stood, for a moment looking like his knees might give out. He exhaled a laugh as shaky as his legs and grinned.

"Thanks for that, man," he said, nodding to Richard. His dark hair was in wild disarray, his lips red from their kisses. "I haven't come that hard in days."

Richard froze, his mouth hanging open.

Days?

He'd given Hunter the best damn orgasm of his life. What the hell was he talking about? In *days*?

"Okay," Brandt said. "We'll see you both on location in two weeks."

Two weeks?

Oh, fuck, that was right. Reduced schedule. The next scene wasn't until the full moon.

He was going to fire Daniel for how poorly this contract had been negotiated. Why would they wait *two weeks* to do another scene? That was a waste of time and a waste of a perfectly good knot that was throbbing to get back into Hunter's ass.

No, not Hunter's. It didn't have to be Hunter's.

Anyone's ass.

Hunter slipped on the robe Everett handed him, covering up all his pretty skin and the marks Richard had left on him, and then he was walking away, stride wobbly but determined, heading to his dressing room.

What the fuck did he think he was doing, just leaving? Shouldn't he want Richard to take care of him, to wrap him up in his arms and hold him? That was what the others had wanted. They'd wanted Richard to stay with them, to not leave them. They hadn't strolled to their dressing rooms as if Richard had only given them the best orgasm they'd had in *days*.

What the actual fuck?

Why didn't Hunter want Richard to cuddle him?

Or to fuck him again this goddamn second?

Could he not see Richard was half-hard?

Wait. Why would he care if Hunter wanted to be cuddled? That wasn't his job.

"You alright there?" Brandt asked, and Richard jumped, belatedly realizing he was staring at the closed door of Hunter's dressing room.

"Fine." Richard forced himself to look anywhere else. "See you in two weeks."

That last part absolutely did not come out as a snarl.

He stalked past Everett, who was holding out his robe for him, and made his way to his own dressing room.

What had just happened?

Why was he feeling the need to care for Hunter? To tuck him into bed and pamper him. Bring him his favorite foods. Chase away anything and everything that worried him. And then, when he'd done that, fuck him, slow and deep. Take his time. Make damn sure it wasn't just the best orgasm he'd had in *days*.

Days.

Fuck that.

He didn't slam the door behind him. An upset person

would do that, and he wasn't upset. Though, once inside, he did growl to himself.

Fucking humans. There was something not right with Hunter. That had to be it. No one casually walked away after Richard knotted them.

He entered the small attached bathroom and cranked on the shower, but when he went to step inside the cubicle, he stopped.

Did he really need a shower? He'd showered that morning, and California was in a drought. Shouldn't he be conserving water?

He pulled a face.

What. The. Fuck?

He sniffed himself and groaned at the combination of Hunter and sex on his skin. God, Hunter's scent was sinful. It'd be a crime to wash it off, to dilute the way it wrapped itself around Richard, soft and strong and so goddamn perfect.

The thought smacked into him like a semi-truck, backed over him, then rammed into him again.

Hunter smelled good. On him.

No.

No, no, no.

Uh-uh.

This wasn't happening.

He forced himself into the shower and scrubbed himself clean.

Mostly clean.

Sort of clean.

He might not have been as thorough about it as he could have been, but that wasn't his fault. He was in a hurry.

After he toweled himself dry, he grabbed his phone and opened the group chat with his two closest friends.

RICHARD

We need to have dinner tonight.

The response was immediate.

MAX

Most people need to have dinner every night.

RICHARD

Fuck you.

The moment Richard sent it, it reminded him of Hunter, and he cursed.

RICHARD

I need to talk to you both ASAP.

HARDIN

You filmed a bonding scene today, didn't you? Did the human catch feelings already?

RICHARD

Meet me at Palacio. 6PM.

MAX

Ask nicely.

Why was everything reminding him of Hunter?

RICHARD

Drinks on me.

MAX

Ah, the magic words. Free drinks.

HARDIN

Did you ever think we might have plans or a date?

RICHARD

With each other?

They sent *NO*s at the exact same time.

RICHARD

If you two aren't sitting next to each other on the couch at one of your apartments playing some shitty video game as I type this, I won't just buy your drinks at dinner, I'll blow you both.

That idea sat low and sick in his stomach, and Richard grimaced. He'd done scenes with both his friends before. But now the thought of touching them was making him queasy.

He breathed through it.

MAX

Eh, you suck at blow jobs.

RICHARD

I do not.

HARDIN

How many people can verify that? Six?

Seven. Now.

RICHARD

Are you assholes available for dinner and drinks or not?

HARDIN

We'll be there. No blow jobs required.

MAX

But bring your credit card. I'm drinking the place dry.

God, he hated his friends.

He huffed and tossed his phone on the vanity while he dressed.

When he was finished, he ran a hand through his damp hair and exited his dressing room... and found himself heading to Hunter's. He hesitated a second before knocking.

After a long stretch, Hunter answered, freshly showered and entirely too clean. The kind of clean that was asking to be dirtied.

His warm brown eyes darted past Richard, then back, confusion on his face.

"Do you need a ride?" Richard asked before he could stop himself.

Hunter frowned. "A ride?"

"To the apartment."

"Oh. I thought MateHub was sending a car for me?"

Like they usually did.

"Right. But my car is here. And we're going to the same place. So, I thought, maybe, you'd want a ride."

Hunter scrutinized Richard like he'd never seen him before, like he suspected Richard might want to speak to him about an extended warranty on a car he didn't own, then answered. "Uh. Sure? Hold on."

He shut the door in Richard's face.

The little ball that was Hunter's presence in his mind was a jumbled, dull buzz that Richard couldn't begin to untangle. But he'd never attempted to read those emotions in the past; there was no reason he should want to now.

He'd heard people talk about their bonds, how they were these beautiful connections that lived and breathed between themselves and their mate. Richard had never felt like that. He'd always pushed the connection as far from himself as possible, kept it compartmentalized, firmly not part of himself, just an annoying mental interloper for a few months. Not something he'd ever wanted to delve into, to explore, to deepen until it tied him to someone so completely there was no separating them.

Who in their right mind would want that?

A few minutes later, Hunter reappeared, looking vaguely suspicious and carrying a large duffel bag.

Richard stared at it.

Oh, shit. He hadn't thought this through, had he? Any of it.

He didn't offer to take the bag, and he didn't want to. Not at all. He didn't take bags for people. Just like he didn't care about their emotions.

"This way." He led Hunter out of the studio.

A significant chunk of forever had passed since he'd stepped onto the sixth floor earlier that day, and it took equally as long for the damn elevator to arrive.

Once they were inside, it crawled down the building.

Richard needed to suggest they pump music into this thing. It was too quiet in there. Who'd ever heard of an elevator without music? And since when did this ride take longer than a direct flight to Australia?

After they passed approximately one hundred stories to get to the ground floor, each excruciating second filling the cramped space with Hunter's scent, they crossed the parking lot to his car.

When Richard hit the button to unlock the doors and the lights on his SF90 flashed, Hunter whistled softly. His eyes traced over its sculpted, aerodynamic contours and velvety red sheen.

"Now that is a fucking car," he said, voice appropriately reverent.

Not for the first time that day, Richard wanted to preen. His car was sexy as fuck. It was good Hunter appreciated it.

But then Hunter tilted his head. "It doesn't have a trunk, right?"

"It has a frunk," Richard said, doing everything in his power not to rub a hand over his neck. "My bag is in there."

"So..." Hunter lifted his duffel and raised an eyebrow at him.

"There's room in the car."

Kind of.

Hunter had to sit with it half in his lap and half spilling over the center console, but at least he hummed in appreciation at the purr of the engine when Richard started it.

That was the only smooth thing about the drive to the MateHub apartment. It was as awkward as the elevator ride, though at least there was music and traffic was light.

Richard had no idea what to say to Hunter. He knew nothing about him, minus how sublime he felt clenching around his cock, and that was not exactly a conversation starter.

He'd never realized how small his car was, but like the elevator, it became saturated with Hunter's scent at an alarming rate. His scent that rubbed up against Richard, stroked over him, filling his lungs.

His co-stars' scents had never been remotely appealing. He couldn't say the same about Hunter's.

It was a feat of willpower not to lean over at red lights, to get closer, to breathe him in. To run his hands all over Hunter and mark him with his scent. He still smelled like

Richard, but not nearly enough, and Richard itched to rectify that.

Not that it'd be easy with the duffel bag in the way.

A couple decades later—though the clock claimed it'd been less than ten minutes—he pulled into the apartment's assigned spot. He grabbed the duffel and opened his door, but as he tried to get out, there was a tug.

"I can get it, thanks," Hunter said.

Richard forced his hand to let go, finger by finger.

He got out, popping the hood to grab his bag.

Hunter peered at it. "You have a custom-made ba—No. Of course you do."

Well, obviously. A regular suitcase didn't fit in a Ferrari.

Richard turned and walked inside, steeling himself for another drawn-out ride up to the fourth-floor apartment he lived in almost as often as his own.

He unlocked the door and let Hunter in.

Hunter looked around, eyes wide as he took in the spacious kitchen and the living room with its massive TV. "This is a lot nicer than my place."

Richard's brow furrowed. It wasn't even close to nicer than his. But he supposed Hunter was still new to the industry.

"So..." Hunter said. "Are there rules I need to know?"

"Rules?"

"About the apartment. The contract said I have to live here, but do I have to be here the whole time? Is it fine if I go out and see friends?"

Richard's frown deepened. "You don't want to be here?"

"Well, I mean, for sleep, or whatever's required? But I'd rather not hang out here all day. Unless I have to. The contract didn't say."

The realization that he didn't want Hunter to leave

settled uneasily in Richard's chest. He wanted to keep him in the apartment, reclaim him until he was so covered in his scent, there was no doubt who he belonged to. Maybe then Hunter could go out.

But there was no way in hell Richard actually wanted that. He didn't fuck his co-stars outside their scheduled scenes. It was forbidden by the terms of their contracts, and more than that, it might give them the wrong impression.

It had to be the new bond acting up—an odd hiccup that would pass. Likely caused by how very human Hunter was. Nothing more.

"It's fine," he said instead. "You can come and go whenever. MateHub insists on adding the clause about living together. I have no idea why. Some bullshit about it being a precaution to avoid adverse reactions if the bonded co-stars are apart too soon. I keep trying to get them to drop it."

"Oh, thank god. I would have lost my mind if I were trapped here for three months. What would I even do? It's a nice place, but no thank you." Hunter carried his bag into the first bedroom. The one Richard always claimed.

Richard didn't list the ridiculous number of things they could do if they were trapped in this apartment for three months.

Not that any of them were appealing in the least.

"Well, I guess I'll see you around," Hunter said, doing a quick three-tap check—phone, wallet, and the keys MateHub must have left in his dressing room—then heading out the door.

As it closed behind him, Richard had to physically restrain himself from following. A bubble of anxiety formed in his chest, but he shoved it aside.

This was what he wanted. He didn't like clingy co-stars

who whined to be with him constantly for the entire three months.

Hunter was perfect.

Too perfect.

With a growl, he tossed his bag into the second bedroom, the one with the view that wasn't quite as scenic, then grabbed his keys and left.

The elevator and his car smelled of Hunter.

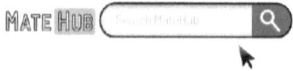

Max and Hardin were already at El Palacio del Gato Crítico when he arrived, sitting at their usual table in the dimly lit restaurant and bar, two drinks in front of them both. A few patrons were casting glances at them, clearly appreciative of their tall, muscular frames and charismatic presence. Max's untamed energy, olive skin, and the black waves framing his face lent him a rugged charm, while Hardin exuded a quiet confidence with his short dark brown hair and tan complexion.

They'd started working for MateHub around the same time Richard had, and the three of them had fallen into an unofficial pack. There weren't many people he could talk to freely about his job, but Hardin and Max were at the top of that list.

Palacio—with its eclectic mix of vintage and cat-themed decor—had become their spot years ago, the place they went to relax and blow off steam, even if Hardin insisted the food wasn't half as good as his abuela's. He had fewer complaints about their extensive drink selection.

Like most nights, a live band was playing, the music

loud enough the human patrons wouldn't overhear them talking about the literal ins and outs of paranormal porn.

Their table was tucked in a corner next to a wall adorned with a mural of a majestic white-and-gray cat who had a whole lot of fluff and a judgmental gaze that silently critiqued Richard's every move as he stalked over to join them and plopped down into a chair.

"Why do you look shell-shocked?" Max asked between sips of a fruity drink roughly the size of his head. His piercing amber eyes glittered in the low light.

"Tell me the human doesn't smell good on me." Richard pretended that didn't sound desperate.

Max and Hardin exchanged a look, their eyebrows climbing in unison, then leaned toward him, inhaling.

Their noses wrinkled.

"First off," Hardin said, "you reek of sex. Did you even shower?"

"Fuck you. I showered after the scene."

Max huffed, muttering, "Not good enough," under his breath.

Hardin continued. "And second, I guess so? Better than anybody else you've bonded before, at least. But that's a low bar. I don't know. Humans have such subtle scents when they aren't bathing themselves in all that shit they wear. It's difficult to tell how he smells on you."

Max nodded. "It's definitely less annoying than everyone else has been, but that's probably because he's human and his scent is so weak to begin with. Less of it to rub off on you."

Richard couldn't have disagreed more. Hunter's scent might be soft, but it was *not* subtle. It was all over him and stronger than any human's scent should have been.

But they weren't wrong. Humans didn't have magic or

75

energy or any supernatural power to amplify their scent. They still had unique scents, but they were less defined.

Maybe Hunter was secretly a mage?

Richard knew that wasn't it. There was no trace of magic on him. That scent was unmistakable.

"Wait." Hardin narrowed his hazel eyes. "Didn't you meet him before the scene to see how he smelled on you?"

"Ah," Richard said, once again feeling the urge to rub his neck. "I may have told Daniel I didn't need to meet him beforehand."

"Dude," Max said. "Seriously? You cocky asshole. Were you trying to play Russian roulette?"

Richard didn't wince; he scoffed instead. "As if there's any chance I'm compatible with a human."

Max snorted in return. "Sure. Which is why you look like your entire world just got turned on its head, then fucked harder than some lucky bastard at a packbang."

Richard wished he could deny it and tell himself Hunter didn't smell good on him, that they weren't compatible in any way, but he couldn't ignore how not knowing where Hunter was and what he was doing was making him restless and twitchy.

His wolf had never given a shit about the people he bonded. It'd never acted like it had today, never stayed so close to the surface, bordering on feral with the instinct to fuck and bite and claim and knot.

Before he could think better of it, he asked, "Have either of your wolves ever reacted strongly to anyone you were filming with? Basically taking over?"

On a new moon, no less.

Their eyes darted toward each other, then quickly away.

"No," Max said as Hardin answered, "Never."

Right. He was a moron. Why had he bothered asking?

Of course they'd never thought about another MateHub performer in a way that wasn't strictly professional. Why else would they, for some reason, never have done a scene with just the two of them? No matter how many requests for one MateHub received from fans. It had to be a coincidence, not years of repressed longing.

He could ask his sist—No. Not worth the amount of shit he'd get for asking how her wolf had reacted when she'd first met her mate.

Hardin cleared his throat, still looking away from Max. "Why? Did your wolf take over? Does it like Hunter?"

Richard shrugged. "Eh. It thinks he's tolerable. You guys are right. It's just how weak human scents are."

Neither of them seemed convinced, but they were also too distracted by not looking at each other to push the issue.

It was fine. Even if Hunter's scent and his were compatible and his wolf had some mistaken ideas about that. Even if it had been the best sex he'd had. In *days*. It was fine. All of that meant nothing. It'd only mean something if they decided it did, and Richard would not be doing that. As long as there were no emotions involved, it'd never go further than this transactional bond.

His career was amazing, and if he were to get involved with his co-star, it would spell trouble for them both. He didn't need a true bond. If he had one of those, he wouldn't be able to perform with anyone else, and who needed a porn star who could only do scenes with one person? That might be acceptable for amateurs, but not for someone like him.

He was a knotting legend. He'd done this a dozen times. There was no chance of him becoming attached to Hunter over the next three months, and after this contract, he'd get that blackout on his bingo card.

It was fine. Not a problem.

He flagged down a waiter.

Max had the right idea about drinking the place dry. It'd certainly be better than going back to an empty apartment.

Not that he cared what the apartment's current state of occupation was.

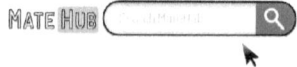

SCENE: *Bonding the Human*

MagicalHWood:
When they advertised this as "Richard Knotz's Hottest Bonding Scene EVER!" I had my doubts. My doubts were decimated. JFC.

KnottyWolf69:
All his growling? I've never heard him sound so pleased and possessive before. He was almost purring.

MagicalHWood:
Fuck, man. I could have come from the sound alone. Where do I find someone to growl over me like that?

snikerdoodleme:
And that snarl when the cameraman went in for a close-up? So fucking hot.

KnottyWolf69:
Richard is always a fucking legend, but this was NEXT LEVEL. New favorite.

jovij405:
I'll be wearing out the replay button on this video, damn.

MagicalHWood:
Same. Can't wait to see what other scenes they do.

BramStroker:
Has Richard ever given anyone a post-knotting rim job? Fuck, that was hot.

KnottyWolf69:
His claws were out at the end. His wolf must have been really into it.

snikerdoodleme:
I wonder if they filmed it on the full moon and were just super slow to release it.

MagicalHWood:
They usually do the hunting scenes on a full moon though, so probably not.

BramStroker:
If this wasn't him at his wolfiest, can you imagine how intense the hunt is going to be? Richard growling while he pins Hunter down and fucks him in the forest?

KnottyWolf69:
I literally came five minutes ago, but I'm getting hard from just the thought of it.

jovij405:
Also, Hunter is FEISTY. Most of Richard's co-stars are ass-up for him in a fraction of the time. Loved seeing him work for it.

HuntMeDown:
I see you losers have come around to the hotness of DickHunt.

MagicalHWood:
We are NOT calling them that.

HuntMeDown:
You will.

KnottyWolf69:
Fuck off, kid.

BramStroker:
I don't know. DickHunt has a nice ring to it.

MagicalHWood:
You're saying that to get spammed with more Richard GIFs, aren't you?

BramStroker:
I would NEVER.

BramStroker:
PS Make sure they're all from this video.

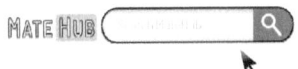

CHAPTER
SIX

"God," Chance groaned for roughly the hundredth time in three days. "You reek like dog. Why do you smell so much like him?"

They were lounging on the floor of their tiny living room, junk food scattered around them as they leaned against the couch—a position far more comfortable than actually sitting on the battered piece of furniture.

"You're imagining things," Hunter said as he started *Beastbound Brawlers*.

They'd already played half a dozen other games that day, but had saved their favorite for last. They could play the arena battle game for hours, and that was exactly what Hunter planned to do.

It was late afternoon. If they played as long as usual, it'd be after nine by the time he returned to the MateHub apartment.

Hunter wouldn't say he was avoiding it. That would be foolish. There was no reason to do that.

"I'm not imagining anything," Chance insisted, calling

on his Starwhisper Sentinel and getting her ready for battle. "Your scents are all mixed and shit."

Hunter sniffed himself. "I guess, kind of?"

It wasn't bad. Almost like wearing a cologne, but fainter. Eau de Richard. MateHub should bottle it and sell it with his other merch.

Not that he was going to say that to Chance. Instead, he busied himself with preparing his Emberlore Phoenix to fight Chance's Beast.

"There's no 'kind of' about it. You reek, and it'll just get worse."

"Get worse?"

"Your scent will be covered even more in dog."

"I figured that much. But why would the dog scent increase?"

"It's the bond. The deeper it goes, the more connected you become and the more you smell like each other."

Hunter laughed. "Yeah, right. That's not happening. Don't worry. This is the most dog-like I'll be smelling."

He had no interest in deepening the bond, whatever that meant. It'd probably require interacting with Richard. Who was clearly a smug asshole he didn't want to be around. One he absolutely wasn't feeling some weird-ass pull toward. One who hadn't landed a starring role in an extensive list of fantasies that were varied and filthy enough, they'd put even the MateHub writers to shame.

Nope. Not at all.

That wasn't something he'd do after a round of... decent sex. Fairly mediocre, passable sex.

It also wasn't the reason he'd been spending most of his time with Chance at his actual apartment instead of the MateHub one. It was just that his things were here.

Chance shot him a skeptical look.

"Why do you have so little faith in me?" Hunter asked. "I'm not going to fall for a guy because he has a nice dick." Even if it was a *very* nice dick. "If that were the case, I would have confessed my love to his merchandise a month ago."

Though, now that he'd had the real thing, the replica wasn't as appealing.

"How is it?"

"His dick?"

"No, you ass. Being bonded to him."

"I don't know." Hunter frowned. "I've got this little bundle of *something* in my head. It's obviously him, but beyond that, I don't feel any different."

"Bonded couples are supposed to feel what their mate is feeling. Emotions and sensations and whatever."

"No, I don't—" Hunter paused, considering. "Okay, after he bit me, during the scene, definitely. It was bizarre, but also insanely hot. You'd love it. You know how much you enjoy being in the middle of a threesome? It's a little like that."

"Fucking while being fucked? I'm listening."

"I was getting thoroughly pounded, but I could also feel what he was feeling. Feel how he felt me. How hot and tight I was around his dick. But after that? Once the scene was over? Nothing, really. Like I said, he's in my head, but sort of distant? It's like seeing someone from far away. You recognize them but can't see their expression or anything. If that makes sense?"

Chance looked thoughtful, then nodded. "That's good. Keep it that way. If you start feeling things when you aren't touching, that means the bond is deepening."

"Seriously, stop worrying about it. I'm not getting attached to some jackass who thinks too highly of himself."

"Okaaaay."

"Okay your ass. I have better taste than that."

"You remember I knew you in college, right?"

"Like you didn't bring home your fair share of losers and assholes."

They started the arena showdown, their Beasts squaring off, as their conversation devolved into a competition over who had brought the worst guy back to their place. The latter was an easier fight for Hunter to win. He'd never brought home anyone who'd fucked him then tried to steal their laptops on his way out, or anyone who'd spent an hour throwing up *near* their toilet before offering them both blow jobs because he 'loved them so much.'

There'd also been the Blue Balls Incident, when Hunter had stumbled out of his room in the small hours of the night to go to the bathroom, only to find himself face-to-face with a naked guy who looked like he'd dipped his balls in bright blue paint. Hunter still wasn't sure that one hadn't been a fever dream, but Chance's lips had appeared to have a slight blue tint in the morning, and he hadn't wanted to ask.

He killed the rest of the evening with Chance, then headed back to his temporary apartment, swinging by the in-house gym for a quick workout that might have taken the better part of an hour.

After an entire day sitting on his ass, it felt good to move again, and he'd never had access to a gym as nice as this before, with all its shiny new equipment to choose from. He ran on a treadmill until he was dripping with sweat and tired enough he'd have no problem falling asleep the moment he was in bed.

When he eventually made it up to the apartment, Richard was reclining on the couch, reading on his phone.

They exchanged nods, and Hunter retreated to his room for the night. At least it had an excellent view.

CHAPTER
SEVEN

For the seventh day in a row, Richard woke to the building buzz of arousal and bit off a curse.

Hunter was at it again. Like he'd been every morning since the new moon.

Richard clenched his hands and tried to ignore it, but that was impossible. Although their shallow bond muffled the sensations, his dick still responded, morning wood coming fully to life as he lay in bed, glaring up at the ceiling.

"I'm not doing this," he muttered.

Even though it'd been a week since he'd gotten off, and the hot ball of need in his mind was making it difficult to maintain that streak.

It was an annoying quirk of the bond. Regardless of how deep the connection was, the sex was amazing, but there was also no way to get off without your bonded co-star feeling it. Which meant, to keep things from escalating to something that was expressly forbidden, it was considered impolite to jerk off during the contract.

Normally, it wasn't a big deal, but that was when they were filming a scene or two a week. Richard could go a few days without getting off. He didn't love it, but it was what it was—part of the whole bonding contract experience. Plus, he used that pent-up energy in his scenes, and his fans loved it.

This time, he had to wait two fuck-less weeks, and apparently, no one had told Hunter how easily physical pleasure transferred through a bond. He hadn't realized it by himself yet, either. With as fresh as their bond was, with them not touching, he likely wasn't feeling much beyond an extra kick to his arousal that he hadn't noticed wasn't his own.

That, or he enjoyed torturing Richard with his regular orgasms.

Richard had zero interest in telling him. That conversation would be entirely too awkward. Just like he had zero interest in taking himself in hand and stroking in time with Hunter's pleasure, letting their orgasms build together, feeding off each other, giving everything that additional edge that made bonded sex so fucking good.

As if reminding him of how neglectful he'd been, his knot gave a dull ache, and he squeezed the base of his dick, groaning.

God, it would be so easy to get himself off like this.

Or better yet, to sink into Hunter's heat, to knot him, to relieve the days-long case of blue balls he'd been suffering.

But he wasn't going to do that. He had no intention of deepening the bond further than necessary. Hunter would get the wrong idea.

If Richard's supernatural co-stars couldn't understand the difference between orgasm-driven endorphins and actual emotions, how would a human ever manage?

Richard kept his co-stars at arm's length for a reason.

They could let their hormones convince them they were in love all they wanted; it wasn't real.

Give it a few more months, after the dopamine and cortisol cocktail wore off, and they'd come to their senses and realize they were in a relationship with someone incompatible, that they had a bond deepened by months of sex but no genuine feelings. That was a recipe for resentment and more pain when the bond was inevitably severed. Richard was doing them a favor, even if none of them appreciated it.

Morning routine aside, Hunter was exactly what he'd hoped for in a co-star. He was in the apartment long enough to sleep, get ready, and leave. Then Richard had the place to himself.

No reason to mess that up.

The pleasure in the back of his mind spiked, and Richard groaned, bracing himself. He fisted his hands in the sheets, his toes curling as he gritted his teeth against the euphoric rush. His dick twitched, precome leaking onto his stomach.

Hunter's orgasm rolled through Richard, leaving him panting, wanting nothing more than to stalk to Hunter's room and demand he take responsibility for the consequences of his actions.

Instead, he breathed through it, trying to think his least sexy thoughts, even if those thoughts kept getting interrupted by the memory of Hunter underneath him, making the sweetest little whimpering sounds as he came, clenching tight on his knot.

Richard groaned again.

Getting bonded to a human was the worst idea he'd had in his life. The next three months were going to be unpleasant.

His dick throbbed in agreement, his balls aching. He growled and threw himself out of bed.

Nothing like an ice-cold multi-jet shower to start the day.

It was fine. He was a professional. He'd get through this, and after they severed this fucking bond, he wouldn't have to deal with any more annoying humans and their annoyingly consistent morning jerk-off sessions ever again.

The moment Richard sat down at their table at Palacio, Max and Hardin started laughing.

"God, I didn't realize blue balls had a scent," Hardin said.

"Funny. I figured you two would know that more than most," Richard bitched back.

"Oooh. The 'I know you are, but what am I?' defense. Haven't heard that one since grade school," Max said.

"I'd like to see how you'd handle being bonded to someone who can't keep his hands off his own dick."

"So... you?" Max asked.

"You wish."

"Did no one tell him you can feel each other get off?" Hardin asked. "That seems like information that should have been shared before he signed the contract."

"Apparently, everyone assumed the human didn't need to be told. You know how these humans are, what with their deep cultural understanding of mating bonds." Richard scrubbed his hands over his face. "Seriously. Every fucking morning."

"So rub one out when you know damn well he'll feel it. That should fix the problem," Max said.

"Or you could tell him," Hardin said.

"That would require seeing him."

"Don't you live together?" Max asked.

"Technically. But I've seen him three times over the last week and a half. And never for longer than five minutes." Not that Richard was bothered by that. If his wolf was more restless than usual, that was simply the fast-approaching full moon, not repressed longing for his damn mate or any ridiculous sap like that.

If anything, it was the fact that he'd never gone this long between scenes before. He had a knot and should be using it, goddamnit.

"Wait," Max said. "Does that mean you have the apartment all to yourself?"

"Pretty much."

"Mind if I come over?"

"Why?"

"Yeah, why would I want to go to a friend's place?"

"It's not my place."

Hardin snorted. "You're there almost as often as your actual apartment."

"The thing is... Uh." Max darted a quick glance at Hardin. "My agent suggested that, after this year's MateHub Games, I should do a transactional bond. And I wanted to check out where I'd be stuck for three months."

Hardin's eyebrows shot up.

"I mean, that's not where you'll be stuck," Richard said with a leer. "But you're welcome to come check the place out."

"Why would you...?" Hardin asked, brow furrowed.

Max shrugged, staring into his drink. "MateHub's been

pushing for more performers who can do them. They're offering good money, and look how far it's taken Richard's career."

"But—" Hardin shook his head. "Whatever. Richard, just tell your human you can feel him jerk off. You shouldn't try to hide it from him."

Richard snorted. "Even idiots eventually figure out the obvious."

Hardin grimaced.

Max cleared his throat, trying to change the subject. "So. What's up next?"

Richard grinned, his wolf almost growling at the thought.

"The hunting scene."

CHAPTER

EIGHT

H unter laughed as Zinnia handed over his outfit for the scene. He held up the red hoodie. "A bit on the nose, don't you think?"

"The fans love the allusion to *Little Red Riding Hood*!" she said, her tone as bright and cheerful as her pink hair.

Well, if he wanted subtle, nuanced filmmaking, he was in the wrong place.

"Besides, it's tradition!" she added, beaming.

She left him to change out of his jeans and into the ones she'd provided. They didn't fit the way he liked, but their sole purpose in life was to get ripped off him, so he couldn't complain.

He stepped out of the trailer they were using for his dressing room and found Brandt waiting for him.

"Ready, Red?" Brandt asked.

"If I were getting fucked by three bears, would you be calling me Goldie?"

"We've never..." Brandt froze, his dark eyes going distant.

"You've never?"

Brandt blinked back to reality. "I just realized we have a blond fox shifter."

"*Goldie Fox and the Three Bears* starring Phil Emupp?"

Brandt nodded.

"I feel bad for the bear who's too small," Hunter said with a snort.

"No such thing," Brandt said, pulling himself up to his full, substantial bear shifter height.

Right. What was Hunter thinking? Unlike some of their wild brethren, bear shifters were big *all over*.

He looked around, taking in the crew and the equipment they'd hauled out to Los Padres National Forest. Someone wandering by might think they were filming an actual movie, not just a werewolf knotting his ass. Though, from what he understood, a mage had enchanted the area to make it unappealing to anyone not in the know, giving them privacy for the day-long shoot.

It seemed like everyone was there and set to go.

Almost everyone.

"Richard isn't here yet," Brandt said. "We have more than enough footage of him stalking through the forest in his wolf form. No point in shooting more. He'll be here in an hour or so."

"I wasn't—" Hunter cut himself off. Fine, he kind of had been. Only because it'd be impossible for him to get fucked in these woods without a co-star there.

"Let's do your interview and then get the shots of you hiking along this trail through the beautiful scenery."

"Enjoying nature before I *enjoy nature*?"

Brandt grinned. "Exactly!"

They kept the interview brief—nothing more than a few questions about how much Hunter had been looking forward to this particular scene, and how it felt wearing the iconic red hoodie. Everett would do Richard's half later while Hunter was filming with Brandt.

When they finished that, they moved on to the opening shots.

The whole process fascinated Hunter. Before working for MateHub, he'd had no idea how much effort went into shooting even simple things. How something that would end up a minute-long clip could take over an hour to shoot. Walking down the path to film one angle, then walking back and doing it again to get a different angle.

And it was all for a video where most viewers would skip straight past the boring parts to get to the boning parts. How much longer must it take on sets where continuity mattered?

But he enjoyed the experience, and it didn't hurt that the weather was as gorgeous as the scenery. He breathed in the fresh pine-scented air, the sun warm on his face.

The perfect day to get knotted outside while a dozen people watched.

He shook his head, not quite believing this was his life.

A crew member handed him a bottle of water as he waited for them to reposition the camera. He took a drink, then paused, his brow furrowing.

He shut his eyes, inhaled, and... *listened*. Not to the world around him, not to the calls of birds and the rustle of leaves. To something inside him.

When he blinked his eyes open, he was certain of one thing.

Richard was there. On set.

That ball of emotion in Hunter's mind was as distant as ever, but now that he'd noticed it, he realized it felt different. Somehow wilder. *Restless.*

He shivered, a thrill rushing through him.

"Okay," Brandt said. "Next up is you running through the trees. Remember, you're a scared human with a ravenous apex predator chasing you."

That wasn't difficult to pretend with the lurking presence inside him, the untamed hunger it exuded, the knowledge that, in another couple hours, that hunger would be turned on him, devouring him.

He repressed another shiver.

It was significantly more difficult to concentrate on what he was doing with that presence stalking him, but he ran as they filmed him traversing a rocky path, then ran some more. When that was over, they filmed reaction shot after reaction shot of him realizing a dangerous animal was hunting him. Then more running, far more than he would have liked with his dick starting to show interest in what came next.

Running was his second favorite form of cardio, but not when his body was primed for the first.

"Alright," Brandt said, what felt like hours later, but had probably only been one. "You go get yourself prepared while we set up everything in the clearing. We'll do some quick shots of Richard stalking you before moving on to the main scene."

"Sounds good." Sounded better than he wanted to admit.

He headed to the trailer and froze as he stepped inside.

Richard was lounging on the bench seat, scrolling through his phone. For all his casual appearance, tension ran through his muscular body, like he was moments away from pouncing.

He glanced up, his light green eyes flashing amber, as

wolfish as he had been during the bonding scene. Maybe more so with the full moon hours from rising.

"Sorry," Hunter said, confused. "I thought this was my trailer."

"For location scenes, we share."

"Oh. Right. Obviously." Hunter had never shot on location. He'd always been in the studios. "Well. I'm going to..." He pointed to the bathroom.

Richard's gaze followed him to the door.

Once inside, Hunter shook himself. He needed to get his shit together.

He undid the button on his jeans, then pulled down his zipper, stopping short when the metallic click of each tooth rang through the tiny room.

Out in the trailer, there was a soft creak, and Hunter realized it'd been Richard shifting his weight on the seat, the sound crystal clear through the paper-thin walls.

He swallowed, hard and audible. If he heard that much with his perfectly normal ears, how much was Richard picking up with his enhanced senses? Heat coiled through him at the idea of Richard listening to everything he was about to do to himself.

His hands wanted to shake as he stripped, but he concentrated on removing his clothes piece by piece, on the feel of the fabric, the whisper of air on his exposed skin.

This was all he had to do. Pay attention to his actions. Ignore the soft rustles Richard was making on the other side of the wall—so loud it was like he was right there. At the door.

Hunter exhaled. Time to get himself prepped for the scene.

While Richard listened.

It was his job. Something he'd done dozens of times before. It shouldn't send arousal curling through him.

He grabbed what he needed from the basket of supplies left by the crew and focused on the methodical work, each step deafening. The snap of the lid, the squish of lube, the squirt of water into him, the rush of it coming back out. Over and over.

The trailer was so quiet, he wondered if Richard had left. But he would have heard that, and he sensed Richard out there. Waiting.

Anticipation sparked along his skin, his dick hardening. He'd known for a while he enjoyed people watching him have sex; he hadn't realized someone eavesdropping was equally as exciting.

Grabbing the lube again, he squelched a healthy amount onto his fingers, then rubbed them against his hole.

For this scene, there'd be no foreplay on camera—once he was caught, he'd be fucked. No words, no warning, no warm-up, just primal fucking. He had to be ready for Richard's thick cock.

He held back a groan as he worked himself open, forcing himself to take his time, to make sure he was prepared for what was to come. The burn was good, but not nearly enough, not remotely what he wanted.

The bench seat creaked, and Hunter swore he heard Richard's breathing hitch, his clothing rustling as he slipped his hand into his pants, fingers curling around the base of his dick, over the hot throb of his knot.

Hunter slid his fingers in deep one last time, then dragged them out. The plug they'd left in the basket was nice and thick, and when he pushed it in, he couldn't stop himself from groaning, from slowly pulling it out just so he could press it back in, from doing it again and again, his legs trembling at the stretch.

To double check he was all set. Any listeners be damned. Even if it did leave him panting for more.

Running through the forest like this—fully hard and filled with a plug—was going to be an experience.

He gave himself a squeeze, biting his lip to keep from groaning.

This was no good. He tried to rein in his arousal, tried to remember he had a job to do.

It wasn't working.

He hadn't planned to jerk off while he was in here—just get himself clean and stretched—but maybe he should. Given how worked up he was, he'd come embarrassingly quickly otherwise. Not much of a hunting scene if he came the moment the big bad wolf ripped his clothes off.

If he did this, he'd be doing it for the betterment of the scene. Nothing wrong with that.

With the utter lack of soundproofing in there, it didn't matter how quiet he was, but if Richard didn't want to hear it, he could leave.

Hunter barely suppressed a shiver, grabbed the lube, and flipped the cap open with a piercing snap.

In the small mirror above the sink, he caught sight of himself. The color in his cheeks was heightened, his eyes almost as wild as Richard's. He wet his lips and gripped himself, thumb rubbing over his tip before he stroked his length with an obscene rasp.

Outside the bathroom, a quiet growl sounded, and Hunter bit back a groan, his eyelids sliding shut. He let out an unsteady exhale and tried to zero in on the sensation of his hand, the familiar motions, but with his eyes pressed closed, all he could imagine was what Richard was hearing.

He kept listening for any noise from Richard, kept stroking himself, his other hand reaching down to tug on his balls.

God, he'd been so horny ever since their first scene together. No matter how many times he got himself off, no matter how intense those orgasms were, he still wasn't satisfied. It was an itch he couldn't scratch, growing worse by the day.

But today, it was like weeks' worth of sexual frustration were being alleviated with every stroke, every pull, every flick of his wrist.

His breathing stuttered as he got closer, each gasp ragged and deafening in his own ears. The slick slide of his hand was so damn noisy, and Richard could hear every sound he made.

Hunter clenched on the plug, wishing it were something more, something hotter, thicker. He groaned and brought his free hand up, grabbing at his shoulder. At the bite mark. It was two weeks old, but still so sensitive. He didn't touch it often. Even brushing his fingers over it brought on visceral memories of Richard's teeth sinking in, his cock buried deep in his ass.

But now, that was exactly what he needed. He dug his fingers into it.

Another growl rumbled through the trailer, louder this time, demanding and hungry, and Hunter came with a choked-off moan. He spilled over his hand and into the sink, his harsh pants echoing off the walls.

His dick twitched as it softened. Aftershocks ran through him, so strong they made his stomach tighten.

It wasn't enough; he hadn't even taken the edge off. He took in a deep lungful of air, then another.

This had not been planned.

He turned on the tap with shaky hands, rinsing them and the sink clean of the mess he'd made.

When he saw his reflection in the mirror, he swallowed. The scene hadn't started yet, and he looked like he'd been fucked five ways to Sunday, his pupils lust-blown, his lips reddened.

As he dressed, each movement drew his attention to the plug.

He didn't know what to expect when he exited the bathroom, but it wasn't Richard sprawled out in the same position, still engrossed in his phone.

Richard glanced up like he hadn't been listening to Hunter finger himself open and jerk himself off.

He stood in one dangerously smooth motion, his dick a mouth-watering bulge in his jeans, a wet patch on the front where precome had soaked through the fabric. He pulled his shirt over his head, then tossed it on the seat before he popped the buttons straining over his cock one by one, studying Hunter's face as he inched his pants and underwear down until his erection sprang free.

The rest of his clothes were cast aside as well, and then he was standing there, naked and hard in front of Hunter, almost like a dare.

"Ready?" he asked, a low growl in his tone.

Hunter clenched down again. Fuck yes, he was.

His eyes traced over Richard's sculpted body, but when he reached his face, Richard was smirking with enough arrogance to knock Hunter out of his stupor.

This fucking bastard. Could he think any more highly of himself?

"Ready when you are," Hunter said.

"Then let's go." Richard turned and headed out the door, his firm, biteable ass on display.

All Hunter could do was follow him out of the trailer.

CHAPTER

NINE

O utside, the production crew milled about in the afternoon sunlight, waiting for them.

Brandt inhaled as they walked up. He cocked an eyebrow at Richard.

Richard smirked. Yeah, Hunter did smell like he'd just gotten off. And for once, Richard didn't mind. Not when he knew what he was about to do to Hunter, that he was going to make sure Hunter got off even harder.

"If you're both ready," Brandt said.

Richard was more than ready. He had been for weeks. Hunter wouldn't be avoiding him this time. He didn't get to jerk off and run away.

Well, he'd run, but today, Richard got to chase.

MateHub had sent a car to pick Hunter up early that morning, to bring him out here and film his scenes. That seemed like a waste. Richard could have driven him. He could have arrived a few hours earlier.

He wasn't willing to chauffeur Hunter around wherever, but he could make exceptions when they were both going to the same place. Though he hadn't done that in years, and Hunter might get the wrong idea.

Whatever. It didn't matter. He had better things to do.

He cracked his neck, rolled his shoulders, and let his wolf take over.

The burn of the transformation swept through him, his body bending and twisting into his other form. He savored the unbecoming and rebirth, the agony and rapture of it like nothing else in the world.

There was a soft gasp, and he turned to find Hunter staring at him in awe and wonder.

That was right. He probably hadn't seen the shift often, and Richard was fucking glorious as a wolf—large and powerful.

He flashed his teeth in a wolfish grin and lowered his head, taking a few slow, predatory steps toward Hunter, enjoying the way Hunter's eyes widened, the instinctual tension lacing through him, the clear readiness to run.

Hunter took a step backward as Richard neared, and Richard growled.

Run, he wanted to say. *Run and let me hunt you. Capture you. Fuck you.*

"OKAY!" Brandt yelled, startling Richard out of stalking his prey. "Let's film these shots so we can move on to the clearing."

Richard wanted to growl for a different reason. He huffed in frustration.

Fine. He'd play nice. For now.

They filmed a sequence of shots of Richard prowling in wolf form behind an oblivious Hunter.

It was tedious—surely they didn't need this from quite so many angles—but Richard stayed a wolf and kept his complaints to himself.

The desire to catch Hunter built, burning in him. In Hunter, too, if the growing bulge in his jeans was anything to go by, or the way his ass would occasionally clench, clearly needing more than that plug in him.

But then finally, *finally*, they were done with the unnecessary bullshit; Brandt had his shots.

A thrill of anticipation ran through Richard. The promise of what they were about to do shivered under his fur. All he could smell was how Hunter craved him, and in his wolf form, it was so much sharper. Like this, the world around him was clearer than it could ever be for a human, and the focal point of all his heightened senses was Hunter. His lust, his need.

The clearing was large enough that it could fit multiple cameras and lights. Some kind of magical barrier dampened the constant hum of the generators used to power them.

The floor in the clearing looked more manicured than the nicest of lawns, its verdant carpeting out of place in the ragged woods. It'd been grown by a company mage, and Richard knew the crew had spent the morning raking the ground, ensuring there were no twigs or rocks that might dig into exposed skin at inopportune moments.

Everything after this was one take. For all the effort they put into setting it up, they wanted this to appear as natural as possible. Which meant once he had Hunter under him, there'd be no more stops, no more delays. Just doing what he did best. Sliding into Hunter and fucking him into the ground.

Richard paced around the clearing as the crew finished their preparations, the grass soft under his paws. Even outside, Hunter's scent saturated the air. The smell of him, of his arousal, hung heavy—an intoxicating, heady blend.

Hunter stepped away from the crew, fading into the trees, and Richard followed on four legs, only to be treated with the sight of Hunter pulling a packet of lube out of his pocket, pushing down his jeans, and reaching behind him. He slowly slid the plug out of his ass, slicked it up with more lube, then pressed it back in a few times like Richard had imagined him doing in the bathroom. Hunter's eyelids fluttered shut, and he stretched himself good and open with the toy.

He was so ready for Richard to fuck him, to reclaim him.

And that was exactly what he'd do.

None of this *days* bullshit.

Hunter pulled the plug out one last time. As he slumped back against the tree, his gaze met Richard's. He froze, terror written on his face, breath caught in his throat, pants around his thighs, dick hard in the fresh air. But then the panic of being feet from a wolf was replaced by the relief of recognition, followed swiftly by the realization of what Richard had watched him do.

They stood there, eyes locked.

Richard stepped forward, baring his teeth, a snarl building, waiting to see if Hunter would run.

Hunter didn't.

"We're all set," Brandt yelled, making Hunter jump and glance in his direction.

He struggled to get his dick back in his jeans, momentarily distracted.

Richard continued his creeping prowl, closing the space between them step by silent step, and when Hunter looked up again, he found Richard much closer.

He jerked in surprise, his back hitting the tree.

Foolish human. Never look away from a predator. Never take your eyes off me.

"Richard?" A tremor wormed through Hunter's voice.

Richard answered with a growl.

Hunter edged sideways, stumbling backward, dropping the plug and lube. He groped blindly behind him for any trees that might be in the way. He shuffled toward the clearing, toward whatever safety it offered, as his focus remained locked on Richard. The pounding of his heart thundered through the forest, and his respiration grew quick and shallow.

Now this was a good little human.

A few more steps, and they'd break the tree line.

Hunter's foot hit a loose rock, and he staggered, almost falling, the noise catching the crew's attention.

Brandt seemed as startled as Hunter, but then he was shouting orders, and cameras were swinging toward them.

Richard didn't care; Hunter was his now. After two long weeks, his wait was over.

"Action," Brandt called, that word seeming to register in Hunter's mind, and he turned, taking off, running into the clearing, breathless, winded, like he'd been chased for miles.

Richard followed, his steps measured and deliberate.

A wild heat filled Hunter's eyes when he looked back— as did apprehension, excitement, and amusement.

Richard's claws dug into the earth with each step as he circled Hunter. He was torn between charging forward to claim his prize and the slower strides that drew out the anticipation.

In the end, his impatience won out. Richard lunged, snapping, catching the leg of Hunter's jeans and pulling. Hunter landed on his ass with a satisfying thud. He tried to scoot away, but Richard closed in.

"Please," Hunter begged, all playacting and far from

how Richard wanted him to sound when he said that word. "P... please, please d... d... don't eat me."

This wasn't supposed to be gentle or nice. This was supposed to be Richard fucking like the animal he was, nothing but raw, primal sex.

But there was no reason he couldn't play with his food first.

Richard shifted to his human form, loving Hunter's genuine shock at seeing the shift so close, how his gaze immediately trailed down Richard's chest, landing on his stiff cock.

He took himself in hand and gave himself a few firm strokes. Hunter twitched.

"Feel that?" Richard asked, low and half-feral from two weeks of Hunter jerking off every single morning.

He saw it register, the panicked realization that Hunter could feel Richard stroking himself in his mind when they weren't touching, feel the transfer of sensation and lust and arousal.

Richard squeezed himself tight, and Hunter let out a breathy moan.

"Wh... what are you going to do to me?" he asked between rapid pants.

Richard's grin was gluttonous, all instinct and vice. "What every big bad wolf does best, Little Red. I'm going to eat you."

And that line, as ad-libbed as it was, would make the MateHub writers proud.

Hunter gave a genuinely startled squeak as Richard yanked him forward by his legs. He didn't give Hunter a chance to compose himself, just pinned him down. He growled as Hunter tried to push him off, though there was no force behind his shoves.

The red hoodie tore apart in satisfying shreds, as did Hunter's jeans, like tissue paper under his claws. He ripped off Hunter's underwear with a snap of his wrist, and Hunter yelped, his dick springing free. Then he stripped him of his shoes and socks, leaving him entirely bare.

The bite mark on Hunter's shoulder stood out against his skin, and Richard couldn't help himself; he leaned in and closed his mouth over it.

Hunter's groan echoed through the clearing, loud and long. He arched into Richard's mouth before he belatedly realized he shouldn't appear to be enjoying this, and he struggled to shove Richard off him.

Richard let himself be pushed away by weak hands, let Hunter scoot out from under him, only to grab him by the ankles and yank him back.

He flipped Hunter over, getting a lovely little surprised squeak, then pressed Hunter's head down, a firm hand keeping his ass in the air.

When Hunter struggled this time, it was merely an excuse to spread his legs wider, to bow his back and angle his hips so Richard had full access.

This would be one delicious meal.

His fingers dug into Hunter's ass cheeks, his claws still out, pricking skin. From the way Hunter pushed back, he didn't mind. Which was good; Richard didn't think he'd have been able to put his claws away even if he'd wanted to, not with how close to the surface his wolf was, with how much it needed this.

Richard nosed Hunter's balls, inhaling deeply. The pull of his scent was as strong as the moon. Stronger even, since the sunlight streaming over them did nothing to dim its allure.

He greedily took one of his balls in his mouth, sucking

until Hunter moaned, then he moved on to the other. Hunter cursed under his breath as he half-heartedly attempted to escape, trying his best to stay in character, to pretend this wasn't precisely what he wanted.

It was time to see how much longer he could keep that up.

Richard licked along Hunter's crack to his hole, flicking his tongue to tease that ring of muscle, and Hunter cried out.

"Not... not there," he begged, his voice cracking with fake fear and real desire. "Please. Please don't eat me."

There was a thread of laughter in his words, and the tickle of amusement sparkled through their bond.

"Don't... stop."

Richard huffed—half growl, half laugh—at the exaggerated pause between the two words. He knocked Hunter's legs farther apart, getting another adorable squeak.

Hunter groaned again as Richard settled in and pleasure inundated him. Richard licked his hole, a long, unhurried, wet drag of his tongue, luxuriating in the taste of his mate, though it would have been better without the lube. Hunter's scent was everywhere, impossible to ignore. He pushed his ass into Richard's face, his cock leaking, though still untouched.

In his mind, Hunter was consumed by impulses and needs. A rumble resounded in Richard's chest as he licked Hunter again, then thrust his tongue inside.

Hunter's reaction was perfect: a muffled scream, a frantic thrashing of his body, his toes digging into the ground.

Richard didn't go easy on him after that; he held him

still and fucked him with his tongue until Hunter cursed, fingers clutching at the grass.

And when Hunter was caught up in a rush of ecstasy so intense it bordered on pain, Richard pulled back, watching his hole clench on nothing, greedy and demanding more.

Fuck, that was a beautiful sight.

"Hungry, Red?"

Hunter nodded, and Richard rewarded him with a final lick. Then he draped himself over Hunter, pinning him to the ground as he dragged his cock along Hunter's slick crack.

"Fuck," Hunter said, the word a low whine.

That was a command Richard was happy to follow. He rubbed against Hunter's hole, teasing him, and Hunter made a frustrated noise, pushing back, trying to fuck himself onto Richard's dick.

Richard pressed forward, breaching Hunter's ass, then pausing because he knew it'd make Hunter curse and rock his hips, trying to force more of Richard's length into him. Richard laughed, a rich chuckle that seemed to brush over Hunter's skin, causing him to shiver.

"Still hungry?" he asked.

Hunter nodded, shook his head, then nodded again, unable to get words out around the desperation running through him—a desperation that was half Richard's own.

Richard drove forward in one quick thrust.

"Yes," Hunter hissed, his whole body arching upward. He'd given up on trying to pretend he wasn't enjoying this, like he wasn't begging for more, hadn't he?

Well, if that was the case, there was no point in Richard holding himself back either. No point in holding his wolf back.

He pulled out, then slammed back in, too impatient for slow and gentle.

Hunter cried out, hands scrabbling for leverage. Richard didn't give him any. He grabbed Hunter's hips and pounded into him, his claws digging into smooth skin, drawing blood.

Through their bond, Hunter's pleasure and pain shimmered. The combination was potent and exhilarating.

He fucked Hunter, fast and relentless, all wolf at that moment, plowing into him without restraint, his thrusts forcing the air out of Hunter's lungs in choked-off sobs.

Richard's feral howl rang out. His arm moved to wrap around Hunter's chest, his hand squeezing at the bite mark. With that leverage, Richard could take him harder, deeper, his knot expanding with every thrust.

The noises Hunter made grew louder, his body shaking. Richard felt every movement, felt Hunter's dick dragging against the ground, leaving a trail of precome in the grass. The prickling brush of the blades was a maddening torture.

With one last forceful thrust, Richard's knot lodged inside Hunter, and that was it for both of them. Hunter's shout hitched into silence as he came, flooding the grass with his release, and Richard milked every drop of ecstasy out of him, making him writhe in pure, unrestrained abandon.

Richard's cock pulsed in Hunter's tight heat, spilling inside him as his orgasm ripped through him like a tidal wave, wild and uncontrollable. He floated, lost in their connection, in the swirling sensations that ricocheted between them.

When Richard returned to himself, Hunter was trembling from the intensity of it, so perfect and sweet.

He caught the curve of Hunter's ear between his teeth and bit down.

"Mine," Richard whispered. "You're mine."

Hunter didn't say a word, but he didn't need to. The way he clenched around Richard's knot said it all. Richard rumbled his approval.

He rolled them over, sitting up with Hunter in his lap, his body lax and boneless as he melted against Richard, his legs splayed wide over Richard's thighs, giving the cameras an excellent view of where they were tied together.

Richard mouthed at his bite mark and got a deep, needy moan for his efforts.

"Sounds like you're still hungry," Richard said, his grin wicked, his fingers curling around Hunter's soft dick.

Hunter shuddered, straining against Richard, a high keening noise slipping from him as Richard stroked him. It was too soon; he was too sensitive, but the wordless cries tumbling from his lips were anything but 'stop.'

He jerked, his head falling back. One of his hands grasped Richard's arm, not to stop him, but to hold on, to anchor himself. His breathing grew louder. His body shook, a fine sheen of sweat glistening on his skin in the late afternoon light, a beautiful picture for the cameras surrounding them.

Richard looked directly into the main camera and smirked as Hunter twitched in his lap, flushed with helpless pleasure. He was doing this to Hunter. No one else could make Hunter feel this good. It was him alone.

He could sense how Hunter was torn between wanting to come and wanting it never to stop, both options too appealing to pick one. Richard decided for him. He shuttled his cock faster as he bit Hunter's shoulder, marking him again, earning a strangled cry.

Hunter wailed, spattering Richard's hand with his second release as he clenched on his knot.

Richard worked him through the tremors racking his body. He nipped his ear, and Hunter quivered.

Euphoria and satisfaction—both his and Hunter's—coiled through Richard in a way that went beyond the physical, beyond anything he'd felt before. Hunter drifted in a hazy bliss, in a feeling of rightness. He sagged against Richard, boneless and sated.

Underneath that satisfaction, something else lingered, something too much like home and family and belonging for Richard to want to examine.

Almost regretfully, he glanced at Brandt and got a nod. Grabbing Hunter's hips gently, he lifted him. Hunter whimpered as Richard's knot popped out. His come gushed out of Hunter, coating his balls and dripping onto the ground.

He held Hunter there, spread open for the close-ups until Brandt called cut.

Hunter slumped to the side, onto the grass. His pupils were blown, his lips red and swollen. He looked wrecked, and the sight of him like that sent raw possessiveness through Richard.

"Leave me here," Hunter said, voice equally wrecked. "I'm dead. I've died. Never moving again."

Richard chuckled. "Was that harder than you've come in days?" he asked, already knowing the answer.

Hunter huffed out a breathless laugh. "Maybe weeks."

"Is that so? Should we see if we can make it months?" He reached over to grab Hunter's softening dick.

Hunter hissed, batting his hand away. "At least a month," he said, a frantic note to his words. "Maybe two."

It was a blatant lie, but Richard was satisfied with it. For now.

He stood and offered a hand to Hunter, but Hunter only laughed. "I was serious about the not moving thing. I ran around for hours, and after that scene, there's zero chance my legs are functioning."

Richard snorted. "Okay." He leaned down and picked Hunter up.

Hunter squeaked again—a sound Richard was really starting to like—and wrapped his arms around Richard's neck.

Brandt shot them a look, but he could go fuck himself. Richard was just helping a co-star out. Hunter was human, after all, and with as thoroughly as Richard had fucked him, helping him to the trailer was the least he could do.

He firmly ignored the speculative glances of the crew and the mistaken romantic notions in Everett's eyes.

When he got Hunter to their trailer, he propped him up in the bathroom. There wasn't enough water in there to shower, not properly, and Richard didn't pretend to be sorry about that.

He grabbed a washcloth from the supplies the crew had left for them and wet it, then used it to wipe Hunter reasonably clean. Hunter was pliant under his hands, almost purring. His eyelids were drooping as Richard helped him into his clothes.

Whenever their skin touched, his exhaustion swept through Richard.

"Do you want a ride to the apartment?" Richard asked.

Hunter cracked his eyes open and hummed a pretty, "Yes, please."

Richard wiped himself down and hurried to get dressed, almost afraid Hunter would fall asleep on his feet. He steered him toward his car, not quite carrying him.

"You know," Hunter said, his words slurring. "I thought

you'd be a complete asshole, but you're actually kind of nice sometimes, aren't you?"

"Not even remotely," Richard said gruffly.

"Liar." Hunter curled up in the passenger seat and dozed the entire two-hour drive home, covered in Richard's scent.

Richard's wolf was disgustingly pleased.

He had to half-carry Hunter again once they arrived at the apartment.

Richard had made people come hard enough that they'd passed out countless times before this, but they were supernatural. They recovered quickly. A couple hours running and then a rigorous fucking didn't wipe them out completely. He'd never fucked someone until they were dead to the world, but he had to say he kind of liked it. Maybe humans had their good points after all.

He tucked Hunter into bed, then went to leave.

And froze, unable to take another step, a sudden panic crawling in his chest at the idea of leaving the room. Of being anywhere other than where Hunter was. Especially when he was this weak and vulnerable.

The warm ball of emotions was more noticeable than before.

"Fuck," he muttered and forced himself to leave, ignoring the little whimper Hunter let out in his sleep as he did.

He took it back. Humans were nothing but trouble.

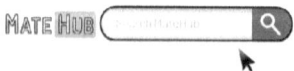

For the first time in weeks, Richard didn't wake up to Hunter jerking off. Hunter also hadn't left the apartment yet. The fact that he was still there soothed Richard more than he was going to acknowledge.

Richard showered—*properly*—then went to make breakfast.

Hunter sat at the kitchen island, poking at a bowl of cereal. His head came up as Richard entered the room.

"Hey," he said. "Thanks for helping me get back here yesterday. I was... out of it."

"I noticed."

Silence fell between them, and Richard turned on a burner, placed a pan on it to heat, and grabbed eggs from the fridge.

"Sooooo..." Hunter dragged the word out. "The bond lets you feel people jerking off?"

Richard's hand twitched, cracking the egg he was holding before he could hit it against the edge of the pan.

"Yep," he said, dumping the mess of egg and shell into the trash, washing his hands, and starting over.

"And I'm assuming I didn't notice before because you... didn't?"

Richard set the second egg he'd grabbed back into the carton and looked at Hunter. "Yep."

"Did I give you two weeks' worth of blue balls?"

"Also yep."

Hunter winced. "I'm so sorry. I'll... not?"

"That's usually for the best."

"Is there an issue when I prep myself?"

"Depends on how you do it."

Hunter's cheeks colored, no doubt remembering how he'd prepped himself the day before.

"But no, in general. It's the pleasure that makes it transfer."

"Got it. Lay off on the prostate stimulation during pre-scene stretching."

Richard shrugged. "Pre-scene isn't going to end with my balls feeling like they're about to explode." Even if Hunter became aroused, it'd only act as foreplay for Richard.

"Sorry. In my defense, that would have been useful to know beforehand."

"It's common knowledge in the supernatural world. The biggest benefit of the bond. Best orgasms you'll have in days."

Hunter's grin was sheepish. "Weeks, even."

Richard snorted. Hunter could say whatever he wanted; they both knew the truth. "Eggs?"

"I didn't know you cooked."

For himself, generally.

"But yes, please."

Richard cracked eggs into the pan, ignoring how much his wolf liked the idea of feeding their mate.

"So what else do I need to know about this whole bond thing? Clearly, I was not fully informed. Can you feel me doing anything else? If I have to pee, do you feel like you have to pee?"

Richard shook his head wryly. "Thankfully, no."

He considered how much he wanted to explain as he placed slices of bread in the toaster.

Hunter was new to this. It was only fair he understood it. It'd help ensure he didn't become attached to Richard. Though his agent was an asshole if he hadn't bothered to spell it all out.

Fine. Richard could do that much.

"Basically, wolf shifters have two types of bonds. Transactional and true. True bonds are this whole bullshit 'true love between compatible people' thing. Transactional bonds are, more or less, business transactions. The couple doesn't need to be compatible; they don't even need to like each other. They just have to want something from each other. Because there's no real emotion involved, the bond between them is shallow. Shallow bonds are easier to sever after the contract is over."

Hunter nodded. "My agent explained that much. He said don't get attached, or severing the bond will be painful."

"Exactly. With a shallow transactional bond, you won't feel much from the person you're bonded to. Certain base, instinctual emotions will transfer no matter what, if they're strong enough. Anger, fear, grief, lust. But that's about it."

"So you can't sense what I'm feeling right now?"

"No. I can sense you in the back of my mind, the same way you can sense me, but I don't know what you're feeling."

Hunter's gaze grew distant, and for one second, an invisible hand stroked along Richard's spine. He repressed a shiver.

"You're hungry," Hunter said.

"I'm hungry first thing in the morning after shifting and fucking for an hour?" Something warm threaded through Richard, but he ignored it. "Good guess," he said dryly.

"What happens with a true bond? How's that different?"

Richard leaned against the counter. "Not my area of expertise. I've heard you're supposed to feel pretty much everything your mate is experiencing, especially when you're touching or have heightened emotions."

"That's the same with transactional bonds, isn't it? During our scenes, I can feel your pleasure and you feeling mine. It sort of echoes between us."

"Right. But that's a base instinct. With true bonds, it's like your mate becomes part of you, not just a little unreadable ball."

Hunter made a face. "That sounds invasive."

"It is," Richard said with a grimace.

"I thought it wasn't your area of expertise." Hunter raised an eyebrow in question.

Richard grimaced again. "Listen, I'm not going to give details, but some people can't separate intense sex and love. It's part of the reason the contract says we aren't allowed to have sex between scenes. It might encourage attachment, and the more attached you are, the more open you become to your mate. The more they can feel your emotions, even when you aren't touching. Whether they want those emotions or not. And if you're feeling their emotions, it means it'll be painful for them when it comes time to sever the bond."

At least he'd never inflicted that on anyone. Months of being bombarded by emotions that weren't asked for and would never be returned was not something Richard would wish on his least favorite person in the industry, Duke Moorhead. Though, none of that bastard's co-stars got attached to him.

Richard couldn't figure out what he was doing wrong, what led so many of his co-stars to think they had a chance. Why, no matter how cold and aloof he acted toward them, he always ended up sitting front row as their attachment to him grew, as they walked straight into pain they should have been able to avoid.

Hunter was scrutinizing him too closely, so Richard turned to flip the eggs.

"But as long as it's only those base emotions, it's easy to sever?" Hunter asked.

"Yeah," Richard replied. "It stings for a few seconds, but that fades fast."

Hunter lapsed into silence for a few minutes as Richard cooked.

"Is there any difference in how they're formed?" he finally asked.

"The mechanics are the same. Biting and fucking," Richard answered, not looking at Hunter.

"So does that mean transactional bonds can become true bonds?"

"Generally speaking, no. People in transactional bonds aren't compatible. I suppose they can grow to feel affection for each other, but it's not the same. True bonds only happen between people who are compatible."

"So wolf shifters have, like, soulmates?"

Richard glanced over his shoulder, but couldn't read Hunter's expression well enough to judge his thoughts on that.

"Not in the traditional sense. It's not some instant connection. There are people we're more compatible with, but it might take a bit to realize how truly compatible two people are."

"But you know it's a true bond? Before you actually bond?"

Richard busied himself with plating up the eggs. "Usually, yes."

"How?"

This conversation was making him increasingly aware of how Hunter's subtle scent lingered on his skin—delicate, but strong. How it combined with his own.

Richard shrugged. "Wolf shifter thing. You just know."

SCENE: *Hunting Down Hunter*

BramStroker:
HOTTEST HUNTING SCENE EVER.

KnottyWolf69:
Seriously. The number of times I just came.

tonythetiger:
I honestly thought I was going to black out.

MagicalHWood:
I knew Richard made his co-stars come hard
enough to do that. I didn't think he could make me
do it through my screen.

HuntMeDown:
That's the hotness of DickHunt for you.

MagicalHWood:
We still aren't calling them that.

KnottyWolf69:
Definitely not. But fuck, that look Richard gave the
camera? It was 100% "Touch him and die" energy.

BramStroker:
Was it? I may need to watch it again to confirm.

tonythetiger:

We should rewatch the whole video to make sure we've got the full context.

KnottyWolf69:

Good idea. I wouldn't want to misinterpret things. Magic, you with us?

MagicalHWood:

I've already hit replay. See you all on the other side of our collective blackouts!

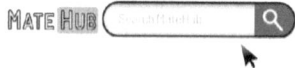

CHAPTER
TEN

The apartment wasn't so bad, actually, Hunter supposed. There were worse places to live for three months.

His bedroom overlooked the lush landscaping surrounding the building's pool, its vibrant flowering plants and strategically placed greenery creating a private oasis that calmed him every time he gazed out the window. The living room had a gaming system that would make Chance weep if he'd ever come over to play a few games—though he was still firmly on Team "Ugh, no, the place will reek like dog." And MateHub kept the kitchen stocked with all the best food. Not to mention the fact that Richard seemed to enjoy cooking.

If Hunter dragged his heels in the morning before he left because he knew he'd get a home-cooked breakfast... well, he didn't think anyone would blame him. Especially not after they tried Richard's pancakes. Or his scrambled eggs. Or French toast. Or...

And if that resulted in Hunter playing a game or two on the drool-worthy gaming setup, well, he'd just had a big meal. He shouldn't be doing strenuous activities like taking a taxi to his friend's apartment on a full stomach.

His apartment. His *real* apartment.

And if those games ended up lasting longer than planned and he happened to be there when Richard was fixing a light lunch, it'd be impolite to turn down the food. Then he really did need to play another game. For his stomach's sake. Which might lead to it being almost time for dinner. And god, Richard's dinners. The man cooked as well as he fucked—an utterly unfair combination.

Hunter and Richard didn't talk or anything, but being in the same room wasn't abhorrent. There was something soothing about gaming while Richard scrolled through his phone or read a book. At the very least, Hunter didn't feel like he needed to escape the asshole's presence.

On the occasions he did leave, it was to hit the in-house gym. He'd exercise and run for an hour, then return.

The one annoying thing about the whole situation was the not-jerking-off part. The number of times he'd apologized to his dick for ignoring it over the last week was verging on pathetic. Not what Hunter would call a good time, but other than that, he couldn't complain.

If he hadn't left the building since the hunting scene, it was fine; Richard hadn't either. Plus, he was so close to clearing this level of *Shadows Veiled*.

The apartment buzzer rang, and Hunter jumped, accidentally hitting a button and nearly giving his position away to the humans he was hiding a coterie of fairies from.

He paused the game, frowning at the intercom. No one buzzed their apartment. The only person who came by was the MateHub employee who delivered their groceries, and he had a key to the building, so he just knocked on their door.

Richard stood, drawing Hunter's gaze with the smooth motion of his muscular body. He wore a simple T-shirt and jeans, both fitting him like they cost more than Hunter's college education.

"Ah," he said, running a hand through his hair, disturbing its perfect styling. "That's a friend. He wanted to check this place out. I didn't think you'd be here when he came over."

Hunter nodded and went back to his game. "It's fine."

"Do you mind if I show him your room?"

"Go for it." It was only mildly messy, and he'd left anything potentially embarrassing at home. The last thing he needed was the real Richard finding the fake Richard in his sock drawer with an almost empty bottle of lube.

Richard showed his friend around, the low hum of their conversation floating through the apartment, but Hunter didn't bother paying attention.

"Is that the new *Shadows Veiled*?" a voice asked.

Hunter hit pause as Richard led Max Thrustwell into the living room. With his Mediterranean good looks, Max was the epitome of a dashing heartthrob, but the usual suave charm he exuded in his scenes was replaced by a glittering excitement as he stared at the massive TV screen.

"It is." Hunter grinned.

"But it's not supposed to come out until next week."

Hunter's grin grew wider. Nice to know Richard's friends had good taste. "Right? Someone at MateHub must have a MysTech connection."

"Damn," Max said, mock-glaring at Richard. "Why didn't you tell me you had an early copy of *Shadows Veiled*?"

Richard stared at him blankly. "Because I don't care?"

Max clutched his chest, his eyes wide and betrayed, but Richard seemed unfazed by his distress.

"Why are we friends?" Max asked, his tone light and teasing. He then walked over and extended a hand to Hunter. "So you're the human. I'm Max. Nice to meet you."

It wasn't the first time Hunter had been called 'the human'—it wasn't even the hundredth—and it wouldn't be the last. He shook Max's hand. "I know who you are. That scene where you're training your new pack recruits to follow your alpha command was super hot. I had no clue that version of Twister existed."

Max's lips quirked in amusement. "And may I say, if you ever want to deliver me a pizza, mess up my order, then offer me your ass as a replacement, I wouldn't say no."

A visceral memory of someone else making a meal out of him rolled through Hunter, but he shoved it down and snorted. "Ah, yes. *My Hungry Customer Gave Me More Than Just the Tip*. Cinematic masterpiece. Right up there with your *Battle of Two Hung Alphas: Who Comes on Top?* Never saw the plot twist of *both* coming."

"It was truly a trope-subverting pioneer," Max said with a snicker. "Two alphas switching? Such madness."

"Okay, I'm curious. Are you really an alpha?"

Max winked at him. "In porn, we're all alphas. Even that jackass." He pointed behind him.

Hunter glanced over to where Richard was scowling at Max, his expression a touch constipated.

"That's what I figured," Hunter said. "People do like their stereotypes. I'll be your scared, virginal human this evening."

"Actually. Funny you should mention that. I'm always part of Richard's 'pack,' so I'll be—"

"Did you want to see anything else?" Richard asked, cutting him off, a hint of a growl coloring his words.

Max blinked at him. "I'm good. This is a nice place." He

turned to Hunter and explained, "My agent wants me to do a bonding contract."

Hunter frowned. "I didn't realize they were already lining up Richard's next contract." It seemed a little soon.

"Oh, fuck no. Not with Richard. There's not enough money in the world for that. I don't know how you haven't killed him yet."

The vehemence of his answer startled a laugh out of Hunter. "Apparently, I won't get paid in full if I kill him."

"Hey!" The growl in Richard's voice was no longer merely a hint.

Hunter shot Max a sly look. "Honestly, he isn't bad to live with. I'd put up with a lot of bullshit for his linguine."

"His... linguine? I've never heard it called that before."

"No," Hunter said, chuckling. "His pasta. It's significantly more impressive than his dick."

"Hey!" Richard said again.

Max's head swiveled slowly toward Richard. "His... pasta?" he asked Hunter as he raised an eyebrow at Richard. "He's cooking for you?"

"Yeah. Have you had his peppery yuzu cream fettuccine? It nearly made me come harder than he has."

"Peppery yuzu cream fettuccine?" The smile spreading across Max's face was, quite frankly, terrifying.

"Okay, if you've seen enough, I'll show you out." There was a dangerous edge to Richard's tone.

"Oh," Max said, "I definitely need to see more." He plopped onto the couch next to Hunter, ignoring the snarl Richard let out. "How's the game?"

Hunter's gaze jumped between them. He'd missed something. Whatever. They could work it out themselves, and he'd ask Chance what was up later.

"I'm barely halfway through, but it's *awesome*. Way too

good to be spoiled. There's a multiplayer mode I've been dying to check out though. Wanna play?"

"Hell yeah. Hardin is going to be so fucking jealous."

Richard huffed and stalked out of the room.

They watched him go, then exchanged a shrug. There was no explaining non-gamers.

Hunter exited his game and handed a controller to Max.

"The first level is wild," he said. "Tons of fun surprises. You're going to love it."

Max snorted. "Who doesn't love the unexpected?"

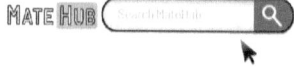

ELEVEN

M ax was getting along entirely too well with Hunter. He'd come over to see the apartment. Why was he still there three hours later, playing this dumb video game?

As far as Richard could tell, they were agents from some secret organization who tried to hide supernatural creatures from humans by using strange combinations of technology, magic, tactics, and flat-out lies. He had no idea how they kept jumping through the few hundred menus to locate ingredients for spells, weapons, and bribe money.

He also didn't understand ninety percent of the words coming out of their mouths.

Scoffing, he turned back to his phone.

Hunter glanced over before returning his focus to the TV, where he was trying to convince a crowd of humans that an actual haunted house was a pop-up guerrilla marketing campaign for an as-yet-unnamed movie while Max was doing something with a magic circle that required bartering with a hermit for his toenail clippings.

Not that he'd been paying attention.

"Did you want to play?" Hunter asked.

"Ooh. No," Max said. "You don't want that. Hardin and I convinced him to play *Beyond the Veil: Spectral Havoc* once, and every single mission we ran with him ended with us all killed by the spirits."

"But that game's so easy."

Max snorted. "Not for Richard. He's only good at one thing, and gaming isn't it."

Richard scowled. He might only be good at one thing, but he was damn good at it.

"Two things," Hunter said cheerfully.

"Ah, right. How could I forget his linguine?"

"I certainly haven't. Oooh. What about *Moonlit Bonds*?"

Max burst into laughter so hard he couldn't play, and Hunter paused the game, snickering as well.

Richard pulled up a browser on his phone and typed in 'Moonlit Bonds game.' Nothing funny showed up in the results.

After Max got himself under control, he said, "But no, seriously. You need to have a soul before you can have a soulmate, and Richard is lacking in that particular area."

Richard suppressed a growl, his irritation building as he scrolled through more search results without finding anything. What the fuck were they talking about?

Hunter studied him, his head cocked, then said, "Go to MysTech.games. It's like MateHub. If you know, you know."

Richard typed in the address and found a website for games aimed at the supernatural community. A vampire-hunter-hunting vampire out for vengeance, a group of mages trying to restore balance to a world on the brink of magical chaos, sirens in a competition to knock off as many sailors as possible. *Moonlit Bonds: The Shifter Chronicles* was under the Adults Only tab.

He blinked at his phone. "'Pick your shape-shifting hero or heroine and fuck your way through the paranormal world until you find your soulmate. Which hole will unlock your knot?'"

That set Hunter and Max off into another fit of giggles, slumping against each other as they shook with amusement.

Richard did not growl. There was no need for him to do that.

"Haha. Very funny. That's not how knots work."

"But that's half the fun," Max said, wiping away tears of unholy mirth. "There are two modes of play. Hard Mode, where you try to find your soulmate in as few fucks as you can. Or Hard Mode, where you fuck as many people as you can before you find your soulmate."

"They're both called Hard Mode?"

"For obvious reasons. You should play Hard Mode."

"Which one?"

"The one you're playing in real life." Max barely got the words out around his laughter. Hunter was snickering again, too.

Richard stood, glaring at Max. "Do you want to stay for dinner or not, asshole?"

"Am I going to get to try this orgasm-inducing fettuccine?"

"No."

"That's disappointing. But sure. Let's see these mad cooking skills of yours."

Not growling was swiftly becoming Richard's default setting. He headed into the kitchen.

It wasn't weird that he was cooking for Hunter; it didn't mean anything. He had to cook for himself, and there were so few good recipes for only one person. It was easier to cook for two.

He opened the pantry and grinned.

No. No fettuccine tonight, but he did have the ingredients he needed for butternut squash ravioli with a nice browned-butter walnut sage sauce.

And if butternut squash happened to be Max's least favorite vegetable, how was Richard supposed to remember that?

Richard stared at the message on his phone.

CHAR

Lunch sometime later this week? If you don't reek too badly of human.

He could imagine how that'd go. His sister would hug him like she always did, pause, inhale deeply, then pull away. Instead of her usual complaints about the scent of his temporary mate, she'd have a shit-eating grin on her face, and Richard would never hear the end of it.

That was the last thing he needed.

RICHARD

You really aren't going to like this one.

Rain check?

CHAR

You couldn't have given me a heads-up for the incubus? Or anyone before?

Fine. See you after the severing ritual, I
guess.

He shouldn't be relieved by that, but he was.

CHAR

Oh, but speaking of heads-up. I saw Mom
yesterday. She's hell-bent on having a pack
dinner soon. Kept muttering something
about making sure "that stubborn boy
doesn't get out of this one."

I'll run interference as much as I can, but
you better come up with a work emergency
that will keep you busy for the next two
months if you don't want her to smell you
when you're all human-y.

Richard winced. He took it back. Lunch with his sister
wasn't the last thing he needed. It'd be a moonlit breeze
compared to dinner with his mother.

RICHARD

Thanks. I'll think of something.

He just didn't know what.

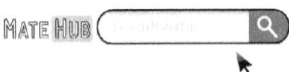

"So," Hunter said as he unbuckled his seatbelt and got out
of Richard's car in the MateHub parking lot. "What is this
scene, anyway? All the contract said was a 'knotting ritual.'
I think I searched through every video on MateHub, but I
couldn't find anything similar."

Richard groaned. "I've seen the script. It's a new idea the writers came up with."

"Uh-oh. That doesn't sound good."

"It never is."

They walked into the lobby.

"How bad is it? Will I be pretending to be a healer who you, a lonely wolf shifter suffering from a dysfunctional knot, go to for help? And then I perform a ritual to remedy your knot problems. A ritual that involves my ass."

Richard snorted and hit the elevator call button. "Are you secretly a MateHub writer?"

"I mean, I don't think I could do any worse. Should I pitch them my Hugo Award-eligible script?"

"Please don't give them any ideas. They have enough of their own."

The elevator arrived, and they got in.

"So what am I in for today?"

Richard huffed. "You were about half right. You'll be a mage who I, a broody pack alpha or some shit, have gone to for a Very Important Ritual. The script glossed over the exact purpose of the ritual, but it's definitely Very Important. Then, during the ritual, you will slip. And fall. And land on my knot."

Hunter was still chuckling when the elevator hit the sixth floor. "No. No, I was wrong. I could *never* be a MateHub writer. That is a level of genius I'll never attain."

When they entered the studio, his laughter was replaced by a surprised little, "*Oh.*"

A twilight glow and the lingering stench of magic filled the room. They wouldn't be outside for this, but that didn't mean they couldn't have the illusion of moonlight spilling over them as they fucked. Perfectly lit for their fans' optimal viewing pleasure, of course, but with some added ambiance.

Richard watched Hunter look around with wide eyes at the otherworldly haze that softened the familiar sharp edges of the studio, leaving it painted in muted purples and blues, lit by a gentle radiance from above.

None of Hunter's previous scenes had featured on-set magic, so this was likely his first time experiencing its full effects.

Not that Richard had seen all of his videos or anything.

The crew was putting the last touches on the set and adjusting the lights and cameras around it.

"What's wrong with your face?" Tristan asked from where he'd been laying out a magic circle on the floor. He straightened up, running a hand through the loose strands of his black hair.

Richard frowned. There was nothing wrong with his face.

"Oh, okay. Never mind," Tristan said. "For a second there, it seemed like you were smiling."

"So glad to see you, too," Richard said flatly. "Hunter, this is Tristan. He's MateHub's resident on-set mage."

"Oh, you're the one who does all the special effects, right?" Hunter asked, holding out his hand.

Tristan shook it. "I am where the magic happens."

"So why aren't you doing this scene? I don't understand why MateHub wants me to pretend I'm a mage when they have mages who work for them."

"First off, I don't work for MateHub like that. And second, literally no mage would do this scene. I think MateHub pitched it to every mage they've ever worked with, and they all said no."

Hunter frowned. "But you're okay with helping me look like a mage?"

"Yeah, but that's significantly different from agreeing to trip, fall, and land on a knot."

"Is it offensive? To mages? Should I refuse to do it?"

Tristan made a dismissive gesture. "The mage council won't like it. But they don't like anything, and it's super amusing when they're pissed off. The rest of us will just think it's stupid. I mean, check out this circle."

Richard took in the circle Tristan had drawn on the studio's floor. Even by MateHub standards, it was a bit much.

"I'm going to assume normal magic circles don't generally feature twelve dicks drawn in glitter, all ejaculating sparkles toward a blank center where I'm guessing we'll be fucking," Hunter said.

"Pretty safe assumptions," Tristan said. "Wait until you see what you'll be wearing and the symbols I'll be drawing on this asshole's chest."

"More dicks?"

"Also a safe assumption. But first, while I have you, can you take your shirt off for me?"

Hunter shrugged and pulled his shirt over his head.

"Let me have your hands."

Richard grabbed Hunter's shirt, and Tristan raised an eyebrow at him.

Before Richard could ask what his problem was, his nose started to itch, and Tristan's eyes glimmered a cool yellow as he gathered his magic.

"All mages have magical tattoos that develop as their magic does," Tristan explained to Hunter as he took his hands. "The shape and color depend on the type of magic the mage has."

Little white lines squiggled up Hunter's arms by the dozens. Hunter stared at them with open fascination, a smile on his lips, wonder lighting up his face.

There was a brief flare of blinding light, and when the afterimage faded, Hunter was blinking at the lines covering three-fourths of his arms, each now complete with an oval head.

"Did you just draw a bunch of magical sperm swimming up my arms?" he asked, face suddenly full of a lot less awe.

"Yep. And wardrobe's waiting for you."

Hunter wandered in that direction, still staring at the glowing sperm on his arms.

"Alright, Mage," Richard said. "Do your worst."

Tristan grinned sharply. "I plan on it."

Richard pulled off his shirt, and Tristan got to work, using a charcoal mixture to draw symbols on his chest, but it was difficult to concentrate on that when Hunter's laughter was drifting out of the door to wardrobe.

"It's stunning alright," Hunter said. "Real pity it's gonna get ripped apart."

"Isn't it?" Zinnia replied. "I tried to make them as realistic as possible!"

"Did you, perhaps, watch *The Sorcerer's Apprentice* before you designed it?"

"I did! I'm so happy you noticed!"

"No hat?"

There was a sigh. "I wanted to make a hat, but Brandt thought it'd look ridiculous."

"Yeah. We wouldn't want it to take away from this spectacular creation of yours," Hunter said in a voice drier than the Sahara. "Well, I better go get myself prepped so I can change into this masterpiece."

He exited the room, something sheer and glittery draped over his arm.

Richard shot him a questioning look, but Hunter just slipped into his dressing room.

When he turned back, he found Tristan finished and staring at him. He glanced down.

Tristan's worst apparently consisted of a series of dicks that formed a circle on his torso in what could only be described as the life cycle of an erection.

"I see your apprenticeship was well spent."

"Fuck off," Tristan said. "Oh, by the way, I've already got you on my schedule for the new moon after next." There was a calculated indifference to his gaze.

"Obviously. Who else would sever the bond?"

Tristan stared him down for a minute longer, then went back to his magical cock circle.

Richard headed toward his dressing room and carefully didn't think about how quickly the last month had passed and that they were already a third of the way through the contract. Not that it mattered. It wasn't like anytime his mind strayed to that thought, a thread of anxiety wrapped itself around his chest. That wasn't something a professional would feel, and if nothing else, Richard was amazing at his job.

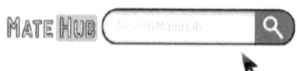

Richard sauntered out of his dressing room naked, half-hard from the building anticipation for the scene they were about to film. It might be patently ridiculous, but his dick didn't care. Bring on the accidental ritual sex.

He made it five steps toward the circle when his eyes caught on where Brandt was towering over Hunter and Everett, pointing to the script as Hunter nodded.

In his mage 'robes.'

Only a miracle kept Richard from choking on his own tongue.

To be fair, he saw *The Sorcerer's Apprentice* inspiration in the long, belled sleeves, the cowl neck, and the heavy cord around the waist. And that was exactly where the similarities ended. Instead of bright colors, it was a barely there black, transparent enough that the definition of Hunter's muscles was still visible. At least where it wasn't covered by more dicks meticulously drawn in silver glitter, exploding sparkling come. God, they even had glittery silver veins drawn on them, didn't they? The soft white glow of the magical sperm tattoos caught the occasional flake, exploding in rainbows of light.

It was definitely something.

Richard was also pretty certain there'd been pants involved in the original costume. Brandt must have decided they, like a hat, would have looked too ridiculous. Plus, who'd ever heard of pants that fell down between when someone tripped and when that someone landed on a knot? That was downright unbelievable.

So instead, the robes split open under the cord, leaving Hunter's dick framed by the sheer fabric falling around it.

Richard swallowed. It'd be so easy to drop to his knees in front of Hunter and suck him off in those robes.

As if Hunter felt that thought, his head jerked up, his eyes zeroing in on Richard. His gaze trailed down his chest, and then he was laughing again. He glanced lower still.

"What? No magic symbols on your wand?"

Richard's lips quirked. "Aren't you the one who'll be

waving around a magic wand? Mine's magic enough on its own."

Brandt's face lit up, and he opened his mouth to speak.

"If you're about to ask me to draw runes on either or both of their dicks, I quit," Tristan called from where he was putting the finishing touches on his magic circle of cocks, somehow enchanting them so the glittery ejaculations were coming out in regular spurts.

Brandt's shoulders slumped. "Fine. Let's start the interview."

He asked them a few things, though Richard wasn't truly listening. How was he supposed to focus on questions like, "If you could do magic, what kind of spells would you do?" when Hunter was wearing such a ridiculous costume?

"Sex rituals," Richard grunted out. Were those drawings of *his* dick? The length and girth looked right in comparison to the size of the balls, and the veins seemed to follow the pattern of his most prominent ones. Had Zinnia drawn a couple dozen of his dick—all at various angles—on Hunter's robes?

His gaze skated over Hunter, landing on how the fabric draped open around his cock. Such an absurd design, leaving Hunter exposed like that. His mouth watered.

"Richard?" Brandt asked, loud enough to cut through the fog of Richard's lust.

"Yes," Richard answered.

"Yes? The most magical sex position is... yes?"

Richard straightened up and leered at the camera. "Of course. They're all magical if you know how to do them right."

Next to him, Hunter snorted.

"How about we get this scene started?" Brandt said. "Richard, if you please." He gestured to the circle.

Richard refrained from rolling his eyes as he took his place, lying on his back in the center of the glittery cocks.

He blinked up at the ceiling. "That's a new angle." They'd rigged a camera up there to shoot straight down.

Everett bounced on the balls of his feet, drawing Richard's gaze. His light blue eyes shone with excitement. "Yes! We learned about top-down angles in film school, and this seemed like the perfect opportunity for an overhead shot to fully capture the magic circle!"

Hunter let out another snort. "I know I appreciate a good top-down angle. Good top-under angles, too."

"We didn't learn about top-under angles." Everett frowned. The confusion on his face was so incongruous on a gay porn set, Richard bit his cheek to keep from laughing.

"The top is Richard. In this scene, Richard is the top-under," Tristan explained dryly, causing Everett's pale cheeks to redden.

"Oh. Yes. I suppose he is."

Richard shook his head. This poor naive kid. His film school needed to add a few courses on the adult film industry to round out their graduates' education.

"Anyway," Brandt said. "We'll see what the fans think about adding a bit of an artistic flair before incorporating more into future scenes. Now, Richard, spread-eagle, please."

Richard stretched out his legs and arms. "Did the writers decide what this ritual is for?"

"Yeah. Last-minute rewrite. You're a broody pack alpha who is afraid your knot doesn't work and you'll never find your fated mate. So you've gone to Mage Savage to perform a ritual that will call forth your mate and your knot."

The lobby was bugged. That was the only explanation.

Off to the side, Tristan handed Hunter a large leather-bound book.

"'Ye Olde Tome o' Seks Magyck?'" Hunter asked.

Tristan nodded gravely. "Passed from generation to generation."

Hunter flipped through it. "All the pages just say 'seks' repeatedly."

"How do you think there were more generations to pass it to?"

"You made this at two in the morning last night, didn't you?"

"Please. Eight in the evening. I'm not losing beauty sleep over this place. The incantation is bookmarked in the middle."

"The incantation?" Hunter flipped to the page in question. His eyebrows climbed as he read.

"For the record," Tristan said, "I had no input."

"I know jack shit about the supernatural, but this doesn't sound like actual magic."

"Congratulations. You officially know more about magic than the MateHub writers."

"Moving on," Brandt said. "Richard, we need to start out with you hard, but Tristan will put a glamour on you so we can reveal it at the most dramatic moment."

Richard shrugged, spit in his hand, and grabbed himself. The crew averted their eyes while he jerked off. He'd always found that amusing. It wasn't like they hadn't watched him jerk off before. But it was sweet they tried to differentiate between when the cameras were and weren't rolling.

Hunter was less courteous. He'd angled himself away slightly and appeared engrossed in reading the prop book, but Richard felt his eyes on him. The presence in his mind burned brighter when Richard thrust into his fist.

You like that, don't you? Richard thought. *Looking forward to me fucking you again?*

Hunter swallowed, his cock twitching and thickening without being touched.

"OKAY," Brandt cut in. "That's enough. Tristan, if you'd please?"

Tristan knelt beside Richard, assessing his length. "Eh."

"What the fuck is that 'eh' supposed to mean?"

"It means 'eh,'" Tristan said, lifting his hands.

Richard's stomach roiled when he thought Tristan was about to grab his cock. But instead, he hovered his hands over it, pale yellow sparking to life in his eyes as his brow furrowed.

A flash of light later, and Richard squinted down at his dick.

His tiny, limp dick.

"Ex-fucking-scuse you," Richard said. Even soft, no one would call him small. Right now, his thumb was bigger.

Hunter was biting his lip, while Tristan radiated smugness.

"Tristan." Brandt sighed. "The fans won't be happy with tha—Oh my god. Do you think any of the mages would be willing to do a scene with a ritual where someone comes to them wanting to magically increase the size of their dick?"

Tristan stared at him flatly. "No."

Crestfallen didn't begin to describe Brandt's expression.

"Wait." Richard pushed himself up on his elbows. "Are *you* the MateHub writers? In the seven years I've worked here, I've never met a single one."

Brandt clapped his hands together. "Right. Tristan, give

him his dick back. Hunter, while you're saying the incantation, make a few 'Let It Go' hand motions, and Tristan will explode magic over your hand. Richard, when Hunter says the final line, arch up like magic is coursing through you, and Tristan will drop the glamour."

"When I drop it, there might be another underneath," Tristan told him, a pleasant threat in his tone, his fingers held less than an inch apart, but he adjusted the spell.

Richard eyed himself; Tristan smiled innocently at him.

Whatever. Eighty percent of impressive was still impressive, and it'd just make the reveal more jaw-dropping.

It was bizarre to see himself soft, yet feel himself hard and pulsing, his dick ready to be done with all this and find a home in Hunter's ass.

He flopped onto the floor.

Hunter stepped into the circle with him. He looked around at the cocks surrounding them. "This is going to end with me having glitter in my ass for weeks, isn't it?"

"Would you rather clean it up?" Tristan asked. "Even with magic, I'm going to be covered in the shit forever." As if supporting his claim, the low studio light caught on a few silver flakes that twinkled in his dark hair.

Hunter grimaced. "Fair point."

Everyone got into position, Hunter standing between Richard's legs, and Brandt called action.

Hunter held up the book and solemnly intoned the first stanza as Tristan made a breeze stir his robes, exposing him further.

"*Zephyrs whisper through midnight veils,*
Twilight glimmers on hidden tails.
Threads of magic intertwine,
Knots of fate in pleasure bind."

He made the requested gesture, and a burst of luminescent sperm exploded above his hand, squiggling in the darkened studio before fading away.

Hunter pressed his lips together, suppressing a laugh before he continued.

"Connections woven, unseen threads,
Lured toward where destiny spreads.
Bonds of glorious fates align,
Awakening stars as futures entwine."

He made a grand gesture in the air that left a swath of sperm trailing behind it, and his eyes took on a manic look as he tried to keep a straight face. In Richard's mind, his presence gleamed with amusement strong enough that it filtered through their bond even though they weren't touching.

"Beneath the moon, a desperate plea,
Magic's touch shall now set free.
With this dance on sacred plot,
Summon forth what's long been sought."

He paused, as if gathering his magic, before declaring,

"Unleash now a euphoric knot!"

Richard had to stifle a laugh of his own as he arched up, and Tristan dropped the glamour, making it appear like his erection went from zero to sixty in a time that would make his SF90 blush. He threw in a few exaggerated moans for good measure.

"CUT!" Brandt yelled. "That was perfect."

"Does everything have to be sperm and dicks?" Hunter asked, unable to contain a snicker.

"YES," basically every crew member answered in unison.

"Fair," Hunter said.

They filmed a dozen more shots. A brief dialog

exchange with Hunter assuring Richard the ritual would work and he'd find his fated mate soon. Hunter dancing around Richard's body in the circle, more magical sperm bursting from his hands. Him tripping over the hem of his slutty robes and falling, arms windmilling, robes having a full-on Marilyn moment as he did. And then a few reaction shots of their shocked faces as he landed.

Hunter's eyes widened comically, his mouth falling open. "Is... is that... your knot?"

Richard grabbed his hips and thrust up, the angle hiding the fact that Hunter was annoyingly not on his dick yet. "My knot for my mate."

Immediately fine with it, Hunter pressed his hand firmly to Richard's heart, little radiant sperm swimming out from beneath his palm, tattooing Richard as his.

Brandt called cut again.

"The mage council will *hate* this." Tristan didn't even try to conceal the glee in his voice.

"Are you sure it isn't offensive?" Hunter asked, still straddling Richard's lap. Richard's cock pressed up against his ass, and fuck, that was distracting.

Tristan waved him off. "There's some offensive shit that could happen between wolf shifters and mages that I've been promised in writing will never, ever happen during a MateHub scene. But this? This is just stupid, and I can see at least a few mages getting off to it. Or at least MST3K-ing it."

Richard wasn't particularly thrilled at the idea of a bunch of mages sitting around roasting one of his scenes, but it was what it was.

"Alright," Brandt said. "Richard, get your knot about half-full. Something you'll be able to get in and out of Hunter a few times before you're tied together."

"Get my—" Richard pushed himself up on his forearms

again, the motion jostling his dick along Hunter's crack. He bit back a moan, then forced himself to focus. "What do you mean, get my knot half-full? You know damn well that's not how that works."

"Oh." Brandt's dark brow furrowed. "I suppose not. I didn't—I mean, *the writers* didn't think this through."

Hunter looked back and forth between Brandt and Richard before the realization clicked. "Oh. Am I going to have to act as a fluffer for my own scene? I didn't even think fluffers were a real thing."

"Do you mind?" Brandt asked.

Hunter lifted his shoulders in a shrug. "It's not like it wasn't going there anyway. Toss me the lube."

The crew members were suddenly fascinated by things everywhere else but them.

Richard's heart kicked up a notch, and Hunter paused, studying him.

"Are *you* okay with this?" he asked, concern written in the furrow of his brow.

"Totally," Richard said, keeping his voice as casual as possible. "Thanks for the assist."

Hunter's eyes narrowed, and Richard could feel the delicate pressure of him sensing Richard, an almost physical brush over his body. Whatever he was doing, whatever answer he got, seemed to be enough. He clicked open the cap on the lube.

"Don't fuck up my artwork," Tristan called.

"Wouldn't dream of it," Hunter replied.

He didn't waste time, just slicked Richard up. That quick motion alone made Richard shudder; he'd already been hard for too long. But then Hunter was reaching between his legs and pulling out the flesh-colored plug he'd been wearing. He groaned before tossing it away. "If they

149

ever make me dance around for an hour with one of those in again, I'm demanding extra pay."

After lining Richard up, he paused with him pressed to his hole and raised an eyebrow, one final check. Richard nodded.

Then he was sliding down, so hot and tight, but taking Richard in like he was greedy for him, like Richard was made to fill him, to fit him better than anyone else could.

Richard refused to think about how no one was watching them, how the cameras weren't on. How he was the only one who'd see Hunter's eyes fluttering shut, his satisfied expression as he bottomed out. He sat there, breathing, adjusting, then started to move.

The realization of how rarely he'd seen Hunter in this position during his scenes hit Richard. There were tons of him getting bent over and railed, and Richard did like that look on him, but it didn't begin to compare to this. Hunter was made to ride cock, and he clearly enjoyed it, fucking himself on Richard's dick in a rhythm all his own and looking devastatingly beautiful as he did it.

Richard kept his hands pressed to the floor. He didn't want to grab Hunter's hips, to find a rhythm that would act as the perfect counterpoint to Hunter's, letting him have control, but giving him a little extra at the same time.

It wasn't long before Richard's knot was expanding, catching on Hunter's rim, making him pant quietly each time he took it in. Richard nearly growled, his claws scraping against the floor. He couldn't stop his hips from moving, meeting Hunter as he pressed down on the swell.

That was it. Just a little more and his knot would be full; they'd be tied together.

"About ready?" Brandt asked, the question crashing Richard back to reality.

Hunter froze, Richard half in him. They both groaned.

"I'll take that as a yes."

Hunter pulled off him completely, and Richard wanted to whine, his knot throbbing in protest. He'd been so goddamn close.

"There's a reason we don't do these kinds of scenes when I'm knotting someone." He was going to make fucking sure Daniel knew he would not be doing anything like this ever again.

"Oh, you're fine. He'll be on your knot again in five minutes. You'll survive. Now, let's get this shot. We need a close-up of Hunter landing on Richard's knot. Rhys," Brandt said to the main cameraman, "you get in there nice and close. Tristan, blow up Hunter's robes again so we've got a clear shot of his ass. Hunter, take his dick as quickly and forcefully as you're comfortable with. We'll speed it up in post. Everyone good to go?"

Richard was more than good. His knot, however, was less than pleased with this situation. He glared up at the camera on the ceiling.

"Ah," Rhys said from where he was kneeling, his camera pointing up under Hunter's billowing robes. "Not sure this is the shot you want. Hunter already looks pretty fucked from this angle."

"Oh." The distress was clear on Brandt's face, but Tristan was shaking his head and stepping forward.

"Seems like *the writers* didn't think of a lot of things. Here. Hunter, can you bend over and hold your cheeks open for me?"

Richard growled, then clamped his jaw shut when he realized what he'd done.

Tristan grinned down at him. "Bend over, Hunter," he said, voice deadpan. "And spread yourself nice and wide so you're ready for me to work my magic. You're going to be so fucking tight."

Richard refused to growl again.

Hunter glanced over his shoulder at Tristan, who rolled his eyes and said, "Glamour."

"Okay." Hunter stuck his ass out and huffed in amusement. "If, two years ago, you'd told me I'd be getting my ass glamoured tight by a mage—Wait. It won't actually be tight, will it?"

"Nah. It'll just look tight for the camera. Getting it actually tight would require healing, which I'm not good at, and I have no desire to get my fingers all up in your asshole in order to attempt it. No offense."

"None taken. And thank god. Can you imagine slamming down on that beast while tight?"

Richard preened. He might be in the worst pain of his life, but hell yeah, he was a beast.

"All set," Tristan said, stepping away.

Hunter frowned down at himself. "But... I want to see. Hold on." He took a step like he was heading to his dressing room.

Richard snagged his ankle, almost whining. Could people not tell he was dying here? That he was the first wolf shifter in the history of the universe to discover that blue knots were a thing? A very lethal and deadly thing.

He needed in his mate *now*.

"Oh, fine," Hunter said, straddling him, and Richard's stomach clenched. "You're no fun."

"I'll be a lot of fun once you get that ass back on my knot."

Hunter scoffed, but he was grinning.

"Action," Brandt called, but Richard couldn't bring himself

to care about anything other than the devilish glint in Hunter's eyes as he lined himself up. A second later, he slammed down, and Richard's entire body arched up, a genuine howl ripping out of him as Hunter's tight heat engulfed his knot.

Fuck, that was perfect. Hunter wiggled his hips, making them both groan.

Brandt's artistic vision or not, there was no way he'd be able to pull out and fuck his knot into Hunter. It'd had enough waiting and had fully expanded as soon as it was back in him.

This was the part of the scene where he was supposed to flip them over, rip off Hunter's robes, and fuck him into the floor.

He brought his hands up to clasp Hunter's hips, grinding into him. "My knot for my mate," he said again, though this time it was a dark, rumbling promise that had Hunter tightening around him. "It's just for you. Do you like it?"

"Yes," Hunter said, voice breathy, not even remotely acting.

"Good." Richard rucked up the fabric of his robes. Hunter took the hint and pulled them off, tossing them aside.

Richard gave himself a few moments to run his hands over Hunter's body, along the lines of his abs and up to pinch at his nipples until his arousal spiked, letting Richard know the exact amount of pressure he needed.

Hunter was staring at him, waiting for Richard to flip them over.

But they'd done that already, and Hunter was too fucking beautiful to waste always being pinned down by some top hammering into him.

Richard smirked up at him. "Now be a good little mate and grind on it for a while. Show me how much you like it."

He sensed how Hunter wanted to roll his eyes at that, but he'd also clenched on him again, and his presence seemed to shimmer, thrilled at being given such a small thing as a chance to control his own pleasure.

They'd *definitely* be doing this again. He'd wanted to do this contract with Hunter because no one was getting him off as hard as he deserved. Richard was man enough to admit that the best way to do that might be by letting Hunter set the pace.

Besides, this way, he got to lie back and enjoy the show.

And what a fucking show it was.

Hunter rocked his hips, hands braced on Richard's thighs. His gaze was locked with Richard's, and when he finally settled into a grinding rhythm that had his eyes glazing over, his mouth parted on near-constant gasps, Richard started to thrust up into him with shallow rolls of his hips that put enough extra pressure on his prostate to transform those little gasps into proper moans.

They moved together until Hunter was shivering and weak from pleasure, his presence a fire blazing in Richard's mind, consuming them both in the most exquisite way.

Hunter leaned forward, his fingernails scraping over his chest, smudging the drawings, his eyes hooded as he returned Richard's smirk. "Now be a good little mate and flip us over and fuck me until the only name I remember is yours."

That, Richard could do.

He had Hunter on his back in record time, fucking into him as much as his knot would allow.

It didn't take much. Hunter had already warmed himself up perfectly. His cries took on a desperate edge, and he clung to Richard, lasting bare minutes before he was coming, his body arching, a groan caught in his throat, gripping Richard so tight it was impossible for him not to follow, not to bury himself deep and release pulses of come inside Hunter.

He had enough presence of mind to roll them over and settle Hunter against his chest before he collapsed against the floor.

Eyes still closed, Hunter hummed with contentment, then wriggled on his knot, drawing a muffled curse from Richard.

"Mmmm," Hunter said, blinking before he focused on Richard's face. When he did, he started chuckling, the sound vibrating against Richard's chest.

He pushed himself up, shaky arms on either side of Richard's head. One hand came up to gently brush against Richard's cheek.

"You've got glitter on your face." Amusement rolled through their bond as he tried to brush it away once more, then gave up. "No use. You'll have to live with being glittery from now on."

He grinned at Richard, his warm brown eyes sparkling with laughter, his dark curls beyond disheveled. Richard had never needed to kiss anyone more in his life.

But he didn't have to do anything; Hunter did it for him, closing the distance between them, licking into Richard's mouth.

Richard closed his arms tighter around Hunter. Some corner of his brain protested that they should end this scene and let Rhys get a nice shot of Hunter's well-fucked hole, but he didn't want to. Not yet. Not when he'd just learned how Hunter liked to be fucked. When he could grind up in the same rhythm Hunter had been riding him and make him gasp, their kisses becoming sloppy. When he could turn Hunter into a quivering mess of desperate moans and clinging hands.

And if it took until his knot was well over half-deflated to wring a second orgasm out of Hunter, MateHub would have to deal with it. They had plenty of footage of him popping his knot out of used holes to go around. Who knew? The fans might enjoy seeing him soften more completely, slide out of his mate more naturally, his come leaking out while they were still tied together.

"Cut," Brandt said, though his booming voice was quieter than usual. Richard glanced over and realized half the crew was looking anywhere but them.

Tristan was staring at them openly though, an unreadable look on his face.

Hunter stretched against him, dragging Richard's attention back to him. "Now that was a good couple months at least," he said, voice rough. "Maybe even half a year."

Damn right it was. Richard ran his fingers over the bumps of Hunter's spine before he could stop himself.

"Any chance you'll carry me to my dressing room this time, too?" Hunter shifted his hips against Richard in a way that threatened to get him hard again real fast.

It hit Richard with a gut-sinking certainty that the actual question was, "Any chance he wouldn't?"

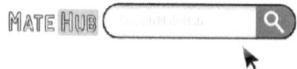

SCENE: A Mage Summoned My Knot and then Fell on It!

MagicalHWood:
This is the stupidest thing I've ever gotten off to. As a mage, I feel like I should be offended. The tattoos. The whole ritual. And those robes? Who would wear that? The lame "magic." Ye Olde Tome o' Seks Magyck? "Unleash now a euphoric knot!"??? But it's SO DAMN HOT. I keep watching Hunter land over and over. The way Richard's knot just pops right in. And then his little surprised face? SO HOT.

KnottyWolf69:
RIGHT? It's freaking stupid and not even remotely how knotting and bonding work, but I need a mage to fall on my knot right the fuck now, please.

MagicalHWood:
I've got an uptight friend who could use a good fuck. Get your dick out, and I'll trip him for you.

KnottyWolf69:
Got two? My alpha needs to get his knot off more than I do.

nuts4knots:
Can we talk for a second about how hot Richard is when he's trying not to laugh?

BramStroker:
For real. It's been forever since he's looked like he's truly enjoying himself during a scene. I mean, obviously he always ENJOYS himself, but this time it seemed like he was having actual fun.

KnottyWolf69:
Seriously, Richard completely zoning out in the pre-scene interview because he couldn't take his eyes off Hunter's cock was unexpectedly delightful.

nuts4knots:
He was almost drooling. Not that I blame him.

HuntMeDown:
I'm telling you. It's all Hunter. DickHunt is meant to be.

BramStroker:
I'm convinced. These last three scenes have been Richard's best, and they've got one thing in common.

MagicalHWood:
Damn, they really did convert you.

KnottyWolf69:
Another scene as hot as these, and they might get me too.

HuntMeDown:
We'll be waiting! You know where to find us!

HuntMeDown:

Though, before I leave, I have to say, I had no idea Richard was such a grower.

MagicalHWood:

That was a glamour! There was one on Hunter's ass too.

KnottyWolf69:

Aaaand he's already gone. Guess you'll have to defend Richard's manhood some other time.

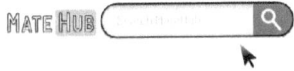

CHAPTER
TWELVE

Hunter stared at the small TV screen and called forth a magical shield, barely blocking an attack as Chance went on the offensive.

It was good to be home, in his own apartment; Hunter kept telling himself that. They'd ordered pizza and were having a gaming marathon.

This was nice. He liked this.

The pizza had been delicious. Really, it had been. He hadn't been thinking about how much nicer home-cooked meals were or anything.

"Is it weird that Richard cooks?" he asked. "Do wolf shifters not normally cook?"

Chance hit pause, whipping his head around to look at him. "You've got a wolf shifter cooking for you?"

"Why do people keep acting like that's strange?"

"Do you not know that food is a big deal for wolf shifters?"

"And why does everyone assume I know anything about this shit? I didn't even know it existed two years ago."

"Probably because you mainline games made for the supernatural community and take supernatural dick like a champ?"

"Ah, yes. That famous conveyor of knowledge. Dick."

"*Supernatural* dick."

"Right. Because sucking you off will lead to enlightenment."

"It's definitely made a few people see god."

Hunter shot him a look, and Chance sighed.

"The thing you have to understand about wolf shifters is that they're all about pack. They have these big-ass meals together. Only people very close to them get invited. Basically, food means family to them. So getting that invite is a huge deal. It's meeting the parents times ten."

"Okay, but he's not inviting me to pack dinners. It's the two of us, and one time, his friend."

"If anything, that's worse. In bonded pairs, the wolf shifter with the higher position in the pack, or the one who could be considered more dominant, will generally want to care for their mate in every way they can. Protect them. Provide for them. All that. Which frequently includes making sure they're well-fed. It's the one cute thing about wolves. These growly, muscular alpha types will suddenly be up to their elbows in flour because their mate has a sweet tooth and they want to make them cupcakes."

"You think Richard is 'more dominant' and 'providing' for me? Fuck off with that. He likes to cook. That's all."

"Wanna bet? Mention some random food you like that he'd never think of making, then wait to see how long it takes before he makes it for you."

Hunter scoffed. "Yeah, right. He's not going to learn how to make laksa because I say I loved that Malaysian restaurant near our dorms."

Chance made a disbelieving noise. "Tell me that next week. But if you end up smelling like dog forever, I'm reevaluating our friendship."

"That's not happening. This is a temporary contract."

"Okaaaay. Enjoy your laksa tomorrow night." Chance unpaused the game.

Hunter frowned.

There was no fucking way.

He stopped the game again. "You're being ridiculous. He isn't *providing* for me."

Chance raised an eyebrow at him. "Is he taking care of you in any other way?"

"No, of course n—" Hunter cut himself off. "Well, I mean, after our scenes, he's helped me get back to the apartment. But considering he fucks me until my brain and bones are liquefied, that's just a professional courtesy."

The look Chance gave him seemed to question whether Hunter's brain had ever regained its solid state. "Richard Knotz doesn't do professional courtesies. When the scene is done, he's done. Everyone knows that."

"I thought that too, at first, but he's not like that at all."

"With you, maybe."

Hunter's phone vibrated before he could protest further.

He opened the message from his agent.

ADRIAN

MateHub wants to move your next scene to this Friday. Are you okay with that?

Hunter shifted. It'd been two days. He was still feeling their last scene, but he'd be good to go before then.

> **HUNTER**
>
> That's fine. Why are they moving it?

> **ADRIAN**
>
> Not sure. They said something about
> wanting to do it before the full moon.

> **HUNTER**
>
> Okay. I'll be ready.

He frowned at his phone.

"Was that your not-mate asking what you want for dinner?"

"No, it was Adrian. MateHub wants to do our next scene a week early. Is there any reason they wouldn't want to film on the full moon?"

Chance's eyes widened in surprise, then narrowed. "How wolfish was Richard during the last one? More animal instinct than human?"

"Extremely. It took a week for the claw marks to heal." Hunter shivered at the memory.

Concern clouded Chance's face.

"Oh, no. That was not a complaint," Hunter assured him.

"What's the scene?"

"It's a group scene. Some bullshit about me being captured by an alpha who then shares me with his pack. They fuck me before he knots me."

"Jesus fucking Christ." Chance slapped a hand to his face.

"It's a dumb concept, but it's far from the stupidest thing MateHub has come up with."

"No. That Jesus fucking Christ wasn't for the concept. I've seen those scenes before. They're moving it because they're worried he'll literally kill whoever was unlucky enough to agree to star in that scene with you two."

Hunter started laughing, then realized Chance wasn't. "Oh. You're serious."

"I'm not remotely kidding. When did the cooking start?"

"I refuse to believe he's cooking to take care of me, but if that's the standard, then the day after the last full moon."

"If he was super wolfish before he started cooking for you, filming a packbang now is a terrible idea. Especially when his wolf will be close to the surface due to the moon. I'm surprised they're trying it at all. Normal wolf shifters get real possessive over their mates. Don't like people touching them, let alone fucking them. Him doing those scenes with his previous co-stars is insane to most shifters. It adds to the whole legend status. Other wolf shifters who do bonding contracts don't do group scenes; Duke Moorhead never has while bonded. But if MateHub has realized Richard is showing more stereotypical mate behavior toward you, I bet they're questioning their scheduling and scene choices."

"You're talking like he can't control his wolf."

"For shifters, when our animal sides are at the surface, we're more primal, less inhibited. There's a lot more 'It's mine' and 'I want it, so I take it.' Our human sides have the ability to override those instincts and impulses. It can be a struggle, but if we want to, we can. Wolf shifters on full moons rarely want to. Wolf shifters with new mates never do."

No way. Richard wouldn't attack someone for fucking Hunter in a scene where they were supposed to be fucking Hunter. He didn't seem possessive or aggressive. Chance's whole 'providing' theory was completely wrong.

He shook his head as they went back to the game, but the idea refused to leave him, prowling through the shadows of his mind.

"Do *you* want to do the scene?" Chance asked with feigned casual interest.

"Of course," Hunter said with a snort. "Why wouldn't I?"

If the thought made something inside him twist, it was because it'd been a while since he'd done a group scene. That was it. There was nothing more to it than that. No matter what Chance might think.

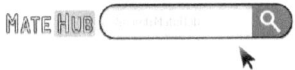

Richard was sitting on the couch again, scrolling on his phone. He seemed to always be doing that.

Hunter picked up a controller and shoved it at him. "Here. I'm teaching you how to play."

Richard looked up. "Why?"

"Because we have four controllers, and Max wants to play one of the *Supernatural Skirmish* games in team mode. *Beastbound Brawlers* is super fun two on two."

"When did you talk to Max?" Richard's brow furrowed.

"He sent me a message yesterday."

"You have Max's number?"

"Yeah. We exchanged contact info while he was here."

Richard grumbled something Hunter didn't quite catch, but he understood the gist.

"Oh. We should too. It's weird we've been living together for over a month and haven't done that. Give me your phone."

Richard grudgingly handed it over, and Hunter entered his number. "Max says he'll get Hardin to come over so we can do some battles."

"You know Hardin?" Richard snatched back his phone as soon as Hunter was finished.

"Never met him, but Max keeps bringing him up. I'm assuming he's Hardin Cox?"

"Yeah, that's him."

"Damn, he's so hot. That cool, mysterious, silent type thing he has going on? I couldn't begin to tell you how many times I've gotten off to his scenes. When Chance showed me MateHub, the first video I watched was this cheesy scenario where Hardin's in a coffee shop and smells his fated mate. They claim each other right there while everyone sips their drinks, like seeing people fuck and bond is a daily occurrence in their world. It was called *Taking My Mate the Way I Take My Coffee: Hot and with Extra Cream*. I'm assuming they were faking the knotting, since there was no close-up, but I couldn't walk into a coffee shop for a year after that without getting hard, imagining him coming in and immediately bending me over the table of some poor grad student working on their thesis."

"That's not how mates work," Richard said, a growl in his voice.

Hunter rolled his eyes. "I'm aware, but I've been told repeatedly it's part of the fun. Anyway, when I tried to convince Chance to come over, he said he'd rather get DP'd by two massive bear shifters than be in a room with three wolves. Which seems a little extreme given the size of some of MateHub's bears. I mean, *Two Bears, One Cub* was hot, but damn, just watching it had me walking funny for days. But to each their own." He wiggled the controller in Richard's face. "So...?"

Richard grabbed it, scowling. "Video games are a waste of time."

"Says the guy who spends hours on his phone."

"At least I'm reading shit. Games can't be that hard."

Instead of commenting on that, Hunter started the *Beastbound Brawlers* training module.

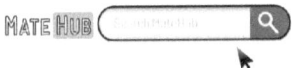

Max hadn't been lying; Richard *sucked* at gaming.

Or, more accurately, he sucked at specific parts. Namely, the fighting parts. Everything up to that was fine. Richard trained Beasts with the best of them, but the moment he stepped into the arena...

Hunter slumped against the couch as Richard died for approximately the three thousandth time. "Why did you take that hit? That's what your Beast is for."

"But she'd already taken two hits. Another one and she'd have fallen below fifty percent, and that would have meant weeks for her to recover."

Hunter's mouth fell open. A minute passed before he managed to get out, "As opposed to you? Who's now dead."

"I can always start a new game."

"You... you sacrificed your avatar to save your Beast?"

Richard crossed his arms over his chest. "She didn't pick the fight. It seems unfair to put her in danger because I challenged this Grand Enchanter Lysandra Moonspell person."

"Who had a level-two Gloomwing Harbinger. You had a level-ten Shadowbound Shade! You should have been able to take out the Harbinger in three hits."

"Now that's unfair to the Harbinger. Why would I hurt them? It's not their fault Grand Enchanter Lysandra Moonspell was unwilling to fight me on their own."

"The entire game is about using Beasts to fight!"

"Making animals fight is unethical." Richard's expression was clearly judging Hunter's entertainment choices.

"Oh my god. You're such a softy. I thought you were some complete unfeeling jackass, but you won't even kill a fictional animal in a video game. You're the softest softy to ever soft. How do you do porn when you're this soft?"

"Hey! There's nothing soft about that."

"And the rest of you?"

"Not wanting to see an animal get hurt, even a fictional one, doesn't make me soft. It's totally normal. There's a reason the website 'Does the Dog Die?' exists."

Hunter stared up at the ceiling. This was not cute. He wasn't finding Richard fucking Knotz *cute*. "Oh! Wait!" He wrenched the controller out of Richard's hand.

"What the—"

"Hold on." Hunter exited the game and pulled up another.

"What is *Enchanted Guardians: Realm Tamer*?" Richard asked as the title loaded.

"It's a world full of magical creatures, and you're their guardian. You create safe havens for them by discovering their abilities, preferences, and personalities. You'll have to build shit for them, gather ingredients for them to stay healthy, and protect them from threats."

"So I have to provide them with whatever they need?"

Hunter blinked, remembering his conversation with Chance. "Uh, yeah. Here. I'll set it up."

"Okay, what—Are you naming that avatar Lord Dick

Softfluff?" He grabbed for the controller, but Hunter held it out of reach until he saved the name.

"Yep. Have fun!" He handed the controller to Richard, who glared at him before turning to the screen and suspiciously starting the tutorial.

"So," Hunter said, clearing his throat. "Chance and I were reminiscing about college. All the things we miss."

Richard grunted, not paying attention to Hunter as he flew through the basic instructions.

"There was this little Malaysian restaurant next to campus. Best laksa I've ever eaten."

Richard made a disinterested noise. On screen, he was coaxing the tiniest baby griffin out from under a bush.

Within fifteen minutes, he'd reunited it with its anxious parents and built them a safer, cozier den—complete with a week's supply of astral gossamer, luminescent nectar, etherleaf fruits, and enchanted frostberries—and was off on a quest to find wispfire ember, the fifth of their special dietary needs.

Hunter let out a breath. Richard caring for adorable mystical creatures and being really fucking good at it was not *cute*. Or attractive. Or any other adjective.

He was a jackass. Not cute. One game didn't change that. Regardless of what Hunter's competence kink was trying to tell him.

And Richard hadn't given a single shit about what kind of food Hunter was craving.

The fact that they had Moroccan food the following night proved it. Chance didn't know what he was talking about. Richard wasn't *providing* for him.

Hunter told Chance as much in a message.

CHANCE

Give it another day or two. He probably had to track down the ingredients.

He wasn't going to drop this, was he?

Whatever. He'd realize soon enough this was just a job for both of them.

Except, when Hunter came in the next night, after a trip to the in-house gym, it was to a familiar scent in the air.

He wanted to curse but couldn't. Richard's laksa was even better than his linguine.

THIRTEEN

Richard didn't know how he'd gotten talked into this —having his friends over to his temporary apartment to play video games with his temporary mate. So he could cook them dinner.

Max hadn't let him forget that.

Whatever he said, it wasn't weird that Richard was cooking. And it wasn't for Hunter.

If anyone doubted that, he'd show them the hundred-plus recipes he'd bookmarked on his phone over the last few weeks. There were way more of them than nights they had left together. If Richard really had been cooking for Hunter, he'd only have another fifty or so saved.

He looked toward the door as the buzzer sounded, then focused again on the TV. He'd nearly convinced the kraken to allow him to treat a nasty cut on one of her tentacles with a poultice. If he didn't help her soon, she'd lose health points and wouldn't be able to properly care for her kraken-lets, and they were too young to take down ships on their own.

The intercom buzzed a second time.

Hunter chuckled, shaking his dark curls as he stood. "I'll get it."

Richard had finished bandaging her up when Hunter opened the apartment door and let Max in.

"Where's Hardin?" Richard asked. "I thought he was coming."

"Ah," Max said, shoving his hands in his pockets. "He couldn't make it, but said he'll see us at the studio tomorrow." He glanced at the TV, then back at Richard. "Are you... playing *Enchanted Guardians*?"

Richard shrugged.

Max stared as Richard did a quick check of his creatures' health and happiness scores. They were set for him to leave them for the night.

"Lord Dick Softflu—Wait a minute. Go back. Is your Pegasus family's happiness maxed out?"

"Yeah."

"*How*? Those prissy bastards are never happy about anything."

"Why would you ask me? I'm terrible at video games. The absolute worst. Only good at one thing."

"Two," Max and Hunter said in unison.

"Well, two plus one very specific instance of a third," Hunter clarified. He looked over at Max. "You should see the number of eggs his dragon has laid. It's disturbing how good he is at this game."

"I take it these newfound skills don't transfer to *Beast-bound Brawlers*."

"Not even remotely."

"Why would I want to play a game like that?" Richard asked, but they ignored him.

"So we're still down one for team battles."

Hunter scanned the room. "Two, apparently. But yeah. I

keep trying to convince my friend Chance to join us, but he refuses. Maybe you know him. Chance Heat?"

"Twunk mountain lion shifter? Does a lot of threesomes?"

"Yep. That's him."

"You think he'll ever let a wolf shifter have a chance at that ass?"

"Nope. If he won't come here because he says it'll reek like dog, I highly doubt he'll let one of you fuck him."

"That's a shame. Waste of a grade A ass."

"I'll let him know."

"Speaking of grade A asses. Did you have this one try *Moonlit Bonds*?" Max gestured at Richard.

Hunter's face lit up, his brown eyes filling with wicked glee. "I think we found what we're doing this evening."

Richard frowned, more than a little concerned about how excited he suddenly seemed. "The knotting game? You want to watch me try to knot someone?"

Hunter looked like he was about to rub his hands together. "Oh, this is going to be fun."

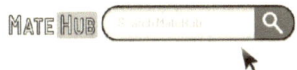

This was the worst game Richard had ever played in his life, and that included MateHub's short-lived attempts to expand their merch into the board game market with Monoporny. Creating a porn empire had been significantly less fun than advertised, but even that hadn't been as tedious as *Moonlit Bonds*.

"How did they manage to make fucking so boring?" He

double-pressed the A and B buttons to change up his angle and speed.

Neither Max nor Hunter was listening.

"How does he keep getting them to sleep with him so fast?" Max asked in an awed whisper, his amber eyes fixed on where Richard's avatar was currently fucking a stable boy up against a tree. "He's averaging one every two minutes. I didn't know you could speedrun this game."

"Speedrun? It's been *hours*!"

"How does he make them come so quickly?" Hunter replied to Max, voice equally quiet, like they thought speaking at a regular volume would mess with his gameplay.

As if on cue, the stable boy came, his groans filling the apartment. Richard hit the down arrow, his softening dick sliding out easily, no knot in sight. He sighed.

"Damn. That was number ninety-two," Max said. "Do you think he'll make it through them all?"

"Statistically speaking, he has to find his mate before he gets through the one hundred fuckable characters, right? I've never heard of anyone fucking all ninety-nine before they get to their mate."

There was a prince that lived in this castle. Might as well have Lord Softfluff fuck him while they were there.

One minute later, Richard had His Royal Highness ass-up in the throne room.

"How does he do that?" Max hissed.

"Is that guard waiting for his turn?" Hunter asked.

"It's not difficult," Richard said. "They have certain needs. You figure out the things that make them feel good, then give them those things. Why didn't they make it more challenging?"

On screen, the prince's pleasure bar was five percent away from full. Richard pressed the B button repeatedly.

Next to him, Hunter made a releasing gesture with both his hands and whispered, "Unleash now a euphoric knot!"

Richard did not snicker at that.

But Hunter's magic didn't seem to be working that evening. Lord Softfluff's dick slid out of the prince. The guard was a similarly quick disappointment.

"Six more to go." Max sounded entirely too pumped.

Richard collapsed against the couch and thrust the controller blindly at him. "You do it then." He'd been fucking for hours; he was done. This game had managed the impossible—making him sick of sex.

"He hasn't fucked his childhood best friend yet," Hunter said.

"Ooh, good idea. He lives around here, doesn't he?"

Richard watched as Max tracked down Lord Softfluff's best friend. "Tell him you've been an asshat for not finding him sooner, and then if there's an option for it, say you want to start over, no years of bitter longing between you."

Both Max and Hunter snapped their heads toward him.

"What?" he asked.

"You read some play guide for this, didn't you?" Max's eyes narrowed.

"Why would anyone need a guide for a game this easy?" Richard asked as he pulled out his phone and started scrolling through a recipe site.

If Hunter liked Malaysian food, how did he feel about Thai? A green curry might be nice this weekend. Or he'd seemed to like the Moroccan food the other night and had said he hadn't had it before. Maybe they should have that again. Richard bookmarked a few recipes.

There were some weak moans from the screen, but he didn't bother looking.

Did Hunter like sweets? Richard hadn't made any desserts yet. He should try baking something.

"Why isn't he coming?" Max mashed a few buttons and got another halfhearted moan.

"He wants you to A-B-B-X him," Richard said offhandedly.

Oh, or these cardamom rose beignets. Hunter might like those. He'd liked the cardamom coconut rice.

"HOLY SHIT," Hunter yelled.

Richard glanced up at the screen where Lord Softfluff's dick was firmly lodged in his best friend's ass, his knot stretching him wide.

As if he needed any more confirmation, Max hit the down button. His dick didn't budge.

Max and Hunter cheered.

Richard scowled as some cheesy happily ever after video played—Lord Softfluff and his new mate literally sailing off into a sunset.

Definitely the worst game ever.

He got up and headed to the kitchen. If he put the barley and vegetable stuffed peppers in now, that'd give him plenty of time to make the salad and skin and cut up the fruit.

A few minutes later, Max and Hunter followed.

Max raised an eyebrow at the high-fiber meal. "Are we all bottoming tomorrow?"

"If one of us is, then we're all eating like we are," Richard said, starting to chop nuts for the salad.

"I mean, it just seems like a waste for me to eat like this and not get fucked," Max said, stealing a few almonds.

Hunter grinned at him. "In that case, feel free to bend

over for me when it's your turn. Between Richard and Hardin, I'm sure my ass will appreciate the break."

Richard chopped harder, refusing to let himself growl.

Max winked at Hunter. "If you ask nicely, Hardin might bend over for you too."

"Nah, I've been imagining him railing me while a bunch of people watch for an embarrassing amount of time."

"The coffee shop scene?"

"Yep."

Richard forced himself to unclench his jaw and stop grinding his teeth.

Max leered at Hunter. "I'll tell you a secret. They offered me that scene, but I turned it down. Thought it'd be too ridiculous. Wanna see if MateHub would be interested in having us—"

"Ah, Richard," Hunter said, cutting Max off. "I think you're supposed to chop the nuts, not pulverize them."

Richard looked at the dusty remnants that had once been walnuts. He breathed out.

Max's gaze ping-ponged between them, a knowing smile creeping onto his face.

"Sorry," Hunter said. "You were saying?"

"Oh, nothing." Max waved a dismissive hand as he stared at Richard. "Just realized they should redo that scene, but with proper knotting this time. Don't you think, Richard? Knot your mate in a café where everyone can see? Is that something you'd want to do? Or are you going to give someone else the chance to do it?"

Richard didn't growl. Instead, he chopped a few more walnuts. *Gently* chopped them.

"Our scenes are already decided though, so he'd have to do it on his next contract." There might have been a hint of disappointment in Hunter's expression, but it wasn't strong enough to filter through their bond.

Richard's stomach dropped at the thought of his next contract. As it was, he wasn't sure he'd survive this one.

But he finished chopping the walnuts and moved on to the almonds.

It was only a job. He didn't want anything more than that. No surprisingly loving public fucks, no hundreds of nights of recipes, no sailing off into animated sunsets.

His life was perfect as it was. He had no desire for any of that. None at all.

FOURTEEN

W hen Hunter and Richard arrived at the studio, a collective unease hung thick in the air, written in tense shoulders and clenched jaws.

They couldn't possibly think Richard would attack someone during the scene, could they? They'd worked with him before, some on scenes exactly like this. But now they were eyeing him like he was about to explode.

If Richard noticed, he didn't seem to care. Instead, he headed straight to his dressing room.

Hunter couldn't retreat to his own so easily. He walked over to where Brandt was standing by the set—a fake dining room featuring a large table. Though Hunter struggled to think of a logical reason why a dining room table wouldn't have a single chair around it. Well, other than the chairs would get in the way of the fucking he was about to receive.

"Everything alright?" Hunter asked.

"All good," Brandt said, though the strain around his dark eyes told a different story.

Hunter leveled a look at him. "Right. Which is why the

usual crew has been reduced by half, and the ones who are here seem to be holding their breath, waiting to see if Richard cuts the red or blue wire."

Brandt winced. "We're just uncertain how this is going to go. We're hoping fewer people on set will present fewer threats to him, though the number of cameramen isn't the real issue."

"He's done scenes like this before."

"He has, but he also has never gotten as wolfy as he does with you. I probably wouldn't even want to do this scene on a new moon."

Brandt seemed legitimately worried, and that was, quite frankly, freaking Hunter out. "Should I be concerned?"

"No. Well. *You* don't need to be."

That was a disturbing way to answer that question. "Do Max and Hardin?"

"That's what we're not certain about."

"You honestly believe Richard might attack them?"

Brandt's grimace was answer enough.

"Then why are we doing this scene?"

"MateHub contacted his agent, who said Richard insists there's no issue."

"But you don't believe him."

"I don't know what to think." Brandt scrubbed a large hand over his face. "I mean, he drove you here today, didn't he?"

"Of course. Why wouldn't he? We were both coming from the apartment at the same time."

"Yeah. He hasn't done that in ages."

Hunter's eyebrows rose. "Why not?"

"My guess? He thinks showing even an iota of kindness

to the person he's bonded to will end up with them becoming attached to him."

"He thinks giving someone a ride will make them fall in love with him?"

Brandt shrugged. "Post-knotting, with all those feel-good chemicals rushing through the body, even the smallest gesture might be confused for more than it truly is."

Hunter's brain decided this was a fantastic opportunity to play him a highlight reel of Richard carrying him, cleaning him up, tucking him in. He shoved down those thoughts. "It's just a contract."

"Right. That's what Richard always says. But instead of his co-stars forgetting that, it's his wolf that doesn't seem to agree. Which is why we're nervous. If Richard's in control, it might be alright. If not..." Brandt grimaced again.

Hunter frowned. When Chance had first brought up the idea, it'd been ridiculous, but with Brandt's obvious concern, it was significantly harder to brush it away.

"Listen. If his wolf does have strong feelings about you, to the point it'll take over if anyone tries to touch you, Richard will not hurt you. You're the safest person here."

"That doesn't reassure me." He wouldn't be alone on set with Richard.

"Max and Hardin can handle themselves. We do this with people who know him well for a reason. They'll be able to read him, and if things get out of control, I'll shift and intervene. No wolf has a chance against a grizzly. Let us worry about that."

Hunter didn't know how that was reassuring either, but before he could process it or reply, Brandt continued.

"More importantly, are *you* good with having them fuck you? You're about halfway through the contract. It's not uncommon for Richard's co-stars to start..." He trailed off, making a vague gesture.

"Feeling attached?"

"Yeah. We give his co-stars an out when they're scheduled for this kind of scene. If you're not okay with other people touching you, we've got a plan B script where the alpha needs to claim his mate in front of his packmates to make it official."

"Oh." Hunter hadn't realized that was an option. But like he'd been telling everyone repeatedly, it was a job. There was no reason he should want an out. "I mean, my ass would appreciate plan B, but I'm fine. No attachments here."

Absolutely none.

"Okay. We'll take your word for it." A skeptical note lingered in Brandt's tone, but Hunter ignored it. "We decided to skip the interview though. Whatever happens, I doubt Richard will be his usual loquacious self."

Hunter snorted and headed to his dressing room.

It'd be fine. Richard was a professional, and he didn't have feelings for Hunter. Everyone was worried for nothing. They'd see that once the scene got started.

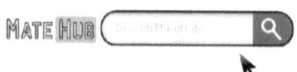

The atmosphere wasn't any better when he returned—stretched, lubed, and ready to go. He'd slipped on his robe, but there wasn't much of a lead-up to this scene, and he wouldn't be wearing anything once they started.

Richard was already out of his dressing room, as were Max and Hardin. The three of them were wearing what

Hunter had come to think of as the Werewolf Uniform: T-shirts all but painted on to show off as many muscles as possible and jeans well-worn and tight enough they molded themselves around dicks and asses. Even while clothed, there was no question about what they were packing. Anyone wearing those jeans outside would get charged with public indecency, and their shirts threatened to burst open with their next deep breath. Not that he was complaining.

They stood off to the side of the set, talking. Richard looked fine.

But when Hunter joined them to introduce himself to Hardin, an ominous thread snaked through the ball of emotion that was Richard in Hunter's mind.

"It's nice to meet you," Hunter said to Hardin, holding out his hand. He was as attractive in person as he was in his videos, positively crushing the tall, dark, and handsome vibe with his black hair and tan skin. His thick lashes framed eyes a person could lose themselves in as they tried to name the mix of colors they held.

Objectively speaking, he was smoking hot. Hunter had figured if they ever met, it'd be a Herculean effort not to immediately climb Hardin like a very wolfy tree. But standing in front of him now, Hunter didn't feel remotely that way. Sure, Hardin was hot. Richard was infinitely hotter.

Hardin glanced at Hunter's hand, but didn't move to take it. "You too."

Hunter dropped his hand.

The tension was unmistakable in Brandt's voice when he spoke. "Are we all good?"

Richard answered with a curt nod. No one else said no.

"Okay," Brandt said. "Let's do this?"

Max and Hardin took their places around the table.

Hunter shrugged out of his robe, handing it to Brandt, then turned toward Richard, expecting to get hoisted up on his shoulder. That didn't happen.

Richard stared at him with an intensity that left him feeling stripped bare, naked in a way he'd never been before. He was about to ask if Richard was okay, when Richard closed the distance between them, his hands stroking over Hunter's neck, then down, over his body.

Marking him, Hunter realized. Covering him with his scent.

The moment Richard's hands were on him, his presence in Hunter's mind jumped forward—half-feral and barely controlled. His green eyes flashed amber, his wolf lurking beneath the surface, a predator seconds away from seizing its prey.

Out of the corner of his eye, Hunter saw Max and Hardin having a heated, silent conversation of subtle gestures and pointed looks. Whatever they'd said to each other, it ended with them switching places so Max would be closer to where Richard tossed Hunter onto the table for the pack.

Richard leaned in, his breath gusting against Hunter's skin. His fingers wound through Hunter's hair, tugging his head to the side so he could run his nose along Hunter's neck.

Hunter's heart thundered in his chest.

The air in the studio pressed down on them, a storm waiting to break.

Waiting for Richard to break.

Richard's hands trailed down his back and along his sides, and Hunter exhaled.

Something sharp spiked through their bond, sour and

jagged. Panic curled like bile on his tongue, and then Hunter felt Richard wrestling control from his wolf, his resolve and determination solidifying.

This was their job. He was going to see it through. He would not be the reason this scene got messed up.

His hands were gentle as they lifted Hunter up and draped him over his shoulder. Taking his mark, he waited for Brandt to call action before striding into the dining room.

Hunter braced to land on the table, but Richard eased him down.

"I've brought some fresh meat for the pack," he said through clenched teeth. He took half a step back—the effort it required clear—but his fingers stayed locked around Hunter's calf, his claws out, digging into Hunter's skin.

"To share?" Max asked, and that was definitely not in the script.

Richard's grip constricted until it was just shy of painful. His chest rose and fell rapidly. Hunter was ninety percent positive he was the only one on set breathing, but he couldn't look away from Richard to check. In his mind, Richard was nothing but chaos and instincts, a battle for control.

"Yes," Richard gritted out.

Hardin was supposed to go first, but he hadn't moved an inch.

Max edged forward and said Hardin's line. "Don't mind if I do, Alpha." The script called for him to grab Hunter and yank him toward him, but he didn't. He casually extended his arm, taking his time, like Richard wasn't rumbling a low warning that built to a snarl as Max's hand crept toward Hunter's leg.

A threat loomed in the air, violence coiled, ready to be unleashed.

Hardin had started to growl too, growing louder as Richard did, as Max got closer to touching Hunter.

Fuck. Chance had been right. They'd all been right.

Hunter risked a glance around the studio. Brandt and the crew were frozen. The only one moving was Max, inching nearer.

He could sense Richard trying to control himself, trying to let go, to step away. Trying not to lash out. Fighting his instincts.

And he was losing.

Hunter reached for him, grabbing Richard's shirt and tugging him forward. Richard's eyes jerked toward him as his body settled between Hunter's legs, his growls momentarily subsiding.

Max backed away quickly.

Hunter looked up at Richard with what he hoped were big, vulnerable eyes that the cameras were catching. He swallowed and shook his head. "I... I only want you, *Alpha*."

He didn't have to wonder if that was the right thing to say. Richard was on him instantly, tongue thrusting into his mouth, a rumble vibrating against his chest, his wolf soothed and smug. Hunter's lips tingled from the force of the kiss.

Richard broke away from his mouth to nip and suck down the side of his neck, decorating his skin with bruises that would be visible for days. Hunter's eyelids wanted to drift shut at the sensation, but he forced them to stay open.

Over Richard's shoulder, he saw Brandt gesture at Max, then Hardin, and back. He made the universal motion for jerking off. Max's eyes jumped to Hardin, though Hunter couldn't see Hardin's reaction.

He turned his head, but Richard's hand found his jaw, a claw scraping along it, gently but firmly returning Hunter's gaze to him. "Only look at me."

Hunter let out a breath. That would not be difficult. Richard's presence filled the room as fully as it filled Hunter's mind. He was everything untamed and beautiful in the world concentrated into one man. The amber glow of his eyes held a feral energy far wilder than in any of their previous scenes. The heat of that stare burned into Hunter, pinning him down. Richard's sculpted body, sun-kissed skin, and tousled hair completed the picture of rugged perfection.

The sound of two zippers opening had Richard snarling, but when neither of them came closer, he seemed appeased.

Richard yanked his shirt over his head and unfastened his jeans, his movements slowed a fraction by his still-clawed fingers. He didn't bother pushing his pants past his thighs before his mouth found Hunter's again. His hands roamed over every inch of Hunter, claws dragging over sensitive flesh.

"You going to be able to put those things away?" Hunter asked under his breath.

Richard shook his head.

Okay then. No extra fingering it was. Not that Richard had the patience for it.

Richard's need to be inside him was an insistent drumbeat thrumming through their bond. With firm and steady hands, he guided Hunter's legs around his waist, his claws sharp pinpricks.

Hunter wrapped a hand around Richard's cock and glided the foreskin up and down, and Richard groaned quietly into his ear.

Richard's grip on him tightened, claws almost piercing his skin, as Hunter lined him up, the head of his dick pressed against his hole. They paused there, panting, need echoing between them, and then Richard was pushing forward, his hips as relentless as his hands were demanding, his pleased noises vibrating against Hunter's neck.

Hunter had never had anyone growl during sex like Richard did. It was all fierce possessiveness, shaking him to his core. He wasn't sure he could imagine getting fucked without that near-constant rumble now.

As if reading his thoughts, Richard's growl transformed into something lower and darker, promising everything he was about to do to Hunter.

When he was completely sheathed inside, a moan slipped from Hunter's lips.

Richard's canines scraped along his throat; his claws trailed burning lines in their wake. It was enough to make Hunter dizzy with arousal. The set, the studio, the world fell away, as it always did when Richard was inside him.

He managed a few controlled, steady thrusts—a brief check to see if Hunter could take it—but that wouldn't last. The need to reclaim Hunter was driving Richard wild. Hunter heard it in his uneven inhales, the rasp of his claws, the grunts that punctuated each motion of his hips. He sensed how going slow was a struggle, how it was costing Richard what little sanity he had left.

And fuck if Hunter didn't need it too, if he wasn't just as desperate for it. For the feel of being taken, for the way Richard wrung more pleasure out of him than anyone had before.

He ran his hands up Richard's back, up the planes of muscle there, until his fingers tangled in his hair.

"Come on," he said, voice breathless, hips rolling, taking Richard deeper inside him. "Show everyone I'm yours."

Richard's hips snapped forward.

It was rough and fast, Richard putting his strength into each thrust, his mouth never leaving Hunter's skin, marking him as his own, but Hunter didn't care. He loved the idea of looking in the mirror and seeing those scrapes and bruises, how Richard's teeth and claws had claimed him.

Hunter wouldn't have been able to stop the sounds he was making if he'd wanted to. His fingers drew bruises of his own where they dug into Richard's muscles. Between them, his untouched cock had leaked enough precome to make him slick with it.

His gaze landed on the juncture of Richard's neck, on the smooth skin there. Too smooth. He should fix that.

The instinct too overwhelming to deny, he leaned forward, his mouth latching onto Richard's shoulder. He bit down, not hard enough to draw blood, but hard enough to bruise. But damn, he wanted to do more than that. He wanted to sink his teeth into Richard, wanted everyone to see his claim etched there.

Richard's head jerked to the side, giving Hunter all the access he could ever ask for. Hunter sucked harder; Richard's harsh breaths were loud in his ears. His hands clamped down on Hunter's hips, his claws digging into his flesh, and Hunter couldn't stop the moan that rose as Richard's knot began to swell. It had his back arching, his ass clenching tight, tying them together.

Ecstasy rippled through him, through Richard, and back.

Hunter whimpered as Richard ground into him. He

sucked on Richard's neck, adding more bruises to the ones he'd already left.

That pushed Richard over the edge. The feel of Richard's dick pulsing inside him, his climax rolling through him, was too much for Hunter, and his own orgasm slammed into him with enough force that his vision went white.

Pleased growls filled the studio as Hunter rode out the aftershocks.

Richard held him, the heat of his body unbearably perfect, his strong arms anchoring Hunter to reality.

He shivered, and Richard adjusted his hold, his hips rocking, milking out every last ounce of pleasure.

Hunter nuzzled his neck, his hands skating over Richard's back and down his arms.

The grind of Richard's hips slowed to a stop, his forehead dropping to rest against Hunter's, his breath ragged.

"Fuck, you feel so good," Hunter murmured, his voice hoarse, wriggling on his knot.

Richard's entire body shuddered at the words, his exhales ghosting across Hunter's face.

They hung there for a blissful moment, Hunter letting Richard make the decision to move or to stay like that forever.

"Can you let them get close enough to come?" Brandt's voice was soft, but both Hunter and Richard jerked at the sound.

Richard gripped Hunter tighter, then gave a short nod.

"Hunter?" Brandt asked.

Hunter also nodded, rubbing soothing circles over Richard's shoulders, his eyes locked on Richard's face as Max and Hardin neared.

Richard growled softly but kept his gaze fixed on Hunter as he lay back on the table.

Max and Hardin jerked themselves until they finished, biting off groans as they came. They either had very bad or very good aim because not a single drop landed on Hunter.

They hastily backed away, but he stayed focused on Richard.

Richard leaned in and kissed him, slow and deep, making damn sure Hunter knew who he belonged to. He broke away to stare down at him.

"Cut," Brandt called, and Hunter blinked.

They hadn't tried to get a shot of Richard pulling out of him, but he couldn't blame Brandt or Rhys. Better not to risk setting Richard off for a close-up, though he seemed calmer, more settled.

Slowly, Richard pulled out, his half-deflated knot and slick head sliding free, and Hunter's muscles trembled in protest, wanting Richard to stay in him longer.

Hunter scooted off the table, his legs less than happy with this whole standing thing, but steady enough to get him to his dressing room by himself.

But he didn't want that, and neither did Richard. Not if the way he looped an arm around Hunter's waist and steered him toward his dressing room was anything to go by.

Hunter didn't bother pointing out that this scene wasn't as demanding as the last two, that he didn't need help.

He let Richard pull him into the shower, both of them flushed and covered in come and sweat.

Richard scrubbed him clean far more thoroughly than last time.

Every brush of Richard's skin sent waves of contentment buzzing through Hunter, and he couldn't begin to untangle how much of it was his and how much was Richard's. He wasn't sure he wanted to.

SCENE: I Only Want You, Alpha

KnottyWolf69:
Okay, I'm convinced. Something's going on between them. I've never seen Richard that possessive before. Also? Hunter marking up his neck? So hot.

demisexlchoklat:
For a second there, I thought Hunter would break skin.

BramStroker:
I'm still salty Hunter HASN'T bitten him properly. Richard's other co-stars did. Like, Hunter, come on! You know you want to sink your teeth into that sexy-ass wolf. Claim what's yours!

MagicalHWood:
It must be because he's human. MateHub probably wouldn't have a mage bite their co-star either.

KnottyWolf69:
I don't care. Mage, human, or otherwise—my mate better bite me in return. He needs to stake his claim all the fuck over me. It wouldn't feel right if he didn't.

MagicalHWood:
Speaking of things feeling off. There were some weird cuts in that scene. Something must have

happened between Richard putting Hunter on the table and Hunter begging for only him.

KnottyWolf69:
My guess? They had it planned as a packbang, but Richard was having none of it.

BramStroker:
Whatever it was, I'm glad they didn't do the usual packbang. This was so much better. I don't want to see Hunter get fucked by someone else while Richard has to watch.

HuntMeDown:
I'm glad you're all coming around nicely. Obviously DickHunt is endgame, but does anyone else think there's something between Max and Hardin too? I had to watch a few times before I could spare them a glance, but when I did...

demisexlchoklat:
Honestly, yeah. They were looking at each other the whole time, not the hotness right in front of them.

MagicalHWood:
That, I can agree with. There was some serious eyefucking going on there.

KnottyWolf69:
Also, the way they managed not to come on Hunter at all? You know damn well they were keeping their scents off him as much as they could for Richard's sake. Friend goals, man.

HuntMeDown:

Okay, Magic, what'll it take for you to finally admit the rest of us are right?

MagicalHWood:

We're halfway through their contract, which means we should start getting side scenes from Richard. If he stops doing those, I'll admit you're onto something.

HuntMeDown:

Scenes with anyone else are not happening. No way. Not when he has Hunter.

BramStroker:

Huh. I never thought I'd be excited for Richard to not do a scene. Weird.

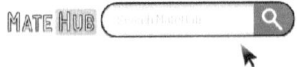

CHAPTER
FIFTEEN

Richard's phone buzzed as he parked in front of Palacio.

DANIEL

You good for next week's scene?

RICHARD

Of course. Why wouldn't I be?

DANIEL

You said that about the pack scene too, and from what Brandt told me, you were very much NOT.

RICHARD

That was a fluke. It won't happen again.

DANIEL

Okay. I'll tell them you're good to go and there won't be any more problems.

Don't make me a liar this time.

196

Richard typed out his reply and stared at it for a full minute before hitting send, unease twisting in his gut.

I won't.

He got out of his car and forced himself to head inside.

Max and Hardin watched him coolly as he walked to their table and sat. Richard couldn't blame them. Palacio's majestic cat mural gazed down on him with an extra dose of judgment.

"Fuck, guys, I am so sorry."

"You're so buying drinks for the rest of the fucking year is what you are," Max said.

Richard winced. "Fair."

"What the shit, man?" Max glowered at him.

"I don't know what's gotten into me."

"Don't you?" Hardin asked.

Richard groaned. He did, but that didn't mean he wanted to admit it. Not fully, anyway.

"My wolf thinks he smells so fucking perfect. It's fixated on him. The thought of him smelling like either of you, both of you. You touching him. Fucking him—" He cut off with a growl. "My wolf couldn't stand it. It wants this shit to be real."

Hardin studied him before asking, "What do you want?"

"There's only a month and a half left. It doesn't matter what I want." He scoffed. "I guess I'll feel what everyone else is talking about when they say severing a bond is painful."

They both jerked their heads toward him at the implied confession in his words. That it wasn't just a physical thing; it wasn't just his wolf.

197

Max opened his mouth to speak, but Hardin beat him to it. "You don't want to keep the bond? To keep him?"

"Why would I? It's a contract. It's our job. He isn't interested in more than that. I felt when everyone else became interested. He isn't. And even if that somehow changed, it'd fuck up our careers. You know that. Performers who get bonded leave the industry. No one wants porn stars who can't fuck other people. MateHub doesn't do exclusive contracts, and after the career I've built up, it'd be embarrassing to have to go somewhere like OnlyMates."

Max shook his head. "Have you checked the message boards lately? Your fans seem highly invested in Hunter and you together. They might be okay with it."

"For how long? A few more months before they're sick of seeing us together, views decline, and MateHub stops giving us work?"

Hardin's gaze flickered over to Max, then back to Richard. "No one did bonding contracts before you. Maybe you could pioneer exclusive contracts too."

Richard grimaced. "Not going to happen. Again, even if I wanted that, which I don't, and even if MateHub would agree to it, which they won't, Hunter isn't interested."

"Shouldn't you ask him that before you assume?"

"I don't need to. Like I said, I'd feel it if he was. I'm getting nothing from him."

"Why not try?"

Hardin was one to talk. "So you're saying I shouldn't silently pine after him for years and refuse to make a move because I'm too afraid it will change the world I've built for myself?"

Hardin's eyes went cold. "You don't have years."

That was a punch to the gut, and it wasn't like he didn't deserve it.

He forced out a slow exhale. "Listen. Neither of you has done a bonding contract. You don't know how shitty it is to have someone constantly pushing their emotions at you, wanting you to return them. To have to sit there and feel the crap they're feeling, whether you want to or not. To have someone convince themselves they're in love with you because the sex is good, even though you aren't remotely compatible. To know it's going to end up hurting them in the end because you'll never have feelings for them. I don't want to put him through that. I think he's already picking up some of my emotions when we aren't touching. If I *try*, I'm going to make it worse for him. He didn't sign up for that."

"But you *are* compatible," Hardin said. "Your scents complement each other well. It was hard to tell at first with him being human, but he smells good on you. *Really good.*"

Richard knew that. It changed nothing. "That might matter to my wolf, but that's not how humans work."

"So find what works for him," Max said. "How did you put it? 'You figure out the things that make them feel good, then give them those things.' Do that."

"He isn't a video game. I can't hit buttons until his pleasure bar is full, then expect him to do whatever I want."

"It's so bizarre to hear you use a video game analogy," Hardin said.

"Right?" Max said. "You need to come with me next time so you can see him play. It's surreal."

Hardin made a noncommittal noise, his focus staying on Richard. "So don't play him. Get to know him. All evidence to the contrary, you're a decent guy. He'll realize that if you let your guard down around him."

"Hardin's right. It pains me to admit this, and you're never going to hear me repeat it, but underneath your whole prickly asshole persona, you're surprisingly not the worst. Sometimes, dare I say, sweet? Stop trying to keep people away. Stop doing everything in your power to keep him from getting attached. He might surprise you."

Richard sighed. "So what do you suggest? I cook for him? Take care of him when he needs it? Or should I take an interest in his hobbies?"

"Or you could, and this might be a radical idea," Hardin said, "talk to him. See if you're compatible in any way other than your scents. Take him out for coffee."

The sudden urge to snarl tore through Richard. Which was ridiculous. There was no need for his wolf to get pissy because Hardin mentioned Hunter and coffee in the same sentence.

"Yeah," Max said with a snort. "Maybe not coffee. But I'm sure you can think of somewhere else to take him."

Richard suppressed another sigh and flagged the waiter down for a drink.

Humans were more trouble than they were worth.

When he got home that evening, Hunter was sprawled out on the couch, his shirt riding up to expose a strip of his abs as he messaged someone.

"Hey," he said, not glancing up.

"Hey." Richard took a step toward his room, then paused.

Would it hurt to try?

Yeah, it probably would.

"Hey," he said again. "I was planning to go to The Original Farmers Market tomorrow morning to grab some ingredients for next week. Would you want to come with?"

Hunter tilted his head back on the arm of the couch to look at him, his dark curls fanning out, his neck exposed, the bite mark peeking out from under the collar of his shirt.

He studied Richard for long enough that it made him want to take back the invitation.

"Sure," he said finally. "That could be fun. I've never been."

"We'll leave around nine-thirty?"

"Sounds good." He went back to his messenger app.

Richard headed to his room. He didn't feel like smiling. He wasn't nervous. This wasn't a date. He was buying groceries. That was it.

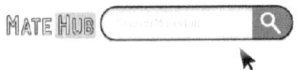

This was not a date, Richard reminded himself for the hundredth time. No matter what it felt like, it wasn't a date.

Talk to him. Get to know him, Hardin's voice nagged in his head as Richard drove toward the Farmers Market, Hunter sitting in the passenger seat, reading on his phone. Like he had been for fifteen minutes.

Richard couldn't remember the last time he'd been on a date. Not that this was one. He also couldn't remember the last time he'd needed to get to know someone in the nonphysical sense. But if he didn't try, the thirty-minute drive was going to drag out longer than it already was.

He latched onto the first topic he could think of. "How did you find out about..." He made a gesture that vaguely encompassed himself and the world. "Us. This. The paranormal."

Hunter looked up from his phone, his brown eyes glittering with amusement. "That's Chance's fault. At college, we shared a dorm room during freshman year and became friends. But there was something weird about him. He was always secretive about certain things, and I couldn't figure out why. He was so open about everything else. Like, he'll happily tell anyone who'll listen how much he enjoys being in the middle of a threesome."

Richard had seen a few of Chance's scenes. 'Enjoys' was an understatement. If Chance relished getting spit-roasted any more, they'd have to rename the Eiffel Tower in his honor.

"And then he'd occasionally say bizarre things like, 'You're not bad for a human,' which, okay. Weird. So I started to assume he was an alien, but I figured whatever. Worst-case scenario, he takes me to his people for a thorough probing. Also, there'd randomly be cat hair on our couch. We didn't have a cat. Though twice I did walk in on him jumping up from the couch, startled and bare-ass naked."

Richard snickered. "Cat naps?"

"I know that now. Apparently, he heard me coming with enough time to shift, but not to get dressed. But weirdness aside, he was an excellent roommate, so we kept rooming together for the following years."

"I take it he eventually told you."

Hunter shook his head ruefully. "All you supernatural types have this aura around you. I don't understand why everyone doesn't notice. You also gravitate toward each other. You find each other in the crowd, even if you don't necessarily like each other's kind."

Richard nodded. He might not be fond of vampires, for example, but he had more in common with them than the average human. There was a natural form of camaraderie in that.

"So we'd go out to clubs together," Hunter said, and Richard had an idea of where this was going. "Some nights, there'd be another hot guy there, or group of hot guys, who'd have that same aura. Something a little wilder or darker about them. Most never seemed particularly interested in Chance, but..." He shrugged.

"They assumed you were fair game if you were friends with him."

"Yeah. Chance never had any issue with me hooking up with guys. Except when they were like him or you. Then he'd go into full-on cockblocking mode. One night, I had this goth guy with cool skin all over me. Now I realize he was likely too old to be dancing with a bunch of college-aged kids, but at the time, I was into it. He asked to do something to me that I misinterpreted. I thought I hadn't heard the 'off,' so I said yes, only to have Chance appear out of nowhere, hiss at the guy, then drag me home."

"That sucks."

"No, it didn't. That was the problem," he said, and Richard chuckled. Hunter continued. "Once we got to our place, we had this huge fight. He was pretty drunk; we both were. I accused him of being a weird alien that didn't want me to fuck other weird aliens. He accused me of being a naive human, which, I mean, not wrong. But how was I supposed to know? It escalated to the point where he ended up yelling that if I insisted on being a dumb human, he'd have to prove how little I knew. Then he was attempting to take off his shirt, but he was still drunk and gave up halfway. Before I could get out a 'what the fuck are you doing,' suddenly he was a cat. A half-clothed cat. And not a house cat either. That made me sober up real quick."

Richard couldn't imagine many humans being okay with having an apex predator magically appear in their apartment. "What happened after that?"

"Some freaking out on my part. When he shifted back, I

had a lot of questions, but he was drunk and mad at me, so instead of answering my questions, he pulled up a website on his laptop, shoved it at me, and said if I wanted to fuck weird aliens, I should do some research first. He then stormed into his room and passed out. The featured video that day was the coffee shop one, so it was on top. It was a fun watch, but with them both moaning about knotting, I figured it was just some fetish I'd never come across before. Then I scrolled down. By the time he woke up, I had even more questions and had also found out how he'd managed to pay for tuition without taking out massive loans. He stumbled out of his room, and I turned around the laptop with a video paused on him."

"In the middle?"

"Yep. He froze, his face the epitome of 'Oh shit, what did I do?' He tried to get out something about special effects and film school projects and some other excuses I was not buying. I'd seen some of yours. No special effects are making that happen."

Richard winked at him. "All real."

"I'm aware." Hunter grinned wryly. "But after some last-minute attempts at denial, we had a talk about it. He got into insane amounts of trouble for telling me without permission, but after I swore a literal blood oath that I wouldn't expose any secrets, people calmed down."

"Even if he'd asked, he wouldn't have gotten permission."

"That's what I gathered. Partners only, right?"

"Generally speaking, yeah. I'm surprised they didn't have a mage wipe your memory."

"That option was definitely on the table."

Hunter explained the interrogation he'd been subjected

to, which would have had most humans running for the hills, but had just left him curious to find out more.

The remainder of the drive flew by, and Richard found himself pulling into the Farmers Market's parking lot. They got out and headed inside.

"Anyway, that was about two years ago, around the start of our senior year. After that, he had less excuse to block my prospects in the club, but he kept saying if I was so attracted to—" Hunter cut off mid-sentence, and Richard belatedly realized they were now surrounded by throngs of humans, bustling between the shops and stalls.

Okay. Well. He had not thought this through. This was not the best place to have any sort of real conversation with Hunter.

Add not-dates to the list of things he wasn't good at.

Hunter shot him a mischievous look. "If I liked... having fun... with certain types of people, I should make it worth my while. Oooh," he said, distracted. "Pumpkin ice cream."

Richard followed Hunter's gaze to an ice cream shop, then had to follow him physically when Hunter wandered in that direction.

As they neared the counter, Hunter pointed to a large sign proclaiming, "Life is short, lick fast."

"Hey. Change two letters, and it's your unofficial motto."

Richard stepped closer to say under his breath, "If you think any of our scenes went too fast, I'll draw the next one out extra long."

Hunter's answering grin was wicked. "You forget. Our next scene? I get to set the pace."

Richard repressed a shiver, not sure how to respond to that, but Hunter's attention had returned to the ice cream.

"One scoop of pumpkin ice cream and a frozen banana, please," he told the man behind the counter.

Richard blinked as a chocolate and nut-covered banana was unceremoniously shoved at him the moment it'd been given to Hunter.

He shot Hunter an unimpressed look.

"What?" Hunter asked, faking innocence. "You don't want my banana? I suppose I could see if someone else wants it."

The need to repress a growl around Hunter was becoming an annoyingly common thing.

Fine. He'd eat the damn banana. And if he flicked his tongue out to catch a couple loose nuts on its tip to watch Hunter's reaction, well, that was Hunter's own damn fault.

Though, considering Hunter responded by licking his spoon clean in a manner that was not safe for market, Richard just had to hope he didn't want anything from the pickle shop.

They strolled through the stalls until Hunter had finished his scoop, getting cream on his lips a distracting number of times in the process.

Richard bought a few hot sauces and some spices before heading to a produce shop.

And immediately regretted all his life choices.

Hunter picked up an eggplant. "Oh, right. I was saying. Chance suggested I make it worth my while. Originally, I thought it was a horrible idea, but then he showed me his latest W-2 and reminded me that only an exclusive audience would ever..." He leered at Richard and squeezed the eggplant, though that was not something a person strictly needed to do before buying one. "So I gave it a shot, and here I am. Seemed easier than getting a normal job."

"Been about a year now?" Richard eyed Hunter with

trepidation as he drifted over to a display of cucumbers and picked up one of the largest.

"Yeah. You?" he asked, fingers running over firm, smooth skin, eyes bright with unconvincing innocence. They were going to get kicked out of this shop if Hunter kept that up.

"I also started right after college, about seven years ago."

Fucking had been the one thing he'd really excelled at, so it'd seemed like the obvious career choice.

Hunter's eyes narrowed, clearly doing the math. "Isn't this your thirteenth contract? Did you start doing this right away?"

"No, actually. This didn't start until a few years in. Before that, we'd pretend, but it was literally all talk with a suspicious lack of close-ups. They did try some... special effects, shall we say, but they never looked right. There have always been a few of that kind of video floating around, but —" Richard realized talking around the next couple sentences would be more trouble than it was worth. So he leaned in and whispered the rest into Hunter's ear. "They were homemade. Real couples, poor quality. Usually with faces hidden. But then a thought hit me. Mages and wolf shifters enter transactional bonds to increase the mage's magic and the shifter's energy. Those kinds of bonds aren't encouraged, but they do come with the same benefits. I figured it might be worth a try. Do a few knotting scenes, but high quality, where people could see everything properly. Not fake moaning about how good it feels, but real close-ups of my knot stretching someone open."

Hunter shivered, his grip on the cucumber going lax, and Richard pulled away, but not before inhaling deeply. God, his scent. He smelled like Richard's.

207

Richard straightened up and kept talking. "I pitched the idea to the company, and they agreed. There were fewer rules back then. Like the three months on, three months off thing. Those have been put in place more recently. The first few years, I... signed more contracts."

"Is that what we're calling it?"

"Signed them hard with a massive pen." Hunter snorted, and Richard grinned at him before continuing. "After the videos were released, they got an insane amount of views, and the company wanted more... contracting, and from there, everything has—"

"Expanded?"

Richard chuckled. "It certainly inflated our views. Helped membership numbers balloon."

"I'm sure that swell enlarged your reach."

"You wouldn't believe how much it's blown up."

"It's good you were able to stretch things further. Spread your... message wide."

"Given how engorged it's gotten, if I were to pull out, I'd leave a gaping hole."

A woman near them jerked her head up, staring at them with raised eyebrows.

"In the market," Richard added, though he doubted it'd help.

Hunter was shaking with silent, repressed laughter, his amusement shimmering in Richard's mind.

Richard put a hand on his back and steered him away from the woman's suspicious stare. He headed toward the fruit, saw the bananas and kiwis, and retreated as quickly as possible, stopping in front of a pile of potatoes.

Potatoes should be safe, right?

After Hunter got himself under control, he asked, "Do your parents know?"

"Hell no," Richard answered. "My sister knows, but my parents are the 'nothing is more sacred and precious than a true bo—relationship' types. My mother wants me to find a nice ma—person to settle down with. I could never tell her how many times I've, uh, settled down. She did ease off when my sister got ma—rried. But she still has expectations."

"What do they think you do?"

"I tell them I've got a boring low-level desk job at a large media company."

"Ah. I've seen the one where you got the desk job. Seriously impressed with your coworker's flexibility. Not everyone could get the hard work done in such cramped quarters."

"Especially considering how much of it there was to do."

Hunter side-eyed him, the hint of a smirk quirking the corner of his mouth.

"What do you tell your parents?" Richard asked.

"Between the nature of the job and being sworn to secrecy and all, there's not much I can tell. With the way I dodge any questions about how my job is going, they think I work for some secret government agency. And they can keep thinking that until I get a normal job or make enough I can retire."

"Which would they freak out over more?"

"That my coworkers exist, or how those coworkers are working with their only child?"

"Yeah, that."

"They both enjoy fantasy movies, so they might think the former is cool. The latter, on the other hand..."

"So they enjoy fantasy movies, but not *fantasy movies*."

209

"And if they do, I'm perfectly happy being kept in the dark."

"Fair." That was something he never wanted to know about his own parents either.

They finished their produce shopping with minimal incidents, though Hunter should have taken the peaches out to dinner first, given how he'd felt them up.

"Okay," Richard said as they exited the grocer's. "I've got everything on my list. Anything you want?"

Hunter looked around, then gestured to a coffee shop. "Shall we?"

Richard raised an eyebrow at Hunter, who blushed slightly, looking more flustered than Richard had ever seen him.

"To get coffee," Hunter clarified. "Not get arrested for... signing contracts in public."

"Right. Of course."

"Should I grab a table?"

Richard was not picturing the things he could do to Hunter while Hunter grabbed a table. "Let's get it to go."

Hunter shrugged. "Works for me."

They got their drinks and sipped them as they walked out to the parking lot.

"How long did it take you to get a car like this?" Hunter asked as they got in.

"Not long after I started the bonding contracts," Richard said, relieved not to have to talk around things anymore. "I'm assuming you got enough for something decent from this contract alone."

"I was able to pay off the education I'm not using. Most of the rest was used to start a retirement fund."

"How responsible of you."

"Hey, I'm living the dream. Debt-free with a nest egg? There are recent grads who'd kill for that."

"Never use the phrase 'nest egg' around Brandt, please? I'm concerned about the scenes it might inspire."

Hunter huffed out a laugh. "He does have some interesting ideas. I know the MateHub Originals division has been working on multiple series after the success of *Howling Hearts & Hidden Heats*. I'm honestly shocked he hasn't proposed a live-action *Moonlit Bonds* yet. How would you like to star in that?" He switched to an announcer voice. "In a village, for some reason populated only by one hundred attractive single horny bottoms, one incredibly well-endowed top searches for true love... by sticking his dick in every hole he can find."

"Pass." If he had to do anything of the sort, he'd rather star in *H4*'s sequel, *Shattered Souls & Secret Scents*. He could pretend to be some knothead alpha prince going into rut over his fated omega's scent if the money was decent. Methodically fucking his way through every bottom MateHub could find without knotting any of them sounded tedious.

"Ah, but think of the suspense and drama. Will it be the tavern boy? The blacksmith? The farrier? The other tavern boy? Or perhaps the mysterious person lurking on the other side of the tavern glory hole?"

"If they ever ask me to do that, I'm quitting. I'm not knotting someone through a glory hole. As much fun as it'd be to stand plastered to a wall, waiting for my knot to deflate."

"Yeah, can't say I'd volunteer my ass for that either."

"Max seems to like the game," Richard said. "He should do it."

"Knot his best friend after fucking half the indust—I mean, village."

"Yep."

"So I'm not imagining it. There's something between them?"

"Has Chance explained shifter scents to you?"

"Not much beyond repeatedly saying you reek like dog, which I haven't noticed. You smell kind of nice. Like a fire?"

The fact that Hunter had noticed his scent was not something he was going to let himself get happy about. "And I'm sure Chance smells like a cat. But that's not what I mean. If two shifters are compatible, their scents complement each other. Both are good by themselves, but together they're even better."

"So you've got shifter A, who smells like peanut butter, and shifter B, who smells like jelly, and if you smoosh them together, they'll be delicious?"

The analogy amused Richard. "Frequently, yes, but it's not always that easy. Sometimes two shifters you'd think shouldn't work together do. Your mango and soy sauce combinations."

Hunter nodded. "French fries dipped in chocolate shakes. It sounds strange until you try it, but once you do, it's the most obvious thing in the world."

"Right. But alternatively, you might have two things you think sound good together, but if you mix them, they aren't greater than the sum of their parts. They're too similar to draw anything new out of the other."

"So dark chocolate is amazing, and adding more dark chocolate would be good, but it won't give you something special."

"But chili might. Or two scents can clash in the worst way."

"Orange juice and toothpaste?"

"Exactly."

"So how do you know?"

"The more two shifters are around each other, the more their scents mix. The more they mix, the more you can guess if they'd truly be good together. But it isn't until they get closer that it becomes apparent. It's the blending that matters."

"What causes the scents to blend?"

"The easiest thing? Touch. Skin-to-skin contact."

"Ooh," Hunter said, sounding like a light bulb had gone off in his head. "When I was a kid, I was out shopping with my mom at this big department store, getting clothes for the new school year. I remember her trying on this perfume. She said she loved how it smelled in the bottle, but when she put it on her wrist, she made the most disgusted face, then spent hours grumbling about how gross it smelled on her."

Richard cocked his head. Huh. He'd never thought of it in terms of perfume or cologne. Shifters weren't big on wearing anything with a scent. But now that Hunter mentioned it, that worked better than the food metaphors. "Yeah. Sometimes, you might like a scent on its own, but it doesn't complement yours. For whatever reason, you aren't compatible. But conversely, the combination might smell like the best thing ever."

"Okay, so what does that have to do with Max and Hardin?"

"Have you ever stood at the base of a waterfall and just inhaled?"

"Again, you're answering my question with another question. But no, I have not."

"I'm getting there. Max's scent is like that. Waterfall mist on mossy stones."

"And Hardin?"

"Hardin is a little more difficult to explain to someone who has never been a wolf. Basically, he smells like the moon reflecting off tranquil waters."

Hunter paused as he considered that. "So together they'd be this moonlit waterfall that spills into a crystal pond surrounded by glistening mossy stones? That sounds... lovely."

"I'd assume the *spilling into* would usually happen the other way around, but yeah."

"Aaand you ruined it. Thanks."

Richard couldn't help his grin. "Anytime. But yes, they smell like they should be compatible, and they're around each other so much, you can guess how their scents might combine if they were bonded."

"So they are compatible?"

"You see, that's the thing. Max and Hardin? They refuse to touch."

"Ever?"

"Ever. Not even a handshake. And they won't do scenes together that would require them to touch."

"Do they not want to know?"

"I've been assuming they're afraid to find out. If they don't know, they can pretend it's not a possibility. It's one thing doing scenes with other people when you aren't sure; it's completely different when you can smell them on your skin and know how perfect they are for you." Richard realized he'd started to grip the steering wheel tighter and forced his hands to relax.

"Would it matter? Why not do scenes only with each other?"

"MateHub wouldn't be okay with that. It might be a fun novelty for a few months, but the fans would get sick of it."

Hunter frowned and looked out the window. "I suppose they would. Do you think they might give it a try after they retire?"

Richard shifted his weight in his seat. "Who knows how long that'll be. Maybe before then, one of them will get tired of waiting and find someone else who's compatible enough. But if that doesn't happen, they've got time to figure it out."

They didn't have an expiration date rushing toward them faster with every passing day.

CHAPTER

SIXTEEN

The moon was hours away from its zenith, and Hunter was already going stir-crazy. His foot tapped a nervous rhythm on the floor.

He tried to focus on the game he was playing, but it was impossible. The mistakes he kept making, the ways he kept dying, would cause Chance to roast him for weeks on end.

And it wasn't even his fault.

Richard lurked in the kitchen, attempting to cook dinner, but it felt more like he was pacing from counter to counter. Stalking the ingredients. Chopping and ripping with more force than could ever be necessary.

In Hunter's mind, he was an agitated ball of instincts, coiled and ready to pounce. His pent-up energy churned beneath the surface with no hope of release.

It was driving Hunter insane.

He'd tried exercising earlier in the day, but it hadn't helped. If anything, running had reminded him of the last full moon.

Running from Richard.

Being caught by Richard.

Being pinned and fucked and knotted by Richard.

He'd cut his workout short before anyone noticed how thoroughly he was enjoying his run.

Games weren't distracting him either. They only proved how dirty his brain truly was. Even Tetris wasn't safe as he slipped his long, straight piece into the tight space he'd left open for it, filling it up perfectly.

He sighed and exited the game. This was not happening tonight. He got up and walked to the kitchen.

"Can I help?" He couldn't cook for shit, but maybe attempting to make something might ease his need to move. Not that it was helping Richard.

But the moment he stepped into the kitchen, Richard spun around, his eyes flaring a predatory amber. He boxed Hunter against the counter and leaned in, breathing deep, that rumble starting low in his chest. He didn't touch Hunter though, just inhaled. His shaky exhale caressed Hunter's neck.

"You smell turned on," he said, his tone dark and rasping with lust.

"In my defense, you only make that noise during sex, so the reaction is Pavlovian at this point. You sounding like that makes me think I'm about to get fucked hard."

Richard growled, then froze. Hunter sensed his struggle, Richard grappling with his wolf. He won, but barely.

"I need you to not talk about getting fucked tonight."

"That's going to be a little difficult considering I can feel how horny you are right now. You're giving me blue balls with your need to get off."

"You're not helping." Richard's jaw tightened.

"This is cosmic punishment for those first two weeks, isn't it?" Hunter grumbled. "Payback for those times I jerked off. Do you go through this every full moon?"

"I almost always have a scene, so I get to fuck out this excess energy. And the few months I don't, I go run with my pack."

"Why didn't you go there this time?"

Richard huffed. "Because they'd smell you on me. Smell that you—that I'm bonded. And they'd have questions."

"Oh," Hunter said, wincing. "Yeah. Sorry. That'd be awkward. But does shifting help? Cause you can do that."

"If I shift, my wolf will have control, and it really wants to fuck right now."

Hunter raised an eyebrow at him.

"Not like that. Well. Maybe like that. My wolf isn't necessarily against it, if that's what it takes. But mostly it wants to stalk you through the apartment, pin you down, then shift to human. At which point, I'd be on top of you. Naked."

The first reply that popped into Hunter's head was, *Don't threaten me with a good time.* He didn't say it though; it didn't seem like a particularly coworker-y sentiment.

"Okay." Richard exhaled forcefully. "Here's what we're going to do. I'll take a step back, you'll walk very slowly to the couch, and I'll do my best not to follow."

Hunter's eyes skated down Richard's body. His muscles were tense with the effort it took to restrain himself, and his jeans didn't need to be skintight to show off that bulge. Hunter's mouth watered. How had he not gotten to suck that thing yet? It seemed downright criminal.

He looked up at Richard. "Okay. We could do that. Or, you could also... follow me. Hard."

Richard's claws scraped across the countertop. "That's against the contract. There's a whole section about no... *following* outside the scheduled scenes."

"MateHub would never have to know."

Every rule deserved an exception or two. Hunter wouldn't object. Richard was a searing presence inside him —an itch that needed scratching. Hunter wanted nothing more than to be the one to scratch it.

But Richard shook his head. "It's a bad idea. I'm not touching you tonight."

It seemed like a hell of a good idea to Hunter, but if Richard wasn't okay with it, even if his wolf was on board, he'd respect Richard's boundaries.

He kept telling himself that on his slow walk to the living room, then repeated it in his head a few thousand times as he attempted to play every video game MateHub had provided—minus *Moonlit Bonds*. He wasn't masochistic enough for that. None of them distracted him from the pulsing need in his mind, or the way that need went straight to his dick. Hunter huffed out a frustrated sigh, throwing his head back on the couch.

"Pretty sure I'm nearing the 'If your erection lasts longer than four hours' point over here," he whined before he could stop himself.

Richard prowled into the room; Hunter swallowed.

Talking about erections was probably also off-limits.

Richard leaned against the wall opposite the couch and stared at him. "I said I wasn't going to touch you, not that you couldn't touch yourself."

"As appealing as that sounds right now, won't that make it worse for you?"

"I put up with it for two weeks. Another night won't kill me."

"You sure?"

"I'll be fine."

Hunter doubted that, but then, it wouldn't take him much to get off. He went to stand.

"I didn't give you permission to leave." The untamed power behind Richard's words had Hunter's head whipping toward him. He was still lounging against the wall, but tension ran through his body, like he was seconds away from springing forward.

"What?" Hunter asked, blinking. "You want me to do it here?"

Richard's eyes flashed, and Hunter had to suppress the urge to squirm as arousal rushed through him. He didn't know whether it was his or Richard's, but it didn't matter.

He ran a hand up his thigh to palm himself through his jeans, nearly groaning. After hours of neglect, the relief of that touch bordered on divine.

"While you watch?" he asked, already breathless.

Richard's snarl was a yes if Hunter had ever heard one.

Okay, then. Alright. Not the first time he'd jerked off in front of someone. Not even close.

He popped the button on his jeans, and Richard's gaze zeroed in on the motion.

This seemed like a violation of the 'no sex outside their scenes' clause, but with the way Richard's presence in his mind kindled to life as he edged down his zipper, Hunter had no interest in following the rules. Besides, they wouldn't be touching, so did it count as sex? As far as he remembered, there hadn't been a no voyeurism or exhibitionism clause.

He felt Richard's eyes on him, tracking his moves. His self-control was holding on by the barest of threads.

Hunter's fingers slid under the band of his boxers and ran over his dick, making him groan and Richard growl. He'd already made a mess of his underwear with the amount of precome he'd leaked. He kept his grip loose as he

220

ran it over his length, enjoying the much-needed relief of his hand against his skin.

His body sparked with electric energy, on fire as pleasure rippled through him from that simple tease alone. The echo he always experienced when Richard was fucking him was there, but fainter without physical contact.

This would be so much better with Richard's hands on him, but even without that, Hunter knew it'd be good.

"Take your cock out," Richard said with a scarcely contained snarl.

Hunter wet his lips. "Is that an order?"

Richard's eyes flicked to his mouth, then back up. His chest rose and fell with each heaving breath. His hands were balled into fists, his claws out and digging into the flesh of his palms. Hunter felt the pain of it, how Richard was using that sting to restrain himself.

They stared at each other, gazes locked, muscles tense, neither of them moving.

Richard looked from his face to his hand in his pants.

"I've seen videos of you with other wolf shifters." Hunter gave himself an exaggerated stroke, as much as he could within the confines of his jeans. "What do you call it? Alpha command?"

Richard's jaw clenched so hard Hunter swore he heard teeth grinding. Eyes glowing amber, Richard let out a stormy rumble that rolled across the space between them, vibrating through Hunter.

"So, *Alpha*, if you want my dick out, command me," Hunter said, insolent tone and cheeky smirk firmly in place as he stroked himself again.

For one moment, Hunter thought Richard might lunge, might pin him to the couch and give him exactly what he wanted. But instead, he growled.

"Take your cock out, Hunter. *Now*."

Hunter's entire body quivered. He had no idea how wolf shifters put that extra authority in their voice. It had no effect on humans, not the way it did on shifters. Hell, he didn't even think Richard could use it since he wasn't an alpha.

None of that mattered. It still made him want to obey. He'd just never been good at following orders.

He inched his pants down and his boxers with them. The drag along his dick was maddeningly slow. Richard's need scorched through his mind, and all it did was make him go slower.

"*Hunter*," Richard ground out, the near-feral warning clear, his patience too far gone for any kind of teasing.

Hunter's erection sprang free, heavy and thick.

"Good. Now, *stroke yourself*."

Hunter shivered at the sound of Richard's command, wild and laced with dominance. As fun as it would be to push him further, to see what he'd let him get away with, Hunter didn't have the patience for it either—not when he was this wound up, not when he felt how hard Richard was, his need for release even stronger than Hunter's own. Richard's desire was a guttural cry in his throat, a tremor deep in his soul.

He didn't try to be subtle or to make it last. He gripped himself tight, thumb swiping over the head. His gaze stayed locked on Richard's face as he shuttled his dick through his fist. He watched lust blaze in Richard's eyes as they fixated on his hand, on his cock.

Arching his back to give Richard a better view, he wished he'd taken the time to undress completely, not just pushed his jeans down around his thighs. That was the only thing that would have made this hotter. Him naked on the couch, while a fully clothed Richard stood over him. But he couldn't bring himself to stop long enough to do that.

Fuck, it was like he was sensing what Richard wanted to see. How he wanted Hunter to touch himself, to fuck into his fist as his other hand played with his balls, to roll his foreskin over his head.

Hunter's breath caught.

He didn't have foreskin.

Richard did.

He wasn't feeling what Richard wanted him to do to himself; it was what Richard wanted Hunter to do to *him*. Because Richard felt every stroke, every twist, every pull.

Hunter squeezed himself harder, and Richard groaned.

Oh, oh, fuck. This was going to be *fun*.

Benefit of the bond, he supposed. He closed his eyes, sinking into that ball of instincts, letting it guide him to what Richard liked. The pressure, the speed. Not just what he wanted, what he *needed*. And Hunter gave it to him.

He forced his eyelids open so he could look at Richard. He was so tempting, so close. Hunter could hear his ragged breath, could feel the heat radiating from his body. He was all wolf—claws and fangs out, a predator seconds from going in for the kill. But somehow, he was controlling himself.

Hunter wanted to break that control.

He sucked two fingers into his mouth, getting them nice and wet, then traced them down until they were teasing at his hole.

Richard's gaze snapped to his face, his eyes full of moonlight and shadows, and Hunter was swept away in the burn of Richard's unsated need.

"Do it," Richard said, his voice rough and hungry.

Hunter pressed the tips of his fingers inside, his pleasure and Richard's mixing in a heady cocktail that made his vision blur, made him push his fingers in deeper, working himself open. Richard moaned in response.

He sensed the buzz of Richard's desire, the ache of his arousal. Every ounce of his attention caressed Hunter like a physical thing, like heat crackling in the charged air between them. Richard's wolf's frustration at not being able to fuck Hunter prowled the room. To have to watch and do nothing about how good he looked. How good he smelled.

Hunter stared him down as he thrust his fingers into his ass harder and faster, loving how Richard shook as he tried to keep his wolf contained, as he tried not to close the distance between them, tried not to come.

"Do you remember," Hunter said between harsh gasps, "when I said it'd been days since I'd come that hard?"

Richard bared sharp teeth, annoyed at the reminder.

Hunter grinned, unrepentant. "The orgasm before that I was talking about? The one where I came so hard? I'd bought this toy from the MateHub shop. Big, long, thick. Filled me right up as I rode it. And that was before I inflated its knot. I almost whited out when I came." He paused for a beat while that sank in—understanding smoldered in Richard's eyes—before he continued. "I just didn't realize how much better the real thing would be."

He pressed against his prostate and imagined himself being stretched wide on Richard's knot.

His climax roared through him, crashing over him in a blinding wave, rushing in his veins, echoing between them, his release an offering to Richard. It had both their hips jerking, their muscles tightening, every nerve ending elec-trified.

Stars exploded inside Hunter as Richard came with a

ferocious howl, his orgasm tearing through their bond as he let himself go, let himself be washed away by the sheer violence of his ecstasy.

Hunter collapsed against the couch, panting, heart racing, shirt splattered with come. He floated in smug satisfaction as he twitched and trembled from aftershocks, trying to recover as euphoria hummed through him, through Richard, and back.

The hottest porn star on the planet had come untouched because of him, and it was more thrilling than anything he'd ever experienced.

He had three seconds to revel in that smugness before Richard was on him, crowding into his space, straddling his lap, trapping him. Not touching him, but so close.

Richard leaned down, inhaling, his lips skimming Hunter's ear. "You were thinking of me as you rode it, weren't you? Wondering how my cock would feel. I can smell how much you want it. How much you need me to knot that pretty little ass of yours again."

Hunter shuddered.

"Do you still have it?"

Hunter nodded, dazed.

"Good," Richard said, his wolf in full control. "Because someday, I'm going to watch you ride it until you beg me for the real thing."

Hunter's ass clenched, and Richard chuckled darkly, breathing Hunter in once more, his presence in Hunter's mind as smug and satisfied as Hunter felt. Then he stalked away, off to his room to clean up the mess in his pants.

Hunter stared after him for a minute before retreating to his own room for the rest of the night, too off-kilter to deal with dinner. Especially if Richard wasn't cooking.

He showered and forced himself into bed, though Richard's wolf continued its restless prowl.

His bed was the exact same as it'd been every night for the last month and a half, but it seemed large and empty.

It took him the better part of forever to fall asleep.

In the morning, when he emerged from his room, Richard was more human again, something sheepish in his expression when he met Hunter's eyes.

"Sorry," he said. "I usually have more control."

Hunter wasn't remotely sorry, and when he concentrated, he could swear he sensed Richard's wolf lurking inside him.

It wasn't sorry either.

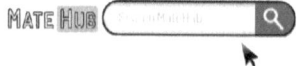

CHAPTER
SEVENTEEN

R ichard stared at the message on his phone. It was from a number he had saved, but had never thought he'd hear from.

STEELE LONGWOOD

Just making sure everything's going alright with my top star.

Steele Longwood—MateHub's founder and sole owner. Richard had only met him a handful of times, but every single one had left him sweating. Steele didn't interfere often with the day-to-day workings of MateHub—he delegated most of it to others—but that didn't mean he couldn't make or break careers.

RICHARD

Everything's great! I'm on my way to a shoot now.

STEELE LONGWOOD

Excellent. I'd hate to have to find a replacement for our biggest moneymaker.

You'll never have to worry about that
with me!

No reply came.

He winced and finished dressing before heading out of his bedroom.

Hunter was sitting on the floor, leaning against the couch, playing *Shadows Veiled*. On screen, he was attempting to convince a group of humans that a full-sized dragon was actually three kids in a trench coat.

Richard cleared his throat, getting Hunter's attention.

"I've..." he started to say, his words catching. He cleared his throat again. "I've got work today."

Saying it made his chest feel tight.

Hunter's brow furrowed, then his mouth fell open. "Oh. Oh, right. You always do scenes with other people during these contracts, don't you?"

"Yeah," Richard said, studying Hunter's face for any hint of what he thought about that—unease, unhappiness, something. "Don't want to let my knot go to waste, you know?"

God, he sounded high pitched to his own ears. He needed to get his shit together.

Hunter gazed at him, his expression impossible to read. His presence loomed large, but also completely devoid of emotions. Nothing pushed at Richard; no unwelcome invasion into his mind.

"Are you... okay with that?" Richard asked.

Hunter cocked his head. "I mean, the contract wasn't exclusive. I came into this expecting you'd have a few side scenes scheduled."

"Oh."

Hunter frowned. "Are *you* okay with it?"

"Why wouldn't I be? Just thought I'd let you know." Richard attempted a grin, but it felt wide and fake.

"Enjoy," Hunter said, tone neutral as he turned back to the game.

Richard nodded, more to himself than Hunter. "I will."

He forced himself out of the apartment. His chest grew tighter with every step his feet took, with every floor the elevator descended, with every mile his car drove.

The traffic was even light, making the trip extra fast.

He parked in MateHub's parking lot and stared out his windshield at the building in front of him, his vision narrowing, his heart pounding, a sour taste on his tongue.

But he breathed through it, taking in deep, steadying lungfuls of air until he didn't feel like he was about to black out.

This was his job. There were no feelings involved. He'd done this before, and it'd never been a problem. It didn't have to be one now.

Hunter didn't care, so why should Richard?

If he didn't do this, his agent would be pissed. MateHub would be pissed. He'd be no better than all the unprofessional people he'd bonded before, letting a few mind-blowing orgasms convince him there was something between him and Hunter when there was nothing. Fooling himself with some imaginary happily ever after that didn't exist.

Because it was just a job.

He got out of his car and entered the MateHub building. His arm was heavy as he lifted it to hit the elevator call button.

When the doors opened, the last person he wanted to see stepped out.

Duke Moorhead looked him over with an icy glare. "Richard," he said as he walked past.

But then he stopped, inhaled, and laughed. The sound of it rang jagged through the quiet lobby.

"A human?" His handsome face twisted into a sneer.

"The contract was for more than you could ever hope to make." Richard kept his reply as cool as possible.

"You know that isn't what I'm talking about." Duke leaned in and inhaled again. He made a tsking noise. "Someone compatible? How careless of you. Are you catching feelings?"

"What's it to you?" Richard growled.

Duke shrugged. "Nothing. Though, however this turns out, it's great for me. Either I get a shot at breaking your record, or you get a taste of your own medicine. Ask me which I prefer." His expression was too vicious to be classified as a smile.

Richard opened his mouth to tell him to fuck off, but Duke was already striding away.

"Have fun with your side scene," he called over his shoulder as he headed toward the exit. "I hope your human doesn't mind sensing you come through the bond. That was always such a treat."

Richard's stomach lurched at the thought. He squeezed his eyes shut until the nausea passed. When he opened them, Duke was gone.

Scowling, Richard hit the elevator button again.

Duke couldn't let it go, could he? Years and half a dozen bonding contracts of his own later, he still blamed Richard for their lack of compatibility.

The elevator smelled wrong—missing a scent he'd gotten used to it holding—but Richard pressed the button for the sixth floor.

Once he reached the studio, he waved at Brandt and the rest of the crew, then made a beeline for his dressing room.

He paced the small room; its white walls closing in around him. His wolf lurked close to the surface, snarling, making it known that this was not where they were supposed to be.

Richard forced himself to stop, to breathe, to ignore the tight bands around his chest.

It was fine. It was a job. He could do this.

He undressed and slipped on his robe, leaving it hanging open as he sat in the chair.

Usually, knowing he was about to knot someone made arousal buzz through him, but his dick wasn't remotely hard.

He gave himself a few strokes.

Nothing. No desire, no pleasure.

He rolled his balls in his hand; he pinched his nipples.

Still nothing.

He closed his eyes and pictured what he was about to do as he stroked his soft dick. He was working with Trick Wilde—coyote shifter, all lean muscle and impressive flexibility. Trick wasn't interested in Richard bonding him, but was always first in line for these side scenes. And damn, could he take a knot. He'd beg for it as he clenched on Richard's co—

Richard flinched away from the thought and swallowed the bile in his throat.

Yeah, that wasn't going to work.

Maybe if he kept it impersonal. Anonymous. Another hole for him to fuck. Hot and tight and not connected to a body he was starting to know more and more, one he wanted to learn every inch of, commit to memory like he'd have forever to explore it.

A shiver ran through him.

He could use that. Imagine that body under him as he fucked Tri—

His stomach twisted, and he thought he might throw up.

That fleeting bit of arousal was gone, his dick still soft and uninterested in his hand.

He ignored the bitter tang in his mouth, the vise grip clamping around his chest.

What the hell was his problem?

His phone vibrated in his jeans pocket, and he sighed and stood, walking over to grab it.

There was one new message.

HUNTER

Are you okay? You don't feel okay.

Richard stared at it for a full minute, his thumb hovering over the screen.

Of course he was fine, and he'd type that out and send it to Hunter. In another minute.

Before he could, his phone lit up with an incoming call.

Richard hesitated but hit answer.

Hunter didn't wait for Richard to say hello. "What the fuck is going on? You do *not* feel okay."

"I'm fi—"

Hunter cut him off. "You're not fucking fine. I've never had a panic attack before, but you're making me feel like I'm having one. So what the hell is going on? Is it the scene? Are they making you do something you're uncomfortable with?"

"No, of course not. There are no hardcore kinks, just me kn—" His throat closed up, and his vision swam.

"Jesus fucking Christ, Richard, breathe. *Breathe*. Can

you hear me? Are you there? Deep breaths. In and out. You're alright. No one is going to make you do anything you don't want to do."

Richard let out a shaky exhale.

"That's good. Just keep breathing," Hunter said, his voice warm and soothing. There was a rustle of clothes on his end. "When's the filming scheduled to start?"

Richard glanced at the clock. "Ten minutes." His lungs refused to work.

"Breathe, Richard," Hunter reminded him. A door slammed; keys jingled. "Interview first?"

"Yes."

"Now, I need you to do something you've never done before. During the interview, *talk*."

"Talk?"

"Yes. A lot."

"Why?"

"Just trust me," Hunter said, his breath rough.

The line disconnected.

Richard blinked at his phone, realizing his wolf had settled, no longer prowling unhappily under his skin. He still wasn't aroused by any means, but he felt calmer. It was going to work out.

Ten minutes later, he exited his dressing room, his robe tied firmly around his waist.

Brandt raised an eyebrow, but Richard just asked, "Where's your pale little shadow today?"

"Everett's working with the MateHub Originals division on the preproduction for the *H4* sequel. If he has his way, *Shattered Souls & Secret Scents* will make *Lord of the Rings* look like a low-budget indie film."

The kid had ambition, Richard would give him that. As misplaced as it might be.

He sauntered over to the love seat to sit next to Trick.

"Hey," Trick said. "Long time, no see. How have you been?"

"Great," Richard said, surprised to realize how true it was. "You?"

"I've got to admit, I've been looking forward to you knotting me again."

"Then let's do the interview," Richard suggested, turning toward Brandt.

Brandt shrugged, and they got started.

"So, Trick," Brandt said. "Tell us how much you've been looking forward to this."

Trick leered at the camera. "I mean, who wouldn't? I only get a chance at that knot twice a year."

Richard glanced at him. "I remember you saying you weren't interested in doing a contract with me."

Trick acted coy, batting his eyelashes at Richard. "Is that an offer?"

He was teasing, but Richard didn't play into it.

"I was thinking, you should do one of your own. I mean, you've got the necessary equipment. Be a shame if it went to waste. If you think it feels amazing getting knotted, you should try it from the other end," Richard said in a light and friendly manner.

Trick narrowed his eyes. "Me? Bond someone?"

"You usually bottom for MateHub, but I know you're vers. You've never thought about it? How it might feel to be the one doing the knotting, instead of being knotted?"

"Well, I mean... yeah. But I figured MateHub wouldn't be interested in me doing that. I'm not their preferred image of a top."

Trick was gorgeous—his body fit, a mischievous glint in his eyes—but he was right. Coyote shifters tended to be smaller than wolves, and MateHub leaned toward casting stereotypical tops.

It was about time that changed.

"Ah, guys, we're getting off topic here," Brandt said.

Richard ignored him.

"You've got to try it. I think it'd be especially good for someone who's vers. When you're bonded to the person you're knotting, you sense what they feel. Not like it's physically happening to you, but a ghost of it."

"So... if I were to bond someone and knot them, it'd be like I was getting knotted too?"

"Not exactly, but as close as you'll get, barring MateHub making throuple bonding a thing. What kind of co-star would you want? I haven't seen you top often. Do you have a type? Would you rather go for some cute twink who'd hang off your knot, or do something a little more appropriately *Wilde* and see if MateHub would let you bond a bear shifter?"

"Ah, guys?" Brandt tried again. "Can we stay on topic?"

"Me knotting a bear shifter?" Trick's eyes were distant, imagining that.

"Can you picture it? It'd be such a fun subversion of the trope. I bet you'd get a bunch of views. MateHub's got some hot bear shifters, and a few of them definitely enjoy getting their asses reamed. How would you like that? Having some big, meaty guy laid out under you, begging for your knot."

Trick wet his lips. "How... how did you say you approached MateHub with the idea of doing a bonding contract?"

"GUYS," Brandt said, attempting in vain to regain control of the interview.

"Oh, that's easy." Richard launched into an overly detailed explanation of the negotiation process.

Five minutes into his long-winded monologue, Hunter busted into the studio, breathing hard, dripping sweat.

"WHERE IS HE?" Hunter yelled, looking around with a frantic stare. "WHERE IS THE... THE FLOOZY WHO WANTS TO SLEEP WITH MY MATE?"

Trick's eyes were comically wide as he mouthed, "Floozy?"

He was justifiably confused. Richard doubted anyone had called Trick a floozy before. Hell, he wasn't sure he'd ever heard that word used in real life.

Hunter spotted them on the love seat and stalked over, pointing a finger at Trick. "YOU! You hussy! Home-wrecker! RICHARD IS *MY* MATE. NOT YOURS. Where do you get off sleeping with other people's mates? You harlot! Adulterer!"

The corner of his mouth was twitching. A shimmering thread wound through their bond, and Richard realized Hunter was about five seconds away from dissolving into a fit of laughter.

He stood quickly, herding Hunter toward his dressing room, shielding him with his body so the crew couldn't see his face cracking into a smile.

"I'll take care of this," Richard said, the words gruff as he stifled his own amusement. Against his side, Hunter shook; his presence in Richard's mind glittered with mirth.

Richard pulled him into his dressing room and shut the door behind them. Hunter collapsed into him.

"God, that was fun," he wheezed, keeping his voice low in case anyone was eavesdropping.

Richard tried to process what had just happened. Hunter had thrown a fit to distract from him having a panic attack at the mere thought of this shoot.

It wasn't the first time someone he'd bonded had

freaked out over his side scenes, but it was the most dramatic and memorable.

No one blamed his temporary mates when they disrupted a filming. They were emotional from the bond; any outbursts were easily forgiven. Richard was held to a higher standard, but Hunter had given him the perfect out, a way to not film this scene while still saving face.

That made a contented warmth want to bloom in his chest, but he refused to let it.

Instead, he said, "You missed your calling. You should have been a real actor."

Hunter shot him a look of mock outrage. "Are you saying my outstanding performances as Broke, Innocent Human were not Oscar worthy?"

"I would never."

Hunter snorted, then grew more serious. "But are you okay? You feel less panicky."

"Yeah, I'm okay." Really okay. More okay than he wanted to think about. "Thank you for calling Trick a floozy. I don't think I'll ever forget the face he made."

"I feel a teeny bit bad about that. I didn't realize you were working with Trick. He's an awesome guy," Hunter said as he grabbed a towel from the bathroom, using it to wipe the sweat off his face and neck.

"Did you run here?" Richard asked.

Hunter gave a dismissive wave. "Seemed faster than calling a car and dealing with traffic. It was only fifteen minutes."

That was the stupidest, most romantic gesture anyone had done for him. It made his entire being feel warm and light.

"Do you want to do this scene?" Hunter asked.

"No," Richard said, a bit disconcerted by how instantly and honestly he could answer that.

"Then get your clothes on. I'll get you out of here."

Richard dropped his robe, and if he took extra time to gather his clothes before leisurely pulling them on, well, that was just a show of appreciation for Hunter. His gaze roaming over Richard's body gave him the thrill of arousal he'd been missing all morning.

When he was dressed, Hunter fisted his hand in Richard's T-shirt and stormed out of the dressing room, dragging Richard behind him.

"I AM TAKING MY MATE AND GOING HOME!" he announced as the crew stared at them. "WHERE NONE OF YOU TROLLOPS CAN SOIL HIM WITH YOUR STRUMPET HANDS AND TARTY WAYS!"

He marched Richard toward the elevator as Richard caught Brandt's eye and made a face he hoped conveyed his sincere regret for not being able to continue as planned. But what could he do? Hunter was not going to let it happen.

"Trollops?" Richard asked after the elevator doors shut.

"Should I have gone with fornicators instead?"

"Whatever you want."

Hunter grinned at him, his face shining with amusement and more beautiful than Richard had been prepared for that day.

"No, seriously. Whatever you want. I owe you and suddenly have an afternoon free. Savior's choice. Say the place, activity, or food, and it's yours."

Hunter considered, then said, "I've never been to the Santa Monica Pier and have been meaning to check it out."

"The pier it is," Richard replied.

Which was how he found himself on his second not-date with Hunter, strolling along the weathered planks, listening to the crash of the waves and the chaotic jumble of sounds that filled the salty air.

Hunter took in the sights, the rides and games, the performers and musicians, but those attractions weren't what held Richard's attention.

The cool ocean breeze tousled Hunter's curly hair, and warm sunlight played over his skin.

His eyes taking on a wicked glint Richard was coming to enjoy more than could ever be healthy, Hunter led him to a food cart and bought a bag of cotton candy.

"Hey," he said as he pulled out a pink wisp. "It's almost as soft and fluffy as you are." He held out the bag.

Richard shot him an unimpressed look, but he still tore off a chunk and ate it.

It was disgustingly sweet. That didn't stop him from wanting to taste the sugary remnants on Hunter's lips.

They'd wandered the length of the pier and were wending their way along the beach when Richard's phone buzzed. He pulled it out, already knowing who the message would be from.

DANIEL

MateHub contacted me about the issues today.

RICHARD

Sorry. I didn't expect Hunter to freak out.

It's probably better if I don't do any side scenes during this contract.

DANIEL

You want me to cancel all the contracts I spent hours lining up?

RICHARD

I think it's for the best. Hunter's not okay with me doing them.

DANIEL

Hunter, huh?

RICHARD

Yeah. It can't be helped. Sorry.

He wasn't sorry, and he didn't care. It felt right.

DANIEL

Fine. I'll cancel the contracts.

Richard exhaled, a weight lifting off his chest.

Hunter was eyeing him as he slipped his phone into his pocket. "Are you going to tell me what had you freaking out so much?"

Richard didn't want to explain that. He made a noncommittal noise.

"You sure it wasn't some kink you weren't comfortable with?"

"Yes."

"Fine," Hunter said. "But if there's anything in our remaining scenes you aren't okay with, you need to tell me."

A sudden sick feeling churned in Richard's gut, and Hunter's head whipped toward him, picking up the emotion. "Which one?"

It wasn't which one so much as it'd been the word 'remaining.' The reminder they only had three left. He'd rather not say that either though.

Hunter studied him for a minute, then said, "You fuck using stripper rules. You do all the touching; your co-stars barely touch you."

240

He wasn't wrong. Richard couldn't deny it. "I like getting people off. I like making them come hard, giving them what they need."

They walked farther down the beach, the lapping of the tide calming Richard.

"You know," Hunter said with a feigned casual tone, "I don't think I've seen you bottom before."

Richard kept his expression neutral, but something must have transferred through their bond.

"That's it, isn't it? You don't want to do that scene."

"Uh…" He didn't want to say he didn't, but…

"Then why did you agree to it?"

"I told my agent he could make concessions to get you to sign the contract."

"And he conceded your ass? I think you need a new agent."

"Nah, he's fine. I could have said no."

"So why didn't you?"

Because he'd wanted to bond Hunter, and he was realizing there was likely a reason for that.

When Richard didn't answer, Hunter asked, "Have you?"

"Not on camera."

"Off camera?"

"A few times when I was younger. Didn't enjoy it."

"Didn't enjoy it because it wasn't for you, or because the people you were with were shit at it?"

"Some of both. But it did make me want to give anyone I fucked the best orgasm of their life."

"Or at least in days," Hunter said, and Richard was amused despite himself.

"MateHub always has you bottom. Do you prefer to top?"

"Eh." Hunter tilted his head from side to side. "It's not so much that I like to top, more that I like control. I don't care if that means I'm doing the actual fucking, or if I'm riding someone's dick. Like, while I'm sure you'd look stunning fucking yourself on my cock, and I'd do it if that's what the scene called for, I'd never choose it for myself. Having you spread out for me while I milked your prostate until you saw stars? That, I'd happily do. I mean, don't get me wrong. Giving up control can be hot, too, and I do enjoy getting bent over and railed. But ideally, the guy will let me have my fun first, then flip me over and drill me into the mattress."

"Best of both worlds?"

"Absolutely," he said with a cheeky grin before sobering. "Are you okay with doing it? I don't think I'll be able to convincingly storm the set of my own scene, call myself an adulterous floozy, then drag you out of there."

Richard laughed at the mental image that conjured up. "I'd like to see you try. But no, I'll be fine."

"When's the last time you've had anything in your ass?"

"A decade ago?"

Hunter looked surprised. "Not even fingers?"

"Ah... no."

"And you were going to jump from that to the scene they have planned for us?"

"I was going to prepare."

Hunter raised an eyebrow at him.

"Eventually. There's a week left. I can... practice." It wasn't like he'd be getting any pleasure from it; it shouldn't cause problems for Hunter.

"Practice?"

"That's what you did, right?"

"Multiple times."

"So has MateHub made your dick into a magical dildo yet? Got any merch I can use?"

Hunter huffed. "Sorry. If you want to practice with my dick, all I can offer is the real thing."

He was joking, but the proposition lodged itself in Richard's brain.

It was a terrible idea for them to have sex outside their scenes. Without the lights and cameras, it'd be too close to something real, too easy to let emotions get involved. And emotions would make the bond deeper, make it more painful to sever than it was already going to be.

But he also didn't want to look like a complete amateur on camera, and if it was just practice...

"Okay," he said.

"What?" Hunter asked. The word came out like a squeak.

"If you're up for it. Literally. We should practice."

Hunter stared at him for long enough, Richard was certain he was searching for a polite way to say no, but then he swallowed audibly. "Let's... let's do that. We should... we should go back ho—to the apartment."

Richard swallowed too. "Okay. Yeah. Let's."

The drive dragged out painfully, anticipation licking along Richard's skin, and only some of it was his own. Hunter was quiet in the seat next to him, but a distracting murmur through their bond as his arousal built.

Richard's whole body was tingling by the time he unlocked the door to the apartment. He scented the air. It smelled like the two of them combined, like it could be home.

He tossed his keys on the kitchen counter. "I should..." He hooked a thumb over his shoulder.

"Do you want help—"

"No. I've got it."

He went into his bathroom. His heartbeat echoed in the small space.

It was practice. Nothing more. No reason for his stomach to feel fluttery.

He took off his shirt, then his jeans and underwear. His cock wasn't quite hard. If anything, it seemed confused, unsure whether it was into this or not. In favor of the sex with Hunter part, less so with the rest.

Turning on the water, he'd never been more grateful that this was a MateHub apartment. Both showers had heads that twisted off and were equipped with everything a porn star could need to get themselves squeaky clean. But even that felt invasive as he flushed himself out before scrubbing his body down.

He dried himself off and entered his bedroom, carrying the bottle of lube from the bathroom and setting it on the bedside table.

Right. He could do this. Not a big deal, and hopefully it'd keep him from making a fool of himself on camera.

He opened his bedroom door. "Hunter?"

Hunter stepped out of his room. He was also fresh from the shower and wearing a towel. "You good?" he asked.

"All good."

Hunter paused, listening, sensing Richard's emotions, and Richard didn't know how he felt about that, about Hunter's regard stroking like invisible fingers over his skin.

"Okay," Hunter said. "Shall we?"

Richard dropped his towel and got on the bed. Hunter followed, straddling one of Richard's legs, his towel riding up on his thighs.

He kept his movements slow as he grabbed the bottle and lubed up his fingers.

"Can you open wider for me?" he asked, and when Richard hesitated, he added, "If it helps, I'll draw a giant circle of glittery dicks around you."

Richard scoffed and spread his legs wider, giving him more access, but when Hunter traced a lubed finger over his entrance, he involuntarily tightened up.

"You don't have to answer," Hunter said, "but were those 'few times' consensual?"

"Yes. Just painful." He'd been young and stupid and hadn't realized it wasn't supposed to hurt. The guys he'd experimented with either hadn't known or hadn't cared. Whichever it was, it'd led to a few less-than-pleasant experiences.

Hunter searched his face.

Richard's eyes darted to the side, uncomfortable under his scrutiny. "I heal fast."

"Physically, maybe," Hunter said. "This won't be like that. Breathe for me."

Richard exhaled as Hunter started to slip a finger inside, but that alone had him clamping down tight around Hunter's fingertip.

"Jesus. How did you think I was going to get in there during the scene?"

"I said I'd stretch first."

"And when you immediately clenched airtight the moment I got near your hole?"

"Grit my teeth and bear it?"

"Because that's how I want someone to feel while I'm fucking them." He went back to teasing Richard's entrance, circling it, applying pressure, but not pushing in. "You can sense it through the bond though, right? When you fuck me?"

"Yeah."

"Do you like how that feels?"

"Yes, but that's because I make damn sure it feels good."

"You don't trust anyone else to do that?"

"No."

"Do you trust me?"

Richard paused. He did. To a startling extent.

"Did it feel good on the full moon when I was fingering myself? I had control then."

"You know it did. You felt how hard I came."

"Okay. This might be a bit awkward, but we'll see if it works. Lube my fingers up." He held out his left hand, and Richard did as told, slicking him up.

Hunter reached his hand under his towel and brought his fingers to his own hole, sliding one in, letting out a hum as he worked it in and out while teasing Richard's entrance.

Desire curled through Richard.

"How's that?" Hunter asked, though he had to know.

Richard nodded.

"Can you breathe for me?"

Richard took in a lungful of air and let it out in a long exhale, bearing down on Hunter's finger as he pressed it in.

There was a little resistance, but it wasn't bad.

"You good?"

Richard's breath was loud in the room.

Hunter paused, waiting for an answer, clearly not willing to go further until Richard gave him explicit confirmation.

"Yeah," Richard managed to get out. "Keep going."

"If it helps, think of how much smaller my dick is than yours."

Richard huffed out a breath. "How is that supposed to help? You're not particularly small yourself."

"It helps because you relax when you laugh."

Richard supposed it did.

"Alright. Most ridiculous scene MateHub has offered you. Go."

Richard's chuckle caught in his throat as Hunter moved both his hands, the odd feeling of his finger sinking into Richard blurring with the pleasure of the finger in Hunter.

"Alpha auction," Richard gasped out. "They wanted me to stand on stage naked while various supernatural creatures bid over who got to take my knot."

"That doesn't sound horrible."

"They wanted my knot out and fully inflated for the auction."

Laughter shook through Hunter's body, through his hands. "Considering how whiny you got during the ritual, that wouldn't have gone well."

"I wasn't whining. I was dying." Richard did not grumble as he said that either.

"Sure," Hunter agreed solemnly.

"But, yeah. That was a no. You?"

"They wanted to do something for the annual MerMay celebration. Get me one of those super elaborate mermaid tails and have a fisherman catch me, then fuck me."

"How would that work with the tail on?"

"Oh, see, that's the thing. They were going to modify the tail so it started at the tops of my thighs. Like I was swimming around in the ocean, ass and dick hanging out of my tail."

Richard shook his head, only to bite back a groan as Hunter stroked over both their prostates.

"I think you need another finger," Richard said.

"Do I?"

"Definitely."

Hunter complied, slipping a second finger inside

himself. The sensations lighting up Richard's mind distracted him from Hunter sliding another finger into him too.

"Still good?"

"Yeah." Surprisingly so.

"Most boring scene?" Hunter scissored his fingers carefully, but it just had Richard pushing back against his hand.

"Blow job contest judge. Sounded fun when I signed the contract. Never realized I'd get sick of having my dick sucked, but somewhere around the three-hour mark, I would have killed for a hand job," Richard said, panting as Hunter's fingers worked him open.

"Am I ready for three?"

Richard nodded again, expecting to feel Hunter do it to himself; he didn't. Instead, he pressed a third finger into Richard gently, like he expected him to tense up. Richard breathed through it and managed not to.

Hunter pulled his fingers out of himself, leaving Richard with the ghost of an empty feeling even as fingers still moved inside him, then wrapped his slick hand around Richard's half-hard cock, grip light and teasing, skating over him.

Richard did his best not to writhe, but as Hunter patiently opened him up, that was a near impossible feat.

"Ready?"

"Yeah," Richard said. If he thought he'd felt empty before, it paled in comparison to the ache of emptiness as Hunter withdrew his fingers to pull off his towel and lube himself up.

Richard watched Hunter line up his dick, but when he attempted to push in, Richard tensed, even though he told himself not to.

Hunter leaned forward, covering Richard's body with his own.

"You're doing great. Now let's see if we can get you to let me in," he said, so close to kissing Richard. Distractingly close, almost enough to keep his mind off Hunter nudging against his entrance, not forcing himself past his resistance, but staying right there, waiting for him to relax.

"Hottest scene?" Hunter asked, sounding as breathless as Richard felt.

"Anything with you," he answered before he could over-think it.

"Same." Hunter groaned. "I mean, is there anyone who hasn't fantasized about doing a ritual to summon a shifter's knot?"

Richard snorted, then gasped as the head of Hunter's cock breached his rim.

He breathed in through his nose and exhaled out of his mouth, not quite managing to relax with Hunter partially buried in him.

"Do you think, if I asked nicely, Zinnia would make me one of those robes?" Hunter's voice was raspy, his eyes trained on Richard's face. "Seems like perfect loungewear."

He was trying to make Richard laugh, and while Richard didn't have enough air in his lungs for that, it still worked. Hunter sank in all the way, buried to the hilt, the stretch and burn almost too much.

"Fuck," Hunter panted, "If you clench me any tighter, knot or no knot, we'll be tied together. Breathe for me?" He stroked a hand along Richard's side. "You'll like this once you relax more, I promise."

Richard inhaled sharply as Hunter rocked his hips, tiny motions that had wisps of pleasure floating in his head. It was better than he would have expected.

"Can you feel how good you're making this for me?" Hunter asked.

"Yeah." Hunter was alight in his mind, bright and blazing and making everything worth it.

He braced his forearms on either side of Richard's head, his body moving in long, slow rolls, Richard's cock trapped between them. Hunter's eyes stayed locked on his face, waiting for Richard to let himself enjoy it. He shifted his hips to press against Richard's prostate, looking pleased when it earned him a moan.

"That's it," Hunter whispered as he leaned in and kissed him.

Richard groaned into Hunter's mouth, but it wasn't in pain. Hunter's heartbeat pounded against his chest.

"You feel amazing," Hunter said, "but damn, this would have been terrible for the cameras."

Richard couldn't argue against that point. As enjoyable as Hunter's slow rocking was starting to feel, it wasn't the sort of thing that would show up well. Still, he couldn't let that comment pass.

"I'm always good on camera." It would have sounded more convincing if he hadn't been quite so breathless.

"Oh, is that so?" The corner of Hunter's mouth quirked up. "If that's the case, I guess we don't need to practice anymore." He pulled away.

Richard grabbed him and yanked him back, the movement driving Hunter deeper, making them both grunt.

"That's what I thought," Hunter said, rocking his hips again, but Richard shifted his own to encourage him to move faster.

Hunter took the hint, and his thrusts picked up speed, his exhales hot on Richard's neck, teeth grazing the skin there. Richard's eyes slipped closed, and the world narrowed down to Hunter's mouth on his unmarked skin. Hunter latched on, sucking where a mating bite would go, making Richard's toes curl.

Fuck, he needed to do that harder. Richard had been bitten a dozen times, but none of them had made him yearn for it like Hunter's mouth currently was. None had made him want to beg for teeth to sink into his skin.

Hunter dragged a line of kisses along his neck. "I can feel you getting close." He gripped Richard tightly, his pace becoming more insistent, pushing Richard closer and closer to the edge.

Richard struggled to breathe around his intoxicating need. He felt Hunter's orgasm, eager and desperate, soaring higher, pulling Richard toward that exhilarating fall.

Every nerve ending sparked to life. Heat ripped through him like wildfire, fanned by Hunter's climax barreling toward him. He choked back a cry of Hunter's name, clutching at his shoulders, spilling between their bodies, his release consuming him until he couldn't think, couldn't see, couldn't remember anything but this moment.

Hunter moaned in his ear, his cock pulsing in Richard. His presence eased from desperation to relief as his mouth found Richard's, their kiss hot and messy as they rode out their orgasms.

They lingered like that for longer than Richard would have expected, but shorter than he would have liked.

Hunter pulled back enough to look at him. "Still good?"

If he couldn't feel how good Richard was, there was something wrong with their bond.

"I can't say I'm going to become an exclusive bottom, but that wasn't the worst orgasm I've ever had." It'd never be his first choice, but feeling how much Hunter had enjoyed it, Richard couldn't say he hated it either.

"Better than you've had in days?"

"Eh, maybe a week."

Hunter grinned at him, and for one heartbeat it seemed like he might kiss him again, but instead, he pulled out, leaving Richard impossibly, achingly empty. Then he rolled to the side, his muscular body glistening with sweat, his limbs loose.

They lay there as their hearts and breathing slowed. It was nice not needing to get up and head to his dressing room so the crew could clean up.

It was nicer to smell Hunter in his bed.

But he wasn't going to think about that.

"I'll admit it," Richard said. "That would have sucked for the cameras. So... what are you doing tomorrow?"

Hunter turned to study him. "Are you implying 'you' is an option?"

"If I have to bottom on camera, I want to be the hottest bottom on that damn site. We've got a week. I'm a fast learner."

He sensed the promise of it sweep through Hunter, his mostly soft dick jerking like it wanted a second round sooner than tomorrow.

"That felt like a yes," Richard said.

"What about the contract?"

Richard shrugged. "It's just practice. MateHub never has to know."

A brief unease wriggled in Richard's mind, but then Hunter was smirking at him. "In that case, hell yes."

He rolled out of bed, took a few steps toward Richard's bathroom, then paused. "Ah. Should I grab you a washcloth?"

His sudden hesitation was understandable. There was no reason for Hunter to help him clean up. Richard wasn't some exhausted, sleepy human who needed caring for. Hunter wasn't some loving partner who'd wipe him down, then cuddle him until they fell asleep.

Richard waved him off. "I'm fine. I'll get up and shower in a minute."

"Right. I'll just…" Hunter pointed toward his room. "Have a good night."

He snagged his towel off the floor and left.

Richard didn't let himself think about it. He pushed himself to his feet, grimacing slightly, and walked to the bathroom.

His eyes caught on his reflection and the dark bruises Hunter had dotted along the juncture of his neck. They'd be gone by morning, washed away by his enhanced healing, as temporary as their bond. He shifted his focus to anywhere but the mirror and got cleaned up.

And when he crawled into bed, he absolutely did not think about what it would have been like if Hunter had wanted to stay.

CHAPTER
EIGHTEEN

Richard really was a fast learner; Hunter had to give him that.

At the start of this contract, he never would have imagined having nightly sex with a guy he'd wrongly assumed was a complete bastard.

Or that the sex would be the best in his life. Not days or weeks or months. His entire fucking life. He hadn't realized how fun it could be to joke around with someone as they fucked, enjoying the breathless laughter he drew out of Richard almost as much as the breathless moans.

He'd never been in a relationship long enough to know anyone's body like he knew Richard's, yet there was so much more he could learn if he had the time.

College had been a series of hookups, and once he'd signed with MateHub, he hadn't known how to navigate a real relationship on top of that.

Finding himself in the same person's bed every night for a week was new. And kind of nice, even if he never stayed in that bed once they were finished.

Richard was this complex ball of emotions in his mind that seemed to get bigger each time they had sex. There was an obvious joke there, and his chosen metaphor might have had something to do with it having been weeks since Richard had knotted him. It'd been too long, and Hunter was starting to crave it.

As good as fucking Richard was, he wanted to ride that knot again. It was like he needed Richard to stretch him wide. To possess him, reclaim him, make Hunter his in every way possible.

It didn't help that he felt how badly Richard wanted that too.

But they didn't need to practice that.

Horniness aside, he couldn't think of a better way to explain how he sensed Richard. Every time he worked Richard open, worked past his automatic barriers, then made him burn with pleasure until they both came, Richard's presence seemed to expand more, filling Hunter fuller.

When Hunter had his hands on him, Richard was an open book. He felt what he liked, what would make him come. What he wanted, what he needed. When they weren't touching, Richard was more confusing. Hunter caught wisps of emotions when they were strong enough, and if he got quiet and *listened*, he sensed more than that. Richard's feelings became clearer and easier to read with each passing day.

Like with Richard's body, that surface-level knowledge left Hunter wanting more, wanting to learn his emotions like a language only he could speak.

Having that constant presence with him, that warmth carried inside him, was more pleasant than he would have expected. He'd assumed it'd be intrusive; it wasn't. It was almost comforting, almost like home.

But it wasn't home.

No matter how much he enjoyed the sex, or how much time they spent together. No matter how many nights they ended up gasping into each other's mouths as he rocked into Richard's tight heat.

It was work.

The best goddamn work week of his life.

Between all the practicing, eating, and gaming, the only reason he left the apartment was to hit the in-house gym. Not that he wasn't getting in a healthy dose of cardio from his more horizontal activities.

Richard had even started to join him.

If the mere memory of Richard running after him, chasing him down, and knotting him in the forest had been distracting, it didn't compare to having Richard on the treadmill beside him, his gray sweatpants doing nothing to hide the bounce of his dick with every stride he took.

Though the bastard didn't need to exercise.

"You have to work out?" Hunter had asked. "Chance never seems to."

Richard shrugged. "It's not so much that I have to. I like to. Running feels good regardless of the form I'm in."

Hunter shot him a disgruntled look. "I don't like to so much as I have to."

Damn shifters and their damn supernatural energy keeping them muscled and hot and flexible and tight and—Ugh. Hunter wanted to groan.

He theorized Richard was exercising for the sole purpose of torturing him with the beads of sweat that slid down the curve of his neck, the flex of his muscles, the way his chest rose and fell with each breath.

And those damn sweatpants. How they fit should be illegal. They weren't safe for Hunter's sanity.

If he'd been asked a week ago whether regular sex would make him more or less horny, this would not have been his answer.

But again, it was just work. Just physical. Just practice.

Tireless, thorough practice.

For their jobs.

They were excellent employees like that. Sacrificing themselves for the company. Putting in the hard time. Going above and beyond, as well as in and out.

And if Hunter slipped into Richard's dressing room when they arrived on set for their fifth scene, he was demonstrating professionalism. He had to make sure Richard was prepared, that he was ready to take the pounding Hunter was about to give him.

They'd filmed the location scenes earlier that morning, out in the woods. This time, the predator had become the prey, Hunter living up to his name by tracking Richard down and tranquilizing him before chaining him up in a cage in his basement.

How Hunter had single-handedly lugged a full-sized man with multiple inches and thirty to forty pounds of muscle on him all that way was conveniently glossed over. They weren't aiming for realism here.

While the scene itself wasn't much more than light bondage, there wouldn't be anything slow or gentle about it either. He didn't want Richard tensing up when he went to fuck him.

So, honestly, simultaneously fingering Richard and himself in the shower while they traded playful kisses was textbook good business practice. A professional courtesy, one might say. As was fucking him slowly with the butt plug the crew had so kindly provided, even if Richard spent that time grumbling about how MateHub should get on with making some merchandise for Hunter already.

Hunter was extra diligent about it, as everyone should be when they had a job to do. Having a respectable work ethic was important.

When they emerged from Richard's dressing room, both naked and hard and eager to get some exemplary work done, Brandt gave them an unimpressed look.

He pointed to the dressing room. "Hunter, you're fine. But Richard, you need to be soft for the start of the scene. You aren't supposed to be enjoying this, remember?"

Oh, right. Hunter had forgotten about that.

It seemed only fair for him to assist a coworker when he'd caused the situation they were in. So he followed Richard to his dressing room, popped out his plug, and milked his prostate until the issue was resolved. If the solution included strings of filthy curses on Richard's part and a slight delay in filming, it couldn't be helped.

Before they left the room, Hunter grabbed Richard's arm, stopping him, then whispered in his ear, "If you can, don't come when I do." He squeezed the base of Richard's dick, eliciting a groan. "I'll make it worth your while."

He then walked away, leaving Richard to stare after him. Without looking back, he knew Richard's eyes were on his bare ass.

Brandt gave an exasperated sigh when he saw them, but Hunter wasn't listening. He was already making his way on set.

It was decked out like a torture chamber, and Hunter thought they might have overdone it. Hopefully no one would click on the thumbnail expecting it to be something hardcore. Everyone had their kinks, and that was fine. Hunter had just never been into anything that caused actual pain. He'd been clear with MateHub from the beginning that he was not interested in doing any scenes of that nature.

That said, there was some appeal to strapping Richard to the table the set designers had prepared. It looked like they were using the same table they used for the scenes where someone went to the doctor to be treated for a vitamin D deficiency. Now with added leather straps and chains.

Richard got on the table and propped his feet in the stirrups, his legs spread wide.

"Ah, guys," Brandt said. "We haven't done the interview?"

"Oh, right," Hunter said, fastening shackles around Richard's ankles. "We should do that."

"*So.* This is a first for both of you. Hunter, how are you feeling about topping on camera?" Brandt waved the crew into place.

Hunter blinked. Huh. When had the crew gotten there? He hadn't noticed them. Whatever, he couldn't focus on that while he skated his fingers up the inside of Richard's legs.

"Hunter?" Brandt prompted.

Wait. He'd asked a question, hadn't he? Something about how Hunter was feeling?

"Great." Hunter gripped Richard's hips, yanking his ass to the edge of the table. Richard leered at him. "Amazing."

Brandt seemed to be waiting for him to add more, but Hunter was too busy slotting himself between Richard's thighs so he could lean forward and fasten the leather straps across his chest. His cock accidentally bumped against Richard's balls as he did.

"...Okay. And you, Richard? Nervous about bottoming on camera?"

Hunter shifted his hips and reached for the second strap, his dick catching on Richard's lubed hole.

Richard hummed. "Not at all."

Hunter grinned at him and gave the tiniest thrust as a reward. Not enough to breach his rim, but enough Richard would feel it. Enough he'd want more.

"Can either of you elaborate on that?"

Hunter would, but all his effort was currently going into hauling himself away from Richard's ass to take both his arms, stretch them over his head, and snap heavy cuffs around his wrists.

He stepped back and admired his work.

It was ridiculous, but Richard made it look good. Strapped down, the flush of orgasm on his cheeks, his legs spread open for Hunter.

Oh, Hunter would meet the requirements of this job with distinction. Earn himself employee of the year with how hard he was about to fuck that ass.

Richard cocked an eyebrow at him, and Hunter smirked. There was no denying how excited he was to do this scene, to top someone on camera. For that someone to be Richard.

Once they got past the cheesy dialog, this was going to be fun.

Brandt sighed loud enough it made Hunter glance over at him.

"Fine," Brandt said. "Let's do the scene."

Hunter stared after him as he huffed his way to his usual place beside the cameras.

What was his problem?

He shrugged and got into position between Richard's legs, and Brandt called action.

"Well, well, well," Hunter said, trailing a hand over the straps and down Richard's chest. "What do we have here? It looks like the hunter became the hunted. By the Hunter."

He might have ad-libbed those last three words, but if the writers hadn't realized how preposterous that line was when delivered by someone named Hunter, it wasn't his fault. Besides, it was making Richard bite the inside of his cheek to keep from laughing, and Hunter liked how his eyes lit up when he laughed.

"Not such a big bad wolf now, are you? Ready for a human to fuck you, shifter?"

Richard snarled and struggled against his bonds, but in Hunter's mind, he was nothing but want, and his dick was already hardening again.

Which meant Hunter needed to get started before that happened. For the sake of the scene, of course.

"Looking forward to your prey making you beg?"

Richard let out a half-feral growl.

This was the part where he was supposed to fuck Richard—ram into him and take everything he wanted—but there was something he'd been dying to do. Another thing he couldn't justify practicing.

He bent down and dragged his tongue from Richard's balls to his tip, finally getting to savor the taste of him. Richard jerked against his restraints, but unlike their first scene, this truly was all about Hunter.

And what Hunter wanted was to take him in his mouth, to feel Richard go from mostly soft to rock hard as he desperately tried to pretend he wasn't enjoying every goddamn second of it, like he wasn't loving every suck and flick and swirl. Like his hips weren't flexing to get deeper

261

down Hunter's throat, like his arms weren't wrenching against the chains so he could twist a hand in Hunter's hair and fuck his mouth.

Maybe they'd do that someday, but for now, Hunter had control, and he wasn't about to waste it.

He traced each vein, licked every inch, then rolled Richard's foreskin forward and slid his tongue inside to swirl over the head. His quick detour to suck Richard's balls had Richard straining against his bonds.

Hunter chuckled, dark and satisfied. Meeting Richard's gaze, he wiped his mouth with the back of his hand.

"You ready to beg, wolf?" He ran a finger along the underside of Richard's stiff cock as he grabbed the lube the staff had tucked in a drawer on the table and slicked himself up.

"Fuck you," Richard snarled. His eyes flashed, his wolf close to the surface even though the moon was new. It didn't always make an appearance when Hunter topped, but it was nice to know it enjoyed it as much as Hunter and Richard did.

"Uh-uh." Hunter lined himself up. "That's not how this is going to go."

He pushed in as roughly as he dared, but he hadn't needed to worry; Richard took his dick like a fucking champ. His body arched as far off the table as the straps allowed, his head falling back. The moan that escaped his lips was more pleasure than pain.

"You like that? Like that human dick filling you up?"

Richard glared at him, but their bond was sparkling with amusement.

"Let's see how much you can take, wolf. You know you're going to come on my cock."

"Never," Richard scoffed, as if he hadn't done that exact thing every night for the last week.

They'd see about that.

Hunter dropped the cheesy dialog. There'd been more, but he didn't care. The script called for him to fuck Richard mercilessly, and he stuck to that. He could be relentless without those lines to make that point.

He exploited everything he'd learned about Richard's body, every place he liked to be touched, which angles were best, the strokes that made him squirm in the most delicious ways. The moves that left him panting, biting his lip to stop himself from begging as Hunter did everything in his power to make him come, to turn him into a writhing mess.

Richard's eyes were bright with a challenge Hunter couldn't resist.

Once he got Richard worked up, he focused on his own arousal, on making damn sure he came as hard as possible, because Richard might be able to deny his own orgasm, but he'd have trouble if Hunter nearly blacked out from his.

Yet another benefit of the bond.

Even though this wasn't scheduled to be a knotting scene, they were filming it the same way they had with the others—apparently too used to that format to think of doing anything else with a bonded pair. Which meant no stopping for different camera angles; there were no interruptions, only Hunter drawing every ounce of pleasure he could out of Richard, zeroing in on the sensations he was making Richard feel.

He did his best to make it last, but he was only human. Not even an incubus would have been able to resist the clench of Richard's ass for long.

His orgasm careened toward him, and he took Richard

in hand, stroking him the way Richard liked, jerking him in time with his thrusts. He might not want Richard to come, but he wasn't going to make it easy on him. Where would the fun be in that?

Richard's hands were balled into fists, his claws out, piercing his skin, the iron tang of blood in the air. His jaw was clamped shut, trying to keep from coming as Hunter's movements grew erratic.

A white-hot tide cascaded through Hunter's veins as he released into Richard. Colors danced behind his eyelids, his breath stolen by the overwhelming sensations that consumed him. The world dissolved into a blissful haze, and he slumped forward, half-collapsed on Richard's chest.

When he returned to himself, Richard's cock was hard and digging into his stomach. He hid a grin against taut muscles before straightening up to watch Richard's eyes roll back as he wrapped a hand around the base of his dick.

Richard's knot was a hot throb that began to inflate when Hunter's fingers closed around it, and Hunter's eyebrows rose. It'd never done that before; he'd thought Richard needed to be in him—in *anyone*—for it to happen. But then, he'd also never felt Richard this desperate to be inside him.

He massaged it, keeping tight pressure around it as he did, and the noise Richard made was like nothing he'd heard before—a needy, animalistic whine coming from deep in his soul. It had Hunter shuddering, his whole body aching with the urge to relieve that hunger in Richard, to give him what he was begging for.

Hunter eased out, loving the way Richard's ass clenched around his softening length, like it wanted Hunter to stay in him longer. The sight of his come leaking out of Richard sent a shiver through his body.

Was this how Richard felt after he knotted someone? That possessive desire to claim momentarily scratched. Satisfaction curled in his gut at the knowledge that everyone would see how deeply he'd marked his mate.

But he didn't let himself dwell on that. He had better things to do.

He leaned in and mouthed along the swell of Richard's knot, feeling it throb against his lips and tongue, earning him another of those broken, guttural sounds.

Time to give Richard what his body was asking for so nicely.

He slicked Richard's cock up with lube before climbing onto the table and straddling him. The head of his dick felt massive as it nudged against Hunter's hole. He hadn't stretched enough for this, but he also didn't care; he wanted to feel Richard for days.

Richard's eyes were blazing as he watched Hunter sink onto his dick. Hunter forced himself to relax as he bore down on his knot until it popped into his ass and he was fully seated. He paused, panting at the burn.

The straps cut into Richard's chest where he arched, and the tendons and muscles of his neck strained with tension.

Hunter's jaw ached. The long line of Richard's neck was so beautiful and perfect. Too perfect, too smooth, too unmarked.

He needed to fix that.

His fingers threaded through Richard's hair and tugged his head to the side. He bit down hard, almost breaking skin.

Richard thrashed under him, howling as Hunter sucked on the juncture of his neck, then nipped at his ear.

"You're mine," he said, fierce possessiveness laced

through the words, and Richard attempted to buck up into him.

Hunter sat back and gazed at Richard, at the dark mark blooming on his skin. This was how Richard's neck was supposed to look. Marked. *His.*

It made Hunter want to rumble the way Richard did, pleased with his handiwork.

He locked eyes with Richard and began to move, pulling off his knot, then plunging down again.

Richard's hands clasped the chains and yanked. It wasn't to take control; he was willing to let Hunter do all the work, to ride his dick until they were tied together, but he wanted to touch Hunter while he did, to make him feel good, to get him off once more.

Hunter wasn't going to let him do that—not yet—but he'd make a few concessions. He felt the things Richard wanted to do, and he did them.

Staring into Richard's eyes, he tweaked his own nipples and stroked his cock how Richard would. It was still soft and oversensitive, but trying to rally for round two.

With as little prep as he'd had, Richard felt bigger than usual. Each time he slammed down stretched him wider. He would definitely be feeling this in the morning, and for days after.

Richard growled low in his throat as his knot caught on Hunter's rim. He tried to move, but his bonds restrained him, his frustration growing with each moment he couldn't touch Hunter.

It didn't take much before Hunter was bearing down on his knot one last time, locking them together.

Fuck, there was nothing else like this. Nothing else that made him feel so full, so owned, so connected.

Hunter ground on his dick, Richard's body shaking as

his orgasm overtook him and echoed through Hunter, leaving him gasping, his spent cock managing a few spurts of its own.

Ecstasy played over Richard's features, his eyes closed, his mouth parted as he pulled in ragged lungfuls of air.

After a minute, his eyes cracked open, and all Hunter saw in them was a deep-seated need.

He didn't hesitate, just reached out, groaning as the motion caused Richard's knot to tug on his rim, and undid the trick latches on Richard's cuffs.

Richard's arms wound around him instantly, pulling him into a kiss that stole all the air from Hunter's lungs, all the thoughts from his mind, all awareness of anything that wasn't Richard's hands on him, the dance of their tongues, the determined grind of Richard's hips up into him, because goddamnit, he should be the one to make Hunter come. Richard's instinctual need to milk a second orgasm out of him was going to kill Hunter someday, but fuck if he wouldn't enjoy his demise, even if it left him whimpering and clinging to Richard as he spilled between them.

There was a little less desperation running through Richard after that, a little more control, and a lot more smugness.

Hunter couldn't say he minded though, not when Richard kept kissing him, kept touching him, his hands roaming over Hunter, trailing off as he softened and slipped out.

"Years," Hunter said. He felt how sated that one word, that one confession, made Richard.

"Best of both worlds?" Richard asked in a low, contented rumble.

"Mmm, absolutely."

Hunter wasn't sure when Brandt called cut. He wished

they could lie there forever, but he got up and finished unstrapping Richard.

They wobbled to Richard's dressing room on unsteady legs.

And if they kissed their way through their post-scene shower, well, Hunter would eventually figure out how to call that professional too.

SCENE: *Hunter and the Hunted Hunter*

KnottyWolf69:
Fuuuuck. Richard bottoming? I never thought I'd
see the day. And it looked like he was ENJOYING it.

BramStroker:
And switching too? MateHub has fed us well
tonight.

lupeybottom:
Did you notice how he was already starting to knot
before he was in Hunter? He must have been
insanely turned on.

KnottyWolf69:
Right? That's so rare. Fuck. I want someone who can
make me knot like that.

MagicalHWood:
That was NOT the first time Hunter has fucked him.
He knew his body too well. Richard wasn't faking it.
He might be the love of my life, but I can admit he
isn't a good enough actor to fake that.

readyorknot:
If they're fucking off camera, do you think their
bond is more than transactional? How hot would it
be if they had a true bond?

MagicalHWood:
Richard hasn't released any side scenes yet. He still has time, but I'm beginning to doubt he will.

BramStroker:
Look how happy they are at the end, when they're tied together and kissing after Hunter undid the cuffs so Richard could hold him. I can't take it. If they sever their bond, I'm going to cry.

KnottyWolf69:
Even if it isn't true, I'm not sure I'll ever be able to watch either of them with anyone else again.

BramStroker:
Seriously. I tried to watch one of Richard's older scenes the other day, and it's just not the same. Couldn't get off to it at all.

readyorknot:
Petition to keep them together longer! I want a couple hundred scenes of them. Seven is not enough.

BramStroker:
They're so good together. Like that callback to their bonding scene? The little "fuck you," "uh-uh, that's not how this is going to go"? They have in-jokes!

MagicalHWood:
I do wonder why there wasn't a pre-scene interview though. I understood no interview for the last scene. Richard was probably too wound up for it.

But they should have asked Richard how he felt about bottoming on camera before the scene.

KnottyWolf69:
I've heard the first few months of a true bond can leave you so caught up in your mate, you barely even notice the world around you. Especially when the bond is demanding you reaffirm it. So my money is on that. Somewhere, there's footage of them too lust-drunk to answer questions.

readyorknot:
Oh god, I need to see that so bad. Release the True Bond Cut!

BramStroker:
My only complaint? Why do they keep teasing us with the biting? Hunter was SO CLOSE to doing it properly this time. I need Hunter's teeth in Richard, biting down, drawing blood NOW. Fuck. Just typing that is making my fangs drop.

lupeybottom:
It would've seemed random to have Hunter bite him during the hunting scene or that ridiculous ritual, but this was the perfect opportunity! Hunter should have bitten him!

BramStroker:
When Hunter finally does break skin, I'm gonna come from that alone.

MagicalHWood:

snort You and Richard both, given how he was thrashing around from Hunter sucking on his neck. Goddamn, it's hot seeing him so desperate.

KnottyWolf69:

If it's a true bond, Hunter DEFINITELY needs to bite him. He needs to show the world who Richard belongs to. There's no way Richard doesn't want that.

BramStroker:

It's a true bond. It has to be. I refuse to believe anything else.

HuntMeDown:

Just so you all know, I've asked the mods to make a DickHunt board. If MateHub approves it, that'll be our confirmation.

MagicalHWood:

Damn, I'm a little impressed. I guess we'll have to wait and see what they do next.

CHAPTER

NINETEEN

R ichard felt Hunter's eyes following him as he
moved around the kitchen.

"How did you learn to cook?" he asked, gaze
fixed on the way Richard was slicing up bell peppers and
cucumbers.

"My mother taught my sister and me. Our pack is pretty
small, but she likes to cook for us and have pack dinners as
often as possible. She says cooking is a skill every good wolf
shifter should have."

He wouldn't mention that the main reason she'd taught
them was so they could use that skill whenever they found
mates. Hunter didn't need to know that. He also didn't
need to know Richard had never cooked for anyone outside
his family before Hunter.

"I'm hopeless in the kitchen," Hunter said. "You should
have seen Chance's and my pathetic attempts to feed
ourselves during college. Honestly, it's a miracle we
survived and never got food poisoning. Or scurvy. Though I
suppose those would have affected me a hell of a lot more
than they'd have affected him."

"Were you the type to live entirely on cup noodles?"

"Of course not." Hunter sounded scandalized. "Are you crazy? Those things are too expensive. Pack ramen all the way, and fast food when we were feeling wild. That Malaysian place near campus was our one splurge. Don't get me wrong, we did eventually figure out such culinary masterpieces as grilled cheese, but it was after some trial and error. FYI, I do not recommend using the iron you borrowed from the only kid on your floor who didn't walk around looking like a wrinkled slob."

"You didn't."

"Oh, yes, we did. And let me tell you, we had neither food nor iron by the time we were done. After that, we just used the microwave."

"You put two slices of bread with cheese in a microwave and called the sad end result grilled cheese?"

"Listen, it wasn't the proudest moment of my life."

"Did you toast them first?"

"What is this 'toast' activity you speak of?"

"And here I was thinking it was a compliment that you enjoyed my cooking. But in actuality, your standards are microwaved cheese sandwiches."

"Yep." Hunter grinned cheekily at him. "I have an incredibly refined palate."

Richard side-eyed him. "Please tell me you've learned since then."

"Of course. I can make all kinds of sandwiches in the microwave now. Cheese, peanut butter and jelly, lunch meat, tuna."

The wicked glimmer of amusement in his eyes had Richard leaning toward that not being true, but he wouldn't put money on it.

"And did you know," Hunter said, "if you take those free ketchup packets from fast food restaurants and spread them on bread, then top it off with a slice of cheese and microwave it, it's indistinguishable from pizza."

He was kidding. He had to be kidding. No one sane would do that... right?

"Oh my god. I can literally sense you squirming in my mind you're so uncomfortable. It's amazing." Hunter cackled.

"Haha, very funny. Now get your ass up and on this side of the counter."

"Why do I have the feeling this won't be nearly as fun as most of the times you've told someone to get their ass up?"

"Oh, believe me. When I'm done with you, you'll be dry-rubbing meat and pulling pork with the best of them."

"You say that like I don't already. I also toss a mean salad, by the way."

Richard huffed. "I have no doubt."

Hunter winked at him. "So what are we making?"

"Baba ganoush."

"I'm going to nod and pretend I know what that is. What's the first step?"

"Roasting the eggplant."

Hunter looked at Richard's crotch, then back up. "Eh, I've had bigger."

Richard leaned in, his mouth against Hunter's ear. "Say that the next time I've got you stretched open on my knot." Hunter shuddered, and Richard smirked. "Thought so."

It took Richard longer than it should have to pull away. Hunter smelled so fucking good.

He tried to focus on the tasks at hand as they worked—preheating the oven, retrieving a baking sheet, cutting the eggplants lengthwise as he explained the dishes they'd be making. He didn't let himself think about how close they were standing, how easy it would be to press himself against Hunter's back, to bend him over the counter as they waited for the eggplants to roast.

Instead, he diced vegetables for the tabbouleh while Hunter attempted to peel the carrots they'd be using for dipping. His peeling technique was only slightly concerning. It seemed decently unlikely he'd lose a finger in the process.

Maybe he'd have Hunter wash the rice for the mujadara next. That might be safer. No sharp objects involved in that.

From time to time, their arms would brush, and he'd get flashes of emotion from Hunter. Nothing major, just a warmth that hinted at happiness.

They managed to make the food without any mishaps. Hunter had even been quite good at tossing actual salad— or tabbouleh, in this case. Probably not as good as he was at tossing more euphemistic ones, but not bad either.

If the meal tasted better than any Richard had made by himself, that had to be a coincidence. It had nothing to do with how pleased his wolf was about cooking with their mate.

To test that theory, he had Hunter help him the next night and the night after that. He'd be happy to never leave this apartment, to spend his days playing video games with Hunter, then cooking with him, in their own little world.

But that world had far too many cracks in it. He'd already left Daniel's latest message unread for two days, only a few words visible in the notification.

DANIEL

I've found a vampire for your nex...

Richard glanced at it again and felt a sudden queasiness in his stomach.

"You okay?" Hunter called out from the living room.

"All good."

A piercing lance of doubt jolted through him, but it was gone just as fast.

Richard took a deep breath and tried to shake off his unease. It lingered.

He couldn't ignore Daniel's message for much longer, but he'd give it one more day.

Tomorrow, he promised himself. He'd get to it tomorrow.

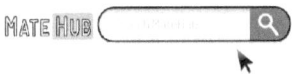

No matter what they cooked, Hunter was the best scent in their kitchen.

No one would blame Richard for finding every excuse possible to get more of that scent. If he stood closer than necessary, if he reached around Hunter to grab an ingredient instead of asking him to pass it over, if he brushed up against him when he showed Hunter how to do something.

Hunter enjoyed it too, judging by the way he pressed back against Richard when he got close, the way he let out hums of pleasure when Richard's fingers brushed against his skin.

Richard lost himself in Hunter's presence, in the movement of his hands over the cutting board—not smooth by any means, but getting better by the day—in the sound of his laughter floating through the kitchen.

Each hit he got of Hunter's scent made warmth curl in

his chest, made his wolf rumble with contentment. Made it impossible to resist the pull toward Hunter. He wanted him, all of him, in whatever way he could have him.

It'd been too long since they'd been together, and it was making him restless with the need to cover Hunter in his scent and reaffirm their bond.

That desperate desire to claim wasn't something he'd experienced before. His wolf had never given a damn about the co-stars they'd been bonded to. Richard had thought people were full of shit whenever they talked about the pull they felt toward their mates, the instinct to be close, to touch, to deepen the bond to the point there was no separating them. It'd sounded like a silly fairy tale. There was no way it could be real.

But he'd been wrong. That pull existed, and with Hunter, it was maddening.

After a week of regular sex, then days of nothing, Richard was crawling out of his skin. The moon was growing in the sky, edging closer to full, but he wasn't sure he'd survive another week without touching Hunter.

He couldn't remember the last time he'd been this horny, this worked up, and he knew Hunter felt it, felt how much he needed to mark him, knot him, do anything Hunter would let him do. It reverberated when they got close and made him want to get closer still—an inexorable, intoxicating pull toward Hunter, leaving his brain clouded with the demands of their bond.

"How are these?" Hunter asked as he crimped the edges of a potato and cheese pierogi.

Richard didn't need to intrude into Hunter's personal space and look over his shoulder to know they were fine, but he did it anyway. "Perfect."

He should move away, but he couldn't deny the temptation. He draped himself along Hunter's back, his hands resting on Hunter's hips, and inhaled his scent.

"You smell so good," he growled into Hunter's ear.

Hunter arched against him. When he spoke, his voice was husky, like he was as affected as Richard. "We've got a scene coming up. Do you think we should practice?"

It was the domestic scene. The softest thing they'd ever film, with ridiculous amounts of sweet foreplay and slow-boning before Richard would get to knot him. It wasn't something either of them needed to rehearse.

Richard wasn't going to let that stop him. He spun Hunter around and pushed him against the counter, kissing him until they were both hard and panting before pulling away.

"We should. But first, we're going to finish cooking and have a nice dinner."

Hunter groaned. "You did not just get me hard, then tell me I have to wait over an hour before you do anything about it."

"Pretty sure I just did."

Hunter leaned forward and nipped at Richard's earlobe. "You won't last that long."

Richard intended to prove him wrong.

And he would have, if it hadn't been for Hunter realizing mid-meal that he had sauce on his hand and deciding, instead of using a napkin, he should lick his fingers clean. Thoroughly clean. Obscenely clean.

If that ended with Richard under the table, sucking Hunter off while he tried to finish his dinner, that was Hunter's fault.

He was a far better dessert than anything Richard knew how to bake.

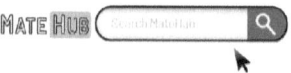

The usual message came five days before the full moon.

MOM

Richard, sweetheart, are you coming to the pack dinner and full-moon run this week?

RICHARD

Sorry, Mom. Super busy at work.

He hated lying to her, but what could he do? She wouldn't understand.

MOM

Are you sure about that? We'd love to see you.

RICHARD

I'll definitely make it next month. Promise.

MOM

Okay. Sooner than that would be better, but if you need until then, I'll wait.

I trust you to make the right decision.

Richard stared at the message, frowning. The right decision? What was she talking about?

"Hey."

The sound of Hunter's voice caused Richard to glance up. He was confused when he saw Hunter in a bathrobe. The only times he'd seen Hunter wearing a robe had been on set, and the sight went straight to his dick. Though, at this point, everything Hunter did followed that same path.

Richard set his phone aside. He'd reply to his mother later. When he replied to Daniel.

Hunter looked sheepish. "Okay, don't make fun of me too much, but I was thinking about the domestic scene and ways we could practice."

Arousal flared through Richard, and Hunter shivered in response.

'Practicing' had become a nightly thing again, though they weren't fucking every night. As long as Richard got to touch Hunter, it didn't matter what they did; it was all good. It'd never not be good with Hunter. Jerking each other off, sucking each other dry, and once humping on the couch until they came in the least porn star way possible— not much of a money shot when they hadn't even managed to get out of their pants first.

Each time deepened the bond between them, etching Hunter onto his soul a little more. He wondered if severing their connection would even be enough, or if Hunter would always be there, this empty ache lurking underneath his breastbone.

Hunter stepped toward him like he couldn't help himself, like there was an inevitable gravity between them. Richard copied the movement.

"Sooo," Hunter said. "It's cheesy, but I ran us a bath. And there are candles. To practice. For the scene."

Richard was dragged forward by the alluring whisper of the bond. His hands fit perfectly on Hunter's waist. "I thought we were going to Palacio tonight."

"Or we could… stay in?" Hunter's breathing was heavy; Richard felt winded too.

They'd tried to leave the apartment three times over the last week. It hadn't happened, particularly once they had so much practicing to do.

"Yeah," Richard said, inhaling Hunter's sweet scent. "Let's stay in."

Hunter tugged him to his bedroom and into the bathroom. Richard followed, desire building inside him.

The room was lit by the warm glow of flickering candles. They cast dancing shadows that softened the marble counters and tiled walls. The steam from the bath filled the air with a balmy intimacy.

But more than the scene before him, Richard couldn't tear his eyes away from Hunter sliding off his robe, revealing his sculpted chest and abs, his hardening cock. A small smile played on his lips, so inviting, beckoning Richard to close the distance between them.

Richard held out for a few more heartbeats, savoring the anticipation and the sight of Hunter silhouetted by candlelight, exposed for only his gaze, a vision of beauty and lust, a masterpiece like no other. His heart raced as time froze, and the few remnants of the outside world faded away. It was them and this irresistible, magnetic attraction between them, the bond drawing them together over and over again.

Hunter's expression held a fierce hunger, but something softer was there too, something that made Richard ache as longing pulsed through his veins.

Their bodies met, their hands roamed, their mouths explored. Richard traced paths over familiar expanses of heated skin.

Breaking apart to undress was torturous—Hunter was addictive and all-consuming, distracting him with hot kisses along his jawline as Richard attempted to unbutton his shirt, to strip off his jeans. But finding he'd already prepared himself was blissful relief, though to make sure,

Richard pushed him up on the counter and fingered him open until he was quivering for more.

Richard lowered them into the hot water and settled Hunter into his lap. Their bodies fit against each other in a way that bordered on divine, and when he sank into Hunter, the only words that existed in the universe were 'home' and 'mine.'

Water lapped against their skin, heightening every touch. They rocked together, moved together, their hearts beating in time. Hunter twisted back to kiss him as Richard's knot expanded and connected them, as their moans mingled and echoed through the room, as they gasped and shook, their passion overtaking them, submerging them, leaving them breathless and spent.

Hunter leaned back against his chest, and Richard held him close, tracing patterns along damp skin. The steamy air in the room was suffused with their combined scent.

They drifted, a tangle of limbs and sated lust.

"Can I ask you something?" The question was quiet to avoid disturbing the tranquil space.

"Anything," Richard said.

"Why do you pretend you're some uncaring jackass in your scenes and interviews?"

Richard winced.

"You don't have to answer that."

He let out a deliberate exhale. "No. It's fine. I, uh, used to be friendlier with my co-stars. If you dig through the MateHub archives, you'll find videos only my biggest fans have seen. Wouldn't recommend watching them though. You'd faint from shock at the sheer number of words I say during the interviews."

"Was it, like, five in a row?"

"Occasionally six or seven."

Hunter snorted. "So what happened? Why did that change?"

Richard shrugged, the water sloshing around them. "I started doing bonding contracts and found out real fast that being friendly was a bad idea."

Hunter didn't speak, just waited for him to continue. Richard wasn't sure why he was telling him this, but it felt necessary.

"The first bonding contract I did was with another wolf shifter. He wasn't a friend, but we were on good terms. I suggested doing a transactional bond with him, and he agreed. I thought we were on the same page. We weren't remotely compatible, but he was a chill guy. A few months bonded to him seemed like no big deal."

"But he caught feelings?"

"Massively. I didn't realize the fact that I could sense his emotions meant the severing ritual would be painful for him. I also didn't realize he wasn't getting any emotions from me. When the bond-severing day arrived, he begged for us to stay bonded and said I could keep doing side scenes if I had to."

"You didn't have feelings for him?"

"No. He was hot, the sex was great, but we had nothing in common. Our personalities clashed whenever we weren't fucking. If we'd stayed together, we would have started to resent each other. I have no clue why he didn't see that."

"So you severed the bond, and it hurt him, but not you."

Richard nodded. "He was in so much pain. I'd had paper cuts that hurt worse. He accused me of leading him on and being a cold, unfeeling bastard."

Hunter turned, trying to look at him. "That wasn't your fault though. You know that, right? You were upfront with what you wanted out of the relationship."

"I was naive and went into the contract not fully understanding bonds or their consequences. I should have researched it more beforehand. Maybe that would have saved him some pain. Instead, he ended up dropping out of the industry for a few years. When he returned, he'd become this chiseled alpha top, out to prove he could do as many bonding contracts as me."

Shock spiraled through Hunter. "You bonded Duke Moorhead?"

"Yeah. Though he went by another name back then."

"I don't think I've seen any of those videos, and I've watched a bunch of yours."

"He got MateHub to take them down. I can't imagine what he paid for that. They're still around. Some of my fans have copies. But unless you know what you're looking for and where to find it, they don't exist."

"I'm surprised you did another bonding contract after that."

"MateHub was offering a lot of money, and I'd done my research. I explained the situation carefully to the shifter I was going to bond. He seemed to understand. I thought if I kept things professional, it'd be fine."

"He didn't, and it wasn't, I assume."

"Nope. And every contract since then. No matter what I do or how much of a cold, unfeeling jackass I am, the people I bond end up getting hurt."

Fucking might be the one thing he excelled at, but apparently that skill didn't transfer to bonding.

"I'm repeating myself here, but that's not your fault. If

you were clear about your intentions from the start, you weren't to blame. You weren't leading people on."

Richard wasn't so sure. Clearly he was doing something wrong if it kept turning out like that. But he'd also never wanted to stop doing knotting scenes.

Hunter shivered, and Richard realized how cold the water had gotten.

He grabbed Hunter's hips, and his mostly deflated knot slipped out of him, making them both groan. They rinsed off and toweled themselves dry.

But the moment they stepped out of the bathroom, their dreamy cocoon was torn apart.

Hunter's presence was as blank as ever now that they weren't touching and the urgency had passed, the bond no longer desperately pulling them together.

No emotions reached out to him; no feelings invaded his mind.

After sharing more of himself than he had with anyone in years, he still felt nothing from Hunter.

The only emotions he got from him were pleasure and arousal and the occasional fleeting burst of something else, if it was strong enough. Which meant it was a physical thing for Hunter, no attachments at all. He obviously enjoyed the sex, but that was where it ended.

Richard had thought he'd be relieved if he found a co-star who felt nothing for him, who didn't bombard him with unnecessary emotions. Another faulty assumption on his part.

They headed to their separate beds, and he repressed a sigh.

Considering how many of these bonds he'd screwed up, Hunter not catching feelings was karma kicking in, but that knowledge didn't lessen the craving for more of his touch, to get as much of him as possible in the limited time they had left.

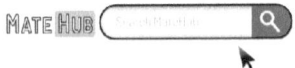

As Max entered the apartment, he inhaled and raised an eyebrow at Richard. He'd come over for games and dinner, but had to smell how mixed their scents had become, how they weren't following the rules of the contract in the slightest. He didn't comment on it though.

Hunter and Max played their arena battle game. Richard wasn't interested in it, but he didn't mind. He might even enjoy hanging out with his mate and one of his closest friends. It felt more perfect than he would have imagined.

He wished Hardin was there too, but he'd been avoiding them for a while. Richard wondered how long that would last. Max and Hardin were never apart for any extended period of time. If Hardin could be there—and Hunter's friend, if he ever got past being around multiple wolf shifters—it might feel more perfect. He might be willing to play stupid battle games if they wanted that.

But the chances of that happening in the next few weeks were slim to none. If Hunter felt nothing for him after two months, two more scenes wouldn't change that.

Richard messed around on his phone, half-listening while Hunter and Max shit-talked each other as they played. He pulled up the MateHub fan forums, clicking on his board. It was something he did more often than he should; he knew that. More than once he'd read comments he'd never be able to unread, but he liked knowing how his fans reacted to his scenes. Frequently they mentioned what they wanted to see him do, and some of their ideas weren't bad.

So he sat there, the scent of his mate saturating the air, the comfort of home draped around him, as he scrolled through page after page of his fans slowly coming to like Hunter almost as much as he did. It shouldn't have mattered; the fact that random people on the internet thought they were meant for each other shouldn't have made a smile play at the corner of his lips. He still didn't think they'd be happy if he stayed with the same person forever, but it was good they saw how amazing Hunter was.

His eyes caught on a comment in the thread about their latest scene.

KnottyWolf69:
If it's a true bond, Hunter DEFINITELY needs to bite him. He needs to show the world who Richard belongs to. There's no way Richard doesn't want that.

The thought of Hunter claiming him for the world to see blazed through him.

When shifters bonded each other, they always traded bites. It was instinctual. He'd never heard of a bonded pair that hadn't. Hell, that was why MateHub had insisted his previous temporary mates bite him. The fans wanted that realism.

Hunter was human though. It was different for him, but that didn't make Richard want it any less. Even if it wasn't real, he wanted Hunter to mark him as his own.

He swallowed, picturing Hunter biting him like he had in a few of their scenes, but harder, breaking skin.

A spike of lust shot through him—Hunter's, not his. He looked up to find Hunter staring at him, breathing accelerated, gaze hooded.

"A CHAMPION IS CROWNED!" the TV declared, and both Hunter and Richard jumped.

On screen, Max's avatar was getting showered with roses, but Max himself appeared disgruntled.

"Concentrate on something other than Richard's dick, please," he complained. "Winning's no fun when you're sitting there slack-jawed, drooling over his knot."

"I wasn't—"

"You totally were."

Hunter glared at Max, but didn't try to deny it again. They started another battle, and Richard watched them play.

"I cannot wait to have full access to the system twenty-four seven," Max said.

"You're assuming I'm not taking it with me when I leave."

Richard tried not to dwell on that comment.

Max gasped in horror. "You wouldn't."

"It'd be a nice bonus, don't you think?"

"I'd never forgive you."

"So you're actually doing it?" Hunter asked.

"I'm considering it. The money's good, and I don't have any reason not to."

"Who would you want to do it with?"

Tension crept into the line of Max's shoulders. "I don't think it matters, as long as it's not someone I'm compatible with."

Hunter frowned. "Why would it have to be someone you're not compatible with?"

"Because it's temporary."

"If you're compatible, does that make it not temporary?"

"No, but it's not a good idea to sever that kind of bond."

That statement felt directed at Richard, not Hunter.

"Is that the whole 'the more you get attached, the more it'll hurt' thing?" Hunter asked.

"Somewhat. But more than that, the real issue is that you'll never have another chance at it if you sever the bond."

"Max," Richard said, a warning in his tone.

Hunter looked over at him, then back at Max. "What do you mean?"

"Shifters don't do second chances," Max said. "We can't. Once a bond has been severed, you can never get it back."

A jumble of emotions coiled through their bond, but Richard couldn't identify them. They were too fast and chaotic—there and gone before he had any idea what Hunter was thinking. Then everything was blank again.

"Not even if both of you want it?" Hunter asked, his brow furrowed.

Max shook his head. "Never. We technically aren't even supposed to bond more than once. There are a good number of shifters who are horrified by the concept of transactional bonds, especially multiple of them. They think you should wait until you find someone truly compatible with you. But that doesn't always happen. Some people get sick of waiting. Sometimes you have to settle for someone compatible enough."

Hunter stared at him for a long beat, then turned back to their game.

Max shot Richard a look, but Richard ignored it. It wasn't Max's place to tell Hunter that. He didn't have any right to judge.

Everyone was quieter for the rest of the evening, their mood more subdued.

Hunter showed Max out. Richard heard them exchange goodbyes in the entryway, but then Hunter stood there, and Richard thought he might not return to the living room at all.

Finally, his soft footsteps whispered over the wooden floors as he was drawn to where Richard sat.

Richard blinked in surprise when Hunter crawled onto his lap, straddling him, working a hand into his hair to tilt his head, and kissing him hard. In Richard's mind, he was nothing but want and need.

He had complete control of the kiss and fucked Richard's mouth with his tongue, only breaking away to say, "Let me top tonight."

Richard didn't hesitate to agree. Hunter wanted it so Richard wanted to give it to him. He wanted to give him everything.

Hunter pulled him into the bedroom so permeated with their scent, Richard could almost fool himself into thinking it was their room, not just his.

Like every time they'd done this, Hunter made it unbelievably good.

He collapsed beside Richard until he regained his breath, then went to roll off the bed, to go to his room, but Richard snared his wrist, holding it tight.

"You should stay," he said before he thought better of it, belatedly realizing how that might sound, so he added, "If we're practicing for this domestic scene, we should give slow morning sex a try."

Hunter stayed, and they did.

And if he stayed the next night too, it was just more convenient for them both. It meant nothing. Richard wouldn't get his hopes up over it.

It wasn't like waking up with Hunter in his arms made him feel complete in ways he'd never believed were possible.

Their sixth scene struck him with its cruel irony. Richard hadn't thought about it when he'd signed the contract. Domestic scenes were all the same. They were boring to shoot. They required too many sweet kisses, too much cuddling. There were a lot more takes, a lot more cuts. It was a day-long affair, and it drove Richard insane every time he had to do it. It was never until late in the evening that they got to the fun part—when they had the cameras set up and there were no more interruptions, just Richard doing what he did best.

The scenes each had a different theme. A glitzy candlelit dinner followed by gentle lovemaking on a ridiculously expensive rug that was not meant to get coated with come. Or they played up the fated mates angle, with them seeing each other and instantly knowing they were meant to be, in awe that they'd found the one person for them. Unlike certain coffee shop scenes he could mention, those relationships were not consummated in front of a crowd. They were taken where no one could see tentative touches by hands shaky with destiny. Other times it was simpler—two people in an established relationship reaffirming their love.

Richard hated them all. They were so painfully sappy.

He didn't hate this one, and his wolf didn't care that they were stuck inside on a full moon. It was thrilled, like *nesting* was something wolves suddenly did.

That didn't make it any easier to shoot, though it was difficult for completely different reasons than usual.

He and Hunter were playing a newly mated couple. They were already in love and were moving in together.

MateHub had rented an empty house for the occasion. Which was how Richard found himself about to move in with Hunter. There'd be shots of them carrying boxes, unpacking, deciding where their belongings would go. In between that would be everything he'd always found annoying about these scenes: tender kisses, stolen caresses, loving glances exchanged at every opportunity.

And he was looking forward to every goddamn second of it.

Even the fucking interview.

Everett had suggested they make it more active than before, and Richard was convinced his whole sweet and innocent persona was an act. Only someone with a sadistic streak would suggest they bake strawberry tarts as Brandt interviewed them.

But not just baking them. No, that'd be too simple. This was a full-blown romantic baking montage, complete with tying each other's aprons, feeding each other strawberries, playfully fighting with flour, using heart-shaped tins, licking whipped cream off fingers and lips, and more.

It was disgusting. He loved it.

He even answered Brandt's dumb questions.

Half the time they did these scenes, it was an effort for

him to get hard for the parts that were foreplay with no guaranteed release for hours in sight. With Hunter, it was so easy. They'd stop for a quick kiss, only it'd never be quick, regardless of how often Brandt told them to keep it brief.

After they'd gotten the opening footage, they moved on to the foreplay, the couple deciding to christen every surface and room in their new house, and not having the patience to do it gradually.

They blew each other in the dining room, fingered each other in the shower, ground against each other on their new couch. And although it wasn't in the script, Hunter bent him over the kitchen counter and expertly tossed his salad.

By the time they made it to the bedroom, Richard's knot was throbbing, and he knew Brandt would want another hour of foreplay in there. It should have made him growl in frustration. It didn't. He was enjoying this way too much. Loving the chance to explore the places on Hunter's body he'd learned over their too-short time together, to use that knowledge to edge him until he was incoherent with desire.

And when he slid into Hunter, when he found his home in him, he'd never felt anything better.

In the past, that'd been his cue to pick up speed, to do exactly what he'd been waiting for. He didn't feel that need now. He was more than content to trade kisses with Hunter as their bodies entwined. Hunter rode him at first, shaking and boneless with pleasure, then he looked down at Richard, and Richard knew what he needed. He rolled them over and made Hunter come hard enough that the echo alone had Richard's vision whiting out.

As they lay there, tied together, paying zero attention to the cameras surrounding them, Richard holding Hunter, all he could think about was how much it was going to hurt to give this up, and he didn't mean the pain of severing the bond. But even knowing that, he couldn't bring himself to stop touching Hunter.

While they were connected like this, while Hunter was relaxed and sated, Richard could almost pretend Hunter wanted it, too.

He could almost ignore the clock ticking in his head, constantly reminding him they only had two weeks left.

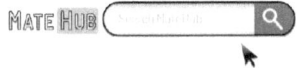

SCENE: *Christening the New House*

BramStroker:
That scene was as hot as always, but THE INTER-VIEW. OH MY GOD. Them cooking together? Bantering? Richard laughing? How are they so cute? SEND HELP. I'M DYING. AGAIN.

KnottyWolf69:
Dudes. Hunter said Richard is an amazing cook. You understand what that means, right? Richard is cooking for him. Not just these tarts. It's a regular thing. FUCK ME. That's a Big Deal. Bigger than Richard big. I need to know what they smell like together. I bet it's something insanely romantic.

knottyornice:
Agreed. The way they were working together? So natural and smooth. They didn't even have to ask for things; it was like they were reading each other's minds. They've done this before.

MagicalHWood:
I can't believe Hunter got him to play video games. Do you remember the interview Richard did with Max back around the time they started? Max said Richard was terrible at video games, and Richard said they were a waste of time and he'd never be caught dead playing the things. But he's playing them FOR HUNTER.

BramStroker:

I think the reason he doesn't like Moonlit Bonds is because he doesn't want to knot anyone but Hunter, even in a video game.

knottyornice:

He's so warm and open around Hunter. I've never seen him like that.

KnottyWolf69:

From one Knotty to another, you've got to watch Richard's old-school interviews. He's completely different in them. He used to be friendlier. Not that this was "friendly" by any means. There was too much eyefucking for that.

MagicalHWood:

Seconded! This was a lot closer to his interviews before his first bonding contract. We got more information about Richard in this one interview than we have in years. But he's never acted the way he does around Hunter. My man is whipped, and it's a good look on him.

HuntMeDown:

So are you finally sailing on this ship with us, Magic?

MagicalHWood:

After this interview and scene, how could anyone not be? But, guys, usually at this point, his co-stars are getting that desperate look in their eyes, like they know it's about to end. This time, they both seemed desperate.

KnottyWolf69:
Fuck. Are you thinking MateHub won't let them keep it? Or they'll have to quit if they want to keep it?

MagicalHWood:
I don't know, but MateHub has never done an exclusive contract.

BramStroker:
Don't say that! If MateHub makes them sever their bond, I'm canceling my membership! I'll watch boring human porn for the rest of my existence in protest!

KnottyWolf69:
Any word on that new board, Hunt?

HuntMeDown:
None yet, but I have faith. DickHunt is meant to be. I don't care who's running MateHub, they have to be able to see that. ~Everyone~ has to.

HuntMeDown:
And if they've somehow missed it, MateHub has a scene suggestion form on their contact page. Just saying.

TWENTY

unter stared at his phone, then hit send.

HUNTER

Are there any bonded couples in the industry?

CHANCE

Fuck, Hunter. You fell for him, didn't you?

Is that why you've been avoiding me for the last month?

HUNTER

I was just curious.

And he hadn't been *avoiding* Chance—not intentionally. He'd been caught up in Richard, and suddenly a day had turned into a week, and then the week had become a month.

CHANCE

There are no bonded couples at MateHub.
You know that.

If someone gets bonded for real, they leave
the industry because bonded couples don't
like to share, even in a professional setting.

That matched up with everything Hunter had researched. He'd found a few on OnlyMates, but they weren't making anywhere near what Richard did, and they usually concealed their faces.

Before he could respond, Chance sent another message.

CHANCE

From what I've heard, true bonds get
intense. Way more than transactional ones.
Doing scenes is one thing, but letting
people see something so personal and
real... Most people wouldn't be
comfortable with that.

After another minute of Hunter not responding, he sent one more message.

CHANCE

You didn't fall for him, right?

Hunter forced himself to reply. His stomach lurched as he hit send.

HUNTER

Of course not. This is just a job.

He collapsed against the couch and pulled up a different conversation.

HUNTER

Can I ask you something about Richard?

It didn't take long for him to get a reply.

MAX

Yes, he's always an asshole.

Hunter snorted. Surprisingly, Richard wasn't, and that was not something he'd have expected three months ago.

HUNTER

What does he smell like? Kind of like a fire?
Is that a thing wolf shifters smell like?

There was a pause before he got a response.

MAX

Why do you want to know?

For the second time in a handful of minutes, he typed the same lie.

HUNTER

I was just curious. He mentioned your
scent, and I realized how differently you
guys process smells.

But also, it seemed weird to ask someone
how they smell? Lol.

MAX

Embers and starry skies.

Hunter hadn't been prepared for the beauty of that answer.

HUNTER

What do I smell like?

There was another pause before the reply came.

MAX

You should ask Richard.

Hunter sighed and tried not to think about how often Richard leaned in to smell him, the pleased growls he let out as he ran his nose along Hunter's neck and inhaled.

If anyone knew what he smelled like, it'd be Richard.

That didn't mean Hunter was ready to ask him.

Their previous scene had been an unexpected headfuck. He hadn't realized something so sweet and domestic could leave him feeling more raw and vulnerable than significantly darker scenes.

The extent to which he wanted that scenario to be real had left him shaken. Richard had felt like he'd wanted it too; he'd seemed as into it as Hunter had been. But that didn't seem to be enough.

He'd been getting a lot of emotions from Richard. For weeks now. None of them indicated Richard thought there was any future for them. Even when they weren't touching, his resignation to it being over pervaded their bond—him preparing for the end.

Richard did like him; Hunter was positive about that. And it was more than just the sex. Hunter sensed that much. Richard telling him about his past had only confirmed that he wasn't treating Hunter the same way he'd treated his former co-stars. From that first ride home, to cooking, to every time they'd ignored the rules of the contract, and more. He wouldn't have done all that if he didn't feel something for Hunter.

The only conclusion Hunter could come to was that Richard was choosing his career over him. His job came first. He might like Hunter, he might enjoy the sex, they might even be compatible, but being together would cause trouble for them at MateHub.

This wasn't the right time for them, and that apparently meant it never would be. He was annoyed no one had bothered to tell him that wolf shifters couldn't bond the same person twice. That seemed like important information. They'd probably assumed he knew, or that it wouldn't matter. And it didn't, not really. Not when Richard seemed dead set on this ending.

It stung. As much as he didn't want to admit it to himself, as much as he would never admit it to anyone else, it hurt. Richard not wanting to keep what they had hurt worse than anything Hunter had experienced. Though that would likely change on the new moon.

But he also couldn't blame Richard. Neither of them had gone into this planning for it to upend their entire life. It was a temporary job. There weren't supposed to be feelings involved.

Even he had no idea what he'd do if he couldn't work for MateHub, and he'd only been doing this for a year, not the better part of a decade. If MateHub wouldn't sign them for an exclusive contract, what would they do? Go to OnlyMates and earn a fraction of what they did now? How would Richard feel about not being able to afford his expensive car and clothes? Was he willing to give that up for Hunter?

Hunter was used to scraping by, living in a cramped apartment with a roommate, not having a car. He could deal with that for a little longer. It wouldn't be so bad to try.

Richard didn't seem to agree.

Squeezing his eyes shut, Hunter held back another sigh.

"Everything okay?" Richard asked.

Hunter jerked in surprise, his attention flying to where Richard was poking his head into the living room. There was a furrow between his brows.

"I'm fine," Hunter said, waving him off.

Richard's gaze grew distant, and it felt like he was brushing against Hunter's mind. But then he shook his head, the resignation returning in full force.

"I was about to start dinner," he said.

Hunter pushed himself to his feet and followed him into the kitchen.

For all he felt Richard, Richard didn't appear to be getting much from him in return, and Hunter didn't understand it. He'd thought the deeper the bond, the more emotions the other person felt. It didn't seem to work that way with humans though. The bond felt like it'd been carved pretty fucking deep, but Richard rarely read his emotions accurately.

The moment Hunter stepped into the kitchen, Richard was backing him against the counter, pulling him into a searing kiss that was so desperate, it seemed like anything should be possible.

They didn't make dinner that night. Instead, they spent it how they'd spent most of their time since their last scene.

Hunter assumed Richard was trying to get him out of his system. If that was the case, it wasn't working for Hunter. He'd never had more sex in his life, but it still wasn't enough. It was like he had this craving inside him, this constant need to touch, to be close, to never let go. He sensed the same need in Richard, and whenever they were near each other, it was impossible to resist the bond drawing them together.

The more time they spent wrapped up in each other, the more their upcoming scene and what would happen afterward loomed. The more Hunter felt Richard's wolf becoming restless, though the moon was waning.

Despite their grasping hands and gasping kisses, the new moon kept creeping closer, its presence in their every touch, leaving Hunter unsure what to say as they lay tied together and the haze of lust momentarily ebbed away.

The remaining days before their seventh scene passed in a blur.

Every day, Richard became a little more resigned, a little more withdrawn.

And every day, Hunter's determination built.

This was right. More so than anything he'd ever experienced. This was meant to be.

Richard might be resigned to letting it go without a fight; Hunter was not.

His stomach sank at the realization he was about to do what so many of Richard's previous co-stars had done to him—pushing feelings at him that he didn't want—but if Hunter didn't try, if he said nothing, he'd regret it for the rest of his life.

He wanted to keep the bond, but couldn't bring it up yet. If Richard said no, it'd make their last few days and final scene awkward. No matter what happened, they wouldn't be able to escape each other until the new moon.

But there was half a day between when they filmed their scene and when Tristan would sever the bond. If Hunter confronted Richard that morning, before Tristan arrived, at least he'd know. One way or another, he'd have closure. And if Richard did turn him down, at least they wouldn't be stuck together much longer.

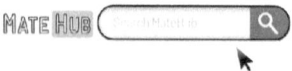

The drive to MateHub was uncomfortable. There were no jokes about the ridiculous things they'd be asked to do. There was no friendly banter. The noise from the traffic filled the silence.

Unease gripped Hunter's stomach, but more than that, nausea rolled through Richard. Each wave crashed over Hunter, shaking him with its force. He wanted to believe that was a sign of hope, but Richard still felt resigned.

The elevator ride up to the sixth floor was equally silent.

As they entered the studio, Richard froze. The tumult of his emotions hit Hunter like a blow to the chest, leaving him winded. He steadied himself and blinked as he took in the set.

It was a bedroom. That part was fairly standard, though they'd decked it out with a nicer bed than usual—this one with a large wrought iron headboard and lush blankets piled high. Everett was fussing with the pillows, his eyes wide as he looked over, his lips pressed together in a worried line.

But Hunter couldn't focus on that when the rest of the bedroom had his breath catching. A banked fire crackled in an ornate fireplace grate, illuminating the room with a flickering glow even under the studio lights, and massive windows lined the back wall. Outside, thousands of stars twinkled, though it was the middle of the day, stars were never that brilliant above the city, and that wall faced the inside of the building.

He knew it was a glamour, but that didn't make it any less stunning.

Brandt walked up to them, his voice and footsteps quiet. "The MateHub writers had a few last-minute changes."

Hunter cocked an eyebrow at him. "Did they?"

"They wanted to try something with a more natural atmosphere."

As he said that, Hunter glanced around. There were hardly any crew members there.

"We aren't doing an interview, and we're only staying to get everything started. Then we'll leave the cameras running, and you can do whatever you want. We're hoping for a homemade video vibe, but with amazing lighting and HD cameras."

"Okay." Hunter didn't know what to think. As far as he knew, MateHub had never filmed a scene like this. In his head, Richard felt oddly numb as he nodded his agreement.

Tension draped itself around them as they walked to the dressing rooms.

Hunter hesitated, unsure which to go to, but Richard took his hand and tugged Hunter into his.

They didn't exchange words, just undressed each other, neither of their hands steady, not quite kissing, but enticingly close to it.

Shivers ran through Hunter as Richard caressed his body, over his chest and down his stomach. Every touch left Hunter breathless, his skin tingling.

He wanted to kiss Richard, to press against him and melt into the warmth of his embrace. But he held himself back, and Richard did too, like they were both waiting for the other to make the first move.

Once they were both naked, Richard inhaled before

looking Hunter in the eye. "Can I get you ready on set?" he asked, his voice a mix of determination and uncertainty.

Hunter agreed without hesitation. Given how much sex they'd been having, he wasn't going to need much, but he always made sure he was good and stretched before any scene. None of his co-stars had been lacking in the size department, and he didn't trust anyone else to do it as thoroughly as he wanted it done.

Anyone but Richard.

Richard led him out to the bed. His body was tense as they sank into the blankets, but Hunter wasn't sure how to alleviate it.

The fire cast a warm radiance over the room. It highlighted the contours of Richard's muscles, the beauty of his features.

They lay there, staring out the fake window as the crew started the cameras, then slipped away.

Brandt didn't call action; he merely raised a hand and stepped back.

They'd been alone in bed a few dozen times. This shouldn't feel special, but it did.

Richard's hand squeezed his thigh before gliding up to his hip. Hunter's breath hitched, and their eyes met. Nothing else mattered. Nothing existed beyond this starlit room.

Leaning in, Richard grazed his lips against Hunter's in the sweetest kiss of his life.

Each of Hunter's senses was filled with Richard. The touch of his lips, the taste of his tongue, the smell of his skin, the sound of that nearly inaudible rumble building in his chest.

Richard's body was made for him. They were meant to

be close, meant to be connected, with no space between them.

Hunter was almost overwhelmed by that kiss alone. Every touch felt like it might break him into pieces.

Richard rolled Hunter beneath him, grabbing the lube under the pillow and slicking up his fingers.

The fire danced and cast shadows on the ceiling as Richard teased his fingers over Hunter's entrance, moving them in slow circles that left him panting, then slipped them inside. Richard worked him open, their shared desire building as he pushed in deeper, spreading Hunter wider.

"You always feel so amazing." Richard's voice was rough, his words an invisible caress that had Hunter arching into him.

Hunter might like control, to be the one to set the pace, but the times like this, when he surrendered himself to Richard, were just as good. When all that mattered was what Richard was doing to him, and his world narrowed to the pleasure only Richard could draw out of him.

Richard kissed down his neck, his mouth finding the mark he'd left three months before.

The sharp edge of his teeth and the slick slide of his tongue dragging over Hunter's skin felt like everything he could ever want. Hunter's eyes fell shut, and he gave himself over to the sensations.

Richard fixated on that mark, sucking and licking and biting until Hunter was squirming on his fingers and clinging to him. It was so sensitive—an erogenous zone meant for Richard alone.

"You smell so damn perfect," Richard said against his skin, sending a shudder along Hunter's spine.

"What do I smell like?" Hunter asked, letting out a trembling exhale, his body desperate for more.

Richard withdrew his fingers and settled between Hunter's legs, descending on him with his mouth and body, soft and hard at the same time. Hunter hitched his legs up, his arms wrapping around Richard's shoulders as Richard bit his earlobe. The head of Richard's cock nudged against his entrance.

"When I knot you," Richard whispered into his ear as he pressed into Hunter in one slow, smooth stroke, "I want you to bite me."

Hunter gasped at the fullness of Richard inside him, the weight of him pinning him down. He tried to concentrate on Richard's words, but couldn't, not with the surge of emotion that came with them. Richard's soul-deep need for Hunter to bite him, to claim him. Even for one day.

He nodded, unable to get words out, unable to do anything but cling to Richard as he moved. His body was on fire, his heart racing, his head spinning. Richard's hands were gentle against his skin, his lips worshiping him.

Hunter tried to get closer, though he'd never be able to get Richard close enough.

Richard pulled back, making Hunter groan—the last thing he wanted was Richard farther away from him—but then Richard was looking down at him with an intensity that stole his breath.

The sweet burn of Richard's movements sent a familiar heat pooling low in his gut. Hunter wanted to let his head fall back, to close his eyes and focus on Richard moving inside him, but he also wanted to watch bliss flicker across Richard's face, mimicking the firelight on his skin.

Richard's shoulders flexed under his hands as he picked up speed, his cock hitting Hunter's prostate, his knot swelling, sending sparks glittering through Hunter. His body felt ready to burst into flames.

Hunter's back arched, his body tensing. His orgasm built, but Richard kept staring at him, his lips parted with ragged breaths. Need blazed so hot and bright behind his half-lidded eyes, it had Hunter reaching for him with demanding hands, pulling him down.

So many things had happened over these three months that Hunter never would have imagined. An entire list of them. Finding Richard cute, loving spending time with him, wanting countless more nights with him, playing games, cooking meals, making love. Anything, everything. It didn't matter as long as it was with Richard.

He added one more thing to that list as his mouth found the juncture of Richard's neck. How natural it felt to sink his teeth into flesh until skin broke and the tang of blood hit his tongue. How right it felt to bite and claim someone, how perfectly connected it made them.

Emotions rushed into him, and Richard's thrusts became erratic, his knot catching on Hunter's rim.

Richard filled every part of him, not only physically, but mentally, until Hunter felt complete in every way.

He knew this feeling, the echo of emotions that had always passed between them as they had sex. It'd become familiar. Now, it was so much more. It wasn't faint; it wasn't just physical, just want and need. Richard's presence was amplified, resonating through him and back.

His emotions swept over Hunter—a whirlwind of love and devotion that flooded into him—but strongest was stunned relief.

"I thought—" The words were gravelly in Hunter's ear. Richard didn't finish the sentence, but he didn't have to. Hunter knew what he wanted to say.

Richard had thought Hunter didn't feel anything for him beyond the physical, that it'd been the bond pulling them together. He'd thought Hunter hadn't wanted more than that. But the truth was written in their bond now that they both wanted it, were both open to it. Now that Hunter had bitten him. Hunter's emotions flowed into Richard, their connection complete, and there was no denying the depth of either of their feelings.

Hunter could drown in those depths, drown in Richard, and he wouldn't care.

The line between where he ended and Richard began blurred to indistinguishable. Richard filling him, stretching him, felt like more than he could handle, more than he deserved.

He looked up at Richard again. Ecstasy and contentment were written on his face. His exhales stuttered over Hunter's skin, his gaze locking on Hunter's as he rocked into him, his wolf flashing in his eyes.

They didn't need words. Richard felt it too—this connection between them, so unbelievably perfect, so incredibly right.

Richard stared at him with wonder, like he was the most precious thing in existence. It sent tingles through Hunter, his heart pounding faster. His nerves were alight, or maybe they were Richard's nerves. It didn't matter; they were one and the same.

Every kiss, every touch, was deeper, fuller, more meaningful. Because it was Richard—the person he wanted to spend his life with.

Hunter hovered on the edge of his orgasm. He clung to Richard, trying to keep from falling apart. He wanted this moment to last forever, to spill into eternity until it was nothing but them and the stars.

But holding on under that onslaught of emotions and sensations was impossible. Hunter let himself fall, and

Richard fell with him. His vision went hazy as their orgasms crashed through them, as they shattered into pieces and were remade into something infinitely more beautiful.

He felt Richard's knot locked tight inside him, felt every pulse of his release as if it were his own, just as Richard could feel his, too.

Richard buried his face in Hunter's neck, his moans almost broken sounding. Hunter let his fingers drift over Richard's shoulders and down his sides, and Richard nuzzled against the skin under his ear, breathing him in. His hand skated up to caress Hunter's face, ghosting across his jaw and cheeks. Happiness swelled in Hunter's chest, taking over his whole body, and he couldn't tell how much of it was his and how much was Richard's.

His body felt light, as if he were soaring, like he might float away with the gentlest of breezes. The only things keeping him anchored were Richard's arms around him, his body warm and heavy atop Hunter's, exquisitely perfect and not something Hunter was ever willing to give up. He was so aware of every touch and every sound, every flutter of his heart. His mind overflowed with Richard.

"Ever," he confessed in the quiet bliss between them. "Not days, or months, or years. *Ever*."

He opened his eyes and found Richard watching him, his smile soft and blinding.

"Same." He leaned down, pressing a kiss to his lips.

Hunter didn't know how much time passed with them like that, curled up in each other, their hearts beating in time. Long enough for Richard's knot to deflate, but still they traded kisses.

When they broke apart, Hunter said, "You didn't answer. What do I smell like?"

"Like home," Richard said, his voice hushed, a caress

against Hunter's skin. "Like the softness of cashmere hiding wrought iron beneath."

Hunter's throat tightened as his hand fell to the cashmere blankets they lay on. His gaze was drawn to the wrought iron grate, cradling the smoldering embers of the fire. Stars gleamed outside the window.

The crew had done this for them. Set up 'them' in the scene with their magical special effects.

"Yeah," Richard said, "I know." The words were a barely formed whisper, feather-soft yet unwaveringly sure, carrying the promise of forever.

Richard held him, and Hunter let his eyelids close, sensing how deeply Richard felt for him. The warmth of his emotions radiated from him like the comforting incandescence of the fire.

"So," Richard said, breathless, nerves creeping through him. "I don't know how to tell you this, but I think I might have caught feelings."

He had nothing to be nervous about. Hunter's lips quirked up. "Yeah. I know."

Richard looked startled for a second, but then Hunter felt him reach for their bond, sensing Hunter through it, relaxing against him.

"In case you need to hear me say it," Hunter said, lacing his fingers together with Richard's. "I don't want to sever this bond. I don't want this to end."

"Same." Richard brushed another kiss against his lips.

"What about MateHub?"

Richard didn't feel remotely resigned anymore. "If they won't give us an exclusive contract, I'm willing to try Only-Mates. Or I'll start my own damn site. I don't care, as long as it's with you."

"Worst-case scenario, you could start streaming. I'm

convinced people would pay to watch you speedrun *Moonlit Bonds*." Hunter chuckled at the horrified look Richard gave him.

"Don't even joke about that. But if that's what it takes to be with you, I'll do it."

Hunter kissed him hard, and Richard covered him with his body again.

The red lights on the cameras surrounding them winked out one by one as they ran out of batteries and their memory cards filled up. But there was no rush. They had all the time in the world.

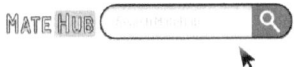

Much later, when they made it to their dressing room, the first thing Richard did was check his reflection in the mirror. Hunter watched him tilt his head to the side, his eyes on the fresh bite mark. He smirked, and smug contentment shimmered through their bond, half Richard's, half his wolf's.

Damn, he looked good claimed.

On the vanity, Richard's phone flashed with a message notification.

Richard opened it and laughed, showing it to Hunter.

TRISTAN

Hey, asshole. Am I coming to the apartment tomorrow or not? The wrong answer comes with a punch to the face.

He typed his reply as Hunter read.

RICHARD

No face punching necessary. We're good.

Thanks for the ambiance.

Tristan's answer was almost immediate.

TRISTAN

Don't blame that cheesy shit on me. I owed
Max a favor.

Hunter squinted at the screen. "Max?"

Richard felt just as shocked as Hunter. His phone vibrated again.

TRISTAN

Congrats.

Richard typed out a quick "Thank you," then set his phone down and went to tug Hunter toward the shower, but another notification flashed on his screen.

He grabbed it, and confusion spiked through him. He turned the phone to show Hunter.

TRISTAN

If Steele gives you shit, tell him my brother
says hello.

Hunter raised an eyebrow. Why would they tell the owner of MateHub that Tristan's brother said hello? He glanced at Richard, but got a shrug in return, and seconds later, it was forgotten as they pulled each other into the shower, hands already eager to touch again.

They kissed under the warm spray, bodies sliding and tangling in ways that surpassed words like perfection and divine.

Richard nuzzled against his neck and rumbled a low,

contented sound. "I'm an idiot. I should have asked you to bite me sooner."

Hunter hummed. "Mmm, yes, you should have."

"You're moving in with me, right?"

The answer was yes, they both knew that, but Hunter had to tease him first. "Max and the crew put together the most romantic thing I've ever seen, and all you've got is, 'You're moving in with me, right?'"

"Sorry. Let me try again." Richard sucked hard on Hunter's bite mark until he was panting and clinging to him. Then he looked him in the eye and said, "You're moving in with me so I can knot that ass of yours on the regular, right?"

Hunter huffed. "Such an improvement. I guess I'll have to go to Max anytime I want some romance in my life."

He half-expected that comment to make Richard growl. Instead, he cupped Hunter's face in his hands, his thumb running over Hunter's bottom lip. He leaned in and kissed him with a slow, devastating tenderness, his emotions flowing through the bond until Hunter felt stretched full with them, possessed completely by them, but also in possession of everything that was Richard in return.

Richard rested his forehead against Hunter's and said, "This isn't what I signed up for, but now, I can't imagine living without you. The idea of an apartment that doesn't smell like you, of not coming home to you, not playing stupid video games and cooking with you, not falling asleep with you in my arms? I don't want to go back to that kind of life. I don't want to live without you. You've made my world complete in ways I never realized it was lacking. So. You're moving in with me, right?"

Maybe Richard could do romance after all.

Hunter let out a shaky laugh. "I wouldn't want to live anywhere else but where you are."

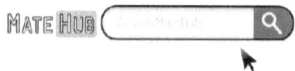

As they drove to the apartment, Hunter opened his messenger app.

HUNTER

So... a funny thing might have happened during the filming today...

CHANCE

Ugh. You're going to smell like dog forever now, aren't you?

HUNTER

Yep. There's no avoiding it now, so you might as well get used to it.

I'll be by the day after tomorrow to pack up my stuff, but I'll keep paying rent until you can find a new roommate.

CHANCE

Don't bother. I already have someone lined up from the first.

Hunter blinked at his phone.

"What's up?" Richard asked, finally reading Hunter's emotions correctly even though they weren't touching.

"I think Chance is kicking me out."

"Good thing you've got a place to go." Richard shot him a sly look.

HUNTER

What would you have done if this hadn't worked out?

CHANCE

Punch that asshole in the face?

Hunter laughed. "Chance is also threatening to punch you in the face."

"So happy to hear my face is so popular," Richard grumbled.

HUNTER

About the roommate situation!

CHANCE

It was always going to work out.

Dog smells good on you.

It's disgusting.

Hunter grinned at his phone. It was nice to know Chance approved.

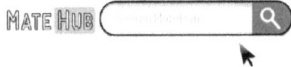

TWENTY-ONE

P acking up the MateHub apartment *with* someone was a first, and for once, his co-star wasn't dragging his feet. Richard felt how ready Hunter was to start their next chapter together, and it wasn't invasive in the least.

He welcomed it—all the little bursts of emotion he got from Hunter, whether they were touching or not, though he had a strong preference for which of those two he'd rather be doing. When his hands were on Hunter, he felt everything.

Their bond was perfect, and it'd just get deeper and better from there as it strengthened between them. He was in awe of it, and it made him more certain that he'd done the right thing with his previous co-stars. He hoped they'd find connections like this in the future and realize the difference too. The transactional bonds they'd had didn't begin to compare.

They were packed in no time, though Hunter did stop in the living room to stare longingly at the gaming system before they left.

Richard wrapped his arms around Hunter's waist from behind. "Yes, they'd notice, but we can get our own. Whatever you want, it's yours."

"I cannot wait to watch you play *Moonlit Bonds* on an 8K microLED wall-size TV."

He was kidding. Their bond said he was kidding. Probably.

It was a struggle to pull away and head to his car. Hunter's duffel bag was still an awkward fit. Amusement glittered through their bond as Hunter adjusted it on his lap so he could buckle his seatbelt.

"There's not much room in here," he said, "but for the record, you need to fuck me in this car. It's so damn sexy."

That idea stroked over Richard's skin. They could make it work. Maybe him sitting in the passenger seat while Hunter had a nice ride. That'd be fun.

"How about we skip this meeting and make that happen? I'll take you up into the hills and show you what my girl can do, and then we can test out her suspension."

He sensed how much Hunter was looking forward to that, but Hunter sighed. "I don't think we should give Steele another reason to be pissed at us, do you?"

Richard winced. No. They should not.

The drive to MateHub was entirely too short. Their agents were waiting for them in the lobby.

"Well," Daniel said in greeting. "Glad there were no more issues."

"I can't say I'm sorry about this," Richard said, "because I'm not. But if this goes well, you'll need to figure out what an exclusive contract with MateHub might entail."

Daniel shot him an unimpressed look. "I've already got the language drafted."

Richard blinked at him. "...What?"

"As soon as you signed on for Hunter fucking your ass, I drew up a contract and the accompanying press release."

"But... but you lined up those side scenes?"

"Fuck no. I lined up *one*. You didn't wonder why you hadn't signed the other contracts yet? I didn't bother looking for a vampire either."

Richard's mouth opened and closed, but he failed to get any form of response out.

Hunter glanced at his agent, clearly wondering if he'd get the same answer, but Adrian shrugged. "News to me. I was preparing ways to hide his body in case you ended up killing him."

"Hey!" Why did everyone think Hunter would want to kill him during their contract?

"There, there." Hunter patted his arm. "I never seriously thought about killing you. I wanted my full paycheck."

Well, that didn't make it better.

Hunter grinned at him.

"But don't worry," Adrian said. "Between the two of us, MateHub has no chance in this negotiation. They're about to sign their biggest contract ever."

Daniel nodded his agreement.

For all their well-earned confidence, it was difficult not to worry as they rode the elevator to the top floor of the building and waited outside Steele's office.

Hunter reached over and squeezed his hand. "Remember," he said under his breath, "we've got a backup plan."

Richard exhaled. Hunter was right. "OnlyMates."

Hunter scoffed. "I was talking about the *Moonlit Bonds* streaming, but okay. We'll try it your way."

Richard shook his head. Whatever happened, they'd make it work. They were going to be fine. He'd known that from the moment he'd woken up with Hunter in his arms and realized he'd do the same tomorrow. That alone made him feel like everything would be alright, regardless of how this went. He'd never felt more sure and settled in his life.

His stomach still churned as they walked into Steele's office though.

Steele sat behind his desk, as intimidating as ever. His slate gray eyes tracked their movements as they arranged themselves in the four chairs in front of him, and his nostrils flared.

There were rumors he'd worked in the human porn industry over a decade ago, before he'd started MateHub, but that he'd quit suddenly.

Richard had never seen any of his videos. He'd been too afraid to search for them. Like Steele would appear out of nowhere and cancel his contracts if Richard typed "Steele Longwood porn" into Google. He certainly hadn't done scenes for his own site.

He had the presence of an alpha, though Richard didn't believe he was one, and his dark hair was graying at the temples. His bespoke suit hugged his broad shoulders and chest. He'd be smoking hot if he weren't quite so terrifying.

"I can't force you to sever the bond if you choose to keep it," Steele said, voice gruff, not bothering with small talk. "But I also can't guarantee you work in the future."

Richard met his gaze, refusing to back down on something so important. "The fans love our videos. Check the message boards. They like us together."

"Fans are fickle. There's no promise they'll stick around."

"There's no promise they won't," Hunter said. "Several have posted about never wanting to see us with anyone else."

"And a few are threatening to cancel their memberships if we aren't allowed to be together," Richard added.

"Sure." Steele regarded them coolly. "And that will last as long as it takes them to realize human porn will never satisfy them."

"We could always go to OnlyMates," Richard said.

Steele snorted. "Could you? I've seen your car. I know the neighborhood you live in. Do you honestly think Only-Mates will pay your rent? There's a reason their best stars end up here, and none of my stars slum it there."

Fuck this guy. Richard didn't care about that. If his choice was between Hunter and his SF90, there was no choice at all. "Speaking of my car. How much would I get if I resold it? Enough to buy a domain of my own and hire a mage to cloak it for me?"

Steele's eyes narrowed.

"None of Richard's contracts have included a non-compete clause," Daniel said pleasantly. "I've made sure of that."

"As have I," Adrian added. "I'd wager Hunter and Richard's first scene after they announce they're keeping their bond would drive a fair amount of traffic to a brand-new site. Fans are fickle, after all."

"What should we call it?" Richard asked.

"YouMate has a nice ring to it," Hunter said.

"It does," Richard agreed. He leveled a look at Steele. "What do you think?"

Steele growled. "The only reason you're here is because your fans started a request campaign for scenes featuring you two. We had to temporarily close our suggestion box, we were getting so many."

That surprised Richard. He hadn't seen his fans organizing that.

"I'll give you a year," Steele said. "A one-year exclusive contract. *With* a non-compete clause. That's it. You'll do regular scenes for us. If other people are in the scene, no touching will be involved. If you're still getting decent views after that, we can talk about an extension."

Richard's relief mingled with Hunter's. That was better than he'd expected. He'd thought they might get a few months, or that the contracts would be offered scene by scene, giving them zero stability. A full year, he'd gladly take.

He looked at Hunter and got a nod, though he'd already known Hunter approved.

"Thank you," Richard said to Steele. "I guarantee you'll be offering us that extension."

Doubt was etched on Steele's face, but they'd prove him wrong.

"We'll leave you three to negotiate the terms," Hunter said, standing and pulling Richard with him.

On their way out, Richard paused. "Oh, right. Tristan said his brother says hello?"

Steele's hand clenched, snapping the pen he was holding in half, and Richard's eyebrows rose in shock.

"Is there anything else?" Steele asked. It was more of a snarled dismissal than a question.

Richard couldn't get out the door fast enough.

The drive to his apartment felt strange. He'd never brought anyone there before. He almost auto-piloted to the MateHub apartment, but that wasn't home anymore. Even if he had been living there for half of the last few years, there was no need to ever go back.

He found himself getting nervous as he unlocked the door to his apartment. Hunter squeezed his arm again, and Richard let him inside.

The first thing that hit Richard was how it no longer smelled right. It no longer smelled like home, not when it lacked Hunter's scent, but they'd fix that soon.

The place was massive, but sterile. Minus the kitchen, it didn't look lived in. Hunter seemed to like it though. As Richard gave him a tour, he sensed him picturing how it would transform over the next few months as they made it their home. After they'd christened every room and surface. After they'd cooked together, played games together, had friends over, and more.

Richard showed him the kitchen last, its ample countertops and cabinets, its spacious stove and large oven. The layout was perfect for preparing meals. It'd been the apartment's main selling point, though he hadn't imagined having someone to cook with him when he'd signed the lease.

But then Hunter's eyes caught on the lone piece of paper hanging on the refrigerator, and Richard cringed. It was a simple black and white printout, large Xs covering most of the squares.

Hunter laughed as he plucked it out from under its plain magnet—another thing that could use more color now that Richard thought about it. "What is KNOTZ Bingo?"

Richard groaned. "My fans made it a few years ago. They wanted to see if I could knot my way through the supernatural community. I was trying for blackout."

"Human isn't even on here." Hunter cocked an eyebrow at him.

Richard stepped closer. "You were too tempting not to make an exception."

"Do you care you won't get your blackout?"

"It's not remotely important anymore." He tugged the

paper out of Hunter's hand and tossed it aside. "There are so many other, more pressing issues."

"Such as?"

"These counters, for instance. They could use some breaking in."

Hunter hummed thoughtfully. "You don't say? I suppose we should get on that. Literally."

That was an excellent idea.

Richard backed Hunter up against the kitchen island. Their bodies brushed, and their eyes locked. Hunter's lips quirked into a wicked smile.

Anticipation sparked between them.

Richard leaned in, their lips a heartbeat apart.

"The things I'm going to do to you in this apartment," he promised, and Hunter shivered. "I'm going to fuck you every way you've ever wanted to be fucked, and then you're going to do the same to me."

Hunter's lust swirled inside Richard, heady and wild. "That's a pretty long list."

"We've got time." He nuzzled against Hunter's throat, getting drunk on his scent.

"Any place in particular you'd like to start?" Hunter asked, breathless.

Richard captured his lips in a kiss. The sparks of anticipation crackled to life, blazing and burning as their mouths devoured each other.

It took the majority of his willpower to break away, but he knew what he wanted. "Let's start at the beginning and make this all about you." He sank to his knees.

Hunter stared down at him. "Only if I get to return the favor."

Richard would never refuse an offer like that.

He popped open the button and unzipped Hunter's

jeans. Slowly, he slid his hand into Hunter's boxers, wrapped it around his hot, hard length, and pulled him out. He teased his fingers along the shaft, reveling in the hitch of Hunter's breath.

Hunter gripped the edge of the counter behind him. "You gonna make me beg for it?"

Richard looked up at him, at the hunger in his eyes, the flush of arousal on his cheeks. "Only if you want to."

That was definitely the right answer. Hunter carded fingers through Richard's hair. "In that case, yes, please."

Richard would do his best. He hooked his fingers into the waistband of Hunter's underwear and pulled them and his jeans down his thighs.

He'd never seen a sight more delicious than Hunter's cock pulsing with need. Leaning in, he inhaled Hunter's scent, his mouth watering, his wolf rumbling in his chest with the desire to taste him.

Hunter's grip tightened in Richard's hair, his hips making little aborted thrusts, wanting the heat of his mouth, and Richard intended to give him precisely that.

He parted his lips, the head of Hunter's dick nudging into—

There was a shriek off to the side.

Richard jumped up, covering Hunter with his body.

"What the actual fuck, Richard?" Char yelled. "*My eyes.*"

He whipped his head around to see his sister standing in the doorway, a shopping bag held up in front of her face, shielding her from the scene she'd walked in on.

"I told you to stop letting yourself in here without my permission, didn't I?" He held back a snarl of frustration. God, he'd wanted to suck Hunter's cock, but from the way Hunter was trying to shove himself into his jeans, that wasn't happening.

"Has he put it away yet?" she asked, not lowering her bag.

Richard huffed. He should have known she'd be stopping by today. But in his defense, his mind had been elsewhere. "Hunter, meet Charlotte, my spare-key-having sister. Char, meet Hunter. My mate."

"Your what?" She jerked the bag down, then back up, then inched it down to check everyone was decent.

Unfortunately, they were.

"Uh, hi," Hunter said, flustered. "Nice to meet you?" It came out as a question.

"Yeah. You too. You'll forgive me for not shaking your hand."

"Understandable." Hunter's voice was higher pitched than normal.

"Explain," she demanded.

"Sooo," Richard said. "You know how you said you wished I'd bond someone who smelled good on me? That happened."

She tentatively sniffed the air, only to wrinkle her nose. "What was that message you sent me? 'You really aren't going to like this one.' Really?"

"About that. You might actually like this one."

"Well, I don't like it right now. Can we crack a damn window?"

Richard was pretty sure this situation was her own fault, but he didn't say that. He didn't want his mate to witness his older sister kicking his ass.

"Have you told Mom?" she asked.

Richard chuckled nervously. "Let's keep it a surprise for the full moon?" He couldn't handle explaining how he'd gotten mated to his mother yet. Maybe he'd be able to think up a good story before then.

"Oh, I'm sure it will be a surprise." She turned her attention to Hunter. "So. You've managed to stay bonded to this asshole for three months without killing him?"

"Hey!"

"He's not bad," Hunter said. "Once you get past the prickly exterior, he's kind of sweet."

"Yeah, he's a real pineapple." She side-eyed them both. "Okay. We're having lunch. But not here. I don't think I'll ever be able to look at these poor counters the same way again."

"Sorry." Hunter cringed, but she waved him off.

"I'll meet you at Richard's judgy cat place in an hour. I don't want to know what you do between now and then." She shoved the bag of groceries at Richard and left.

There were moments when he sort of loved his sister.

Hunter stared at him with wide eyes. "Chance said meeting a wolf shifter's pack is a big deal. Please tell me it won't be more traumatic than that?"

Richard laughed and gathered Hunter close. "I make no promises."

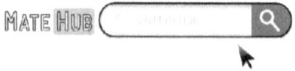

The better part of a week later, when a highly edited version of their seventh scene was released on the same day their exclusive contracts were announced, it crashed the MateHub server for half a day and ended up as the most watched video on the site.

They'd even added a post-scene interview. It'd been odd going in to film that and the announcement video. They'd been fully clothed the entire time and hadn't gotten off, though they'd rectified that once they got home.

What Richard hadn't expected was for Brandt to include a special Behind the Scenes Best of DickHunt Director's Cut video as well, complete with all the highlights of their relationship that had been caught on camera— Richard carrying Hunter off after the hunting scene, Richard growling as Max reached for Hunter's leg, Hunter storming the studio to keep his mate unsullied by tarty ways, them completely failing at the interview before the switching scene, and more. To Richard's horror, it became the second most watched MateHub video.

In order to celebrate their success, they unwrapped themselves from each other long enough to have friends over.

As Richard let him in, Max scrunched his nose. "You couldn't have aired the place out before we got here?"

"Why? It smells perfect."

Max scoffed. "I've been in MateHub studios that smell less like sex."

"You only have yourself to blame," Richard said.

"Aw, shit. Who told you?"

"Tristan."

"Ugh, that bastard. Listen, Brandt and Everett tried to be subtle about it during your domestic scene, but you can't take a hint to save your fucking life, so I merely told them you'd need to be hit over the head with how compatible you are so you didn't do anything irreversibly moronic."

"And whose idea was the bedroom scene?"

Max glared at him. "I might have mentioned how, when two people smell right for each other, when their scents combine so well you can envision it in your mind, it's impossible to ignore, no matter how hard you try. They took it from there."

Richard led him toward the living room. "You do realize this gives us full rein to meddle in your life, right?"

Maybe he could bribe Tristan to set up a whole water-fall-pond situation, and they'd see how Max and Hardin responded to that.

Max tried to play it off. "Only you would fall ass-back-ward into a true bond."

"Hey," Hunter said from where he was setting up the gaming system that'd been delivered that morning. "He did it perfectly. Richard is even better at true bonds than he is at fucking and cooking."

Richard grinned. He was excellent at the important stuff. That was all he needed to be good at. Screw the rest.

Chance showed up a while later, grumbling about how the apartment reeked of dog. Hunter pulled him into a hug just to be an ass.

"Ugh." He pushed Hunter away. "I knew it'd get worse. Congrats, I guess. I wish you a happy lifetime of smelling like dog."

Hunter beamed at him. "Speaking of dogs, how's the new roommate?"

"Trick's fine." Chance glowered at Richard. "My best friend and my apartment are covered in canine, and it's your fault."

Richard was more than happy to take the blame for that.

Chance might complain about wolf shifters, but he was willing to be on their team when they played the advanced copy of *Enchanted Guardians: Sanctuary Defense* that MysTech had sent them. Apparently, their sales had spiked after he and Hunter had discussed their titles in the domestic scene interview.

It was a new version of the only game Richard considered valid, now with more battles. He didn't think he'd ever enjoy fighting in games, but he wasn't half-bad at it when he was protecting the creatures he was raising from shit-heads who were out to exploit their magic. Hunter and their friends handled the offensive end of the fighting, while Richard focused on the defensive, ensuring none of their dragon's eggs got cracked and the baby griffins were out of harm's way.

Hardin even showed up later that night, right before dinner. He was still avoiding Max, but he was there. They'd work on the rest. If there was one thing Richard had learned over the last three months, it was that there was no use denying the inevitable.

Having their friends over for dinner and games, with his mate by his side, was exactly as perfect as he'd thought it would be.

Now he had to figure out how to explain said perfection to his mother.

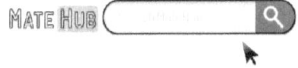

BREAKING NEWS: *Richard Knotz and Hunter Savage Announce Exclusive Contract!*

KnottyWolf69:
We, my dear DickHunters, have reached the pinnacle of porn. No video will ever be better than that; there will never be a hotter scene. The world can end now. It might as well quit while it's ahead.

BramStroker:
Truer words have never been spoken. Today, I saw the face of god, and their name is DickHunt. Also, finally! Hunter bit Richard! Man, did they edge us with that.

theconnoisseur:
It felt special this way though. Like we got to see them bond all over again.

BramStroker:
It really did. They looked so happy in their announcement video!

KnottyWolf69:
It's so romantic, I didn't even mind that they were fully clothed. Though, I mean, I wouldn't have complained if they'd wanted to do the post-scene interview naked.

mage4u:
All that behind-the-scenes footage was AMAZING! I know they said they didn't plan this, but clearly they were meant to be together from the moment they met.

MagicalHWood:
Agreed, but did MateHub have to call this board DickHunters?

HuntMeDown:
Yep. You're welcome!

BramStroker:
Look, I made them a logo to celebrate!

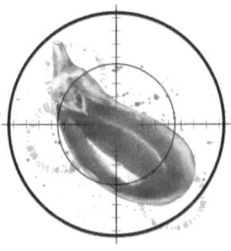

MagicalHWood:
...where can I get that made into a keychain?

mage4u:
While we're at it, I need a strawberry tart sticker that says, "Soil me with your strumpet hands and tarty ways!"

KnottyWolf69:
Put me down for one of everything. I can't believe they're actually staying together. I never imagined the day Richard Knotz would sign an exclusive contract and definitely never imagined I'd be thrilled about it. Just think of it. A year's worth of DickHunt scenes.

BramStroker:
MateHub is making sure we eat well all year round.

theconnoisseur:
I can't wait to see the scenes they do!

HuntMeDown:
Whatever they do, it'll be glorious.

MagicalHWood:
I do have to wonder though. Now that Richard's out of the game, MateHub is going to want someone else to do bonding contracts for them. Who do you think will be next?

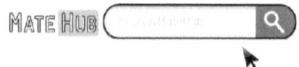

CHAPTER

TWENTY-TWO

H
unter tried not to fidget as Richard's car crawled along the 210 East. Richard placed a hand on his thigh and squeezed.

"You have nothing to be worried about." He'd said the same thing a few dozen times over the last week.

"Are you sure they won't care that I'm human?"

"Positive. They're going to love you."

Hunter forced out an exhale.

"If it helps," Richard said, "focus on how next week, your parents are going to decide whether I'm good enough for their secret agent son."

Hunter chuckled. "We could pretend you're a secret agent too. You've got the double-O down."

"But I'm definitely more than seven."

Hunter snorted. That he was.

Not that it helped when they pulled up to the pack house in the San Jacinto Mountains two hours later. The wooden house was nestled among towering pines, but Hunter didn't have time to appreciate its charming, rustic look. They'd barely taken five steps toward the front door when a tall woman he had to assume was Richard's mother came striding out.

She headed straight at them, though instead of going to Richard first, she yanked Hunter into a crushing hug. He froze, blinking at Richard from over her shoulder.

"It's so good to finally meet you, Hunter," she said. "I can't believe it took Richard this long to bring you to a full-moon run. I'm Anne, but you can call me Mom."

"What?" Hunter asked, at a complete loss as to what was happening. Richard looked and felt equally shocked. He hadn't told her he was bringing someone home with him.

She inhaled deeply. "I knew you two would smell perfect together." She hugged him tighter, and Hunter squeaked.

"Um, Mom," Richard said, "could you try not to break my mate?"

She eased up on the hug so Hunter could breathe again, though she didn't seem willing to let him go anytime soon. That didn't stop her from turning toward Richard and pointing.

"You. You should have brought him months ago. I raised you better than that."

"Ahhh, I... wanted to surprise you?"

"Richard Alexander Knox. I am your mother and your alpha. Do you really think I don't know when you're bonded to someone? Especially when it's a true bond."

Hunter had to fight back a snicker. It would never not amuse him that Richard's real surname was so close to Knotz.

"Wait. You can tell when I'm bonded?" There was panic in Richard's voice and in their bond.

"Anyone you're bonded to is technically in my pack, so yes, I notice when we go from eight members to nine."

"Uh... I can... explain? At work... we... uh..." He floundered, glancing at Hunter for help, but Hunter was enjoying this wreck too much to stop it from happening.

Anne huffed. "Richard, my darling boy. What kind of low-level desk job pays enough for a car like that?"

The sheer amount of horror on Richard's face was glorious. Hunter pulled out his phone and snapped a picture to capture the touching moment. He'd be sending it to Max later. Richard scowled at him.

"I don't want to know about or see any of it," Anne said. "I just want you to be happy, and clearly you and Hunter are perfect for each other. But that doesn't mean you shouldn't have told me when you realized it was a true bond."

"It took me a while to realize what I had," Richard said, heat in his eyes as he looked at Hunter.

Anne tsked, but Hunter jumped in to defend Richard. "Neither of us was open to the bond in the beginning. It felt completely different than it does now."

"Well, of course it would. You'll never have a truly complete bond if you aren't ready for it, if you don't open yourself up and let your mate have all of you. To claim and be claimed in return. The bond can't deepen properly if someone is holding back. But the important thing is you got there in the end. The how doesn't matter."

Hunter supposed she was right, though it might have gone smoother if they'd developed feelings first, then bonded. That seemed to be the more traditional order of operations.

"Okay," she said. "Now to introduce Hunter to the rest of the pack."

339

Hunter attempted a smile, but only managed to show his teeth.

She grinned at him. "Don't worry, dear. The pack will be having way too much fun roasting Richard to harass you. This time."

That was not particularly reassuring, but he followed her inside.

Dinner was less traumatizing than Hunter had feared; everyone was more welcoming than he could have hoped. Growing up, it'd just been him and his parents, so he wasn't used to rowdy family dinners, but this had been nice, if a little overwhelming. Still, slipping outside with Richard into the cool twilight air was a relief.

Richard's wolf was getting restless, though being with his pack and his mate had kept it content for most of the evening. Now it wanted to run. As well as do a few other things. The intensity of those urges crackled in Hunter's veins.

"Please tell me my pack hasn't scared you off," Richard said, pulling him close.

"Never. You're stuck with me."

"I will be." Richard leered at him, and Hunter shook his head fondly.

"Looking forward to it."

Richard leaned in like he was about to kiss Hunter, his lips hovering, tempting, but then he stepped away.

Hunter watched as Richard stripped off his clothes piece by piece, baring his muscular body under the moonlight. He moved with a sinuous grace that transfixed Hunter. His eyes were locked on Hunter, a predatory gleam in their depths.

He let Hunter look his fill, then something rippled through him, twisting him, changing him. The pleasure-pain of the transformation rushed through their bond, leaving Hunter breathless.

Richard was beautiful in his wolf form, majestic and powerful. Hunter crouched and reached out to touch him.

Even though he knew it was Richard, part of his mind still screamed at him to flee as the large wolf slowly stalked toward him. But Richard nuzzled against his hand and let Hunter run fingers through his soft fur. That low rumble built in his chest, reminding Hunter of the first time they'd been in a forest together.

Hunter shivered. Maybe he should listen to his instincts after all.

The moon was so bright that night, he could see well enough. He stood and stretched, looking down at Richard with a smirk. Then he took off, running into the trees behind the house.

He felt Richard's surprise, felt him start to follow.

It didn't take long for Richard to catch him, but that was exactly what Hunter wanted.

End of MateHub: Legend (MateHub Book One)

Thank you for reading!

"Good," Richard said, his wolf in full control. "Because someday, I'm going to watch you ride it until you beg me for the real thing."

Sign up for my mailing list to see Richard fulfill his promise. You'll also be the first to hear information about my upcoming releases and get an occasional free short story.

MATEHUB: KING

You've seen a legend fall. Now it's time to dethrone a king.

Duke Moorhead's story.
Coming soon.

ELEMENTAL BONDS

KnottyWolf69:

I need a mage to fall on my knot right the fuck now, please.

MagicalHWood:

I've got an uptight friend who could use a good fuck. Get your dick out, and I'll trip him for you.

KnottyWolf69:

Got two? My alpha needs to get his knot off more than I do.

Want to see KnottyWolf69, his alpha, and MagicalHWood get their HEAs? Check out *Elemental Bonds*, starting with *Accidental Bonds*.

Accidental Bonds (Elemental Bonds Book One)

Victor Mills may detest magic, but the mage he's hired to protect his pack smells like everything his wolf has ever wanted. As an insidious rot creeps through his territory, he must learn to trust the mage and the growing bond between them. If he fails, his pack will pay the ultimate price.

Available now on Amazon and in Kindle Unlimited.

Impulsive Connections (Elemental Bonds Book Two)
KnottyWolf69's Story

After a run-in with a malicious spirit leaves Kade Mills reluctantly bonded to a bookish mage, he struggles to resist the heady pull of their unwanted connection. But he soon discovers that bond could be the key to saving everything he holds dear... and it might not be as unwelcome as he thought.

Available now on Amazon and in Kindle Unlimited.

Unexpected Alliances (Elemental Bonds Book Three)
MagicalHWood's Story

Coming soon.

Soil Me with Your

Strumpet-Hands and Tarty Ways

ACKNOWLEDGMENTS

The idea for *MateHub* came to me while I was writing my debut novel, *Accidental Bonds*. It popped into my head, grabbed me by the throat, and would not let me go until I wrote it. What started as a throwaway joke about 'a mage slipped, fell, and landed on my knot' just kept expanding and expanding and expanding. Appropriate, I suppose, given the subject matter. 'Secret supernatural porn site' is a supremely ridiculous concept for a book, but it was so much fun to write, and I now have a dozen side characters demanding books of their own.

I'd like to take a moment to thank my amazing beta readers, Amy Pittel and Megan Dischinger, for their work on this novel. It would not exist without their encouragement, support, and excellent feedback.

Amy read this back when half the characters weren't even named yet and a few of the scenes were just 'I'll write this part later,' for which I am thankful. I'd also like to express my gratitude for her playing telephone with one of her other authors to help me find the best location for MateHub in LA, and many thanks to that author as well.

Megan was also great to work with, as always, and her feedback helped me put the finishing touches on this book. If I ever start selling a sticker about 'tarty ways,' it will be thanks to her.

Additionally, I'd like to thank Kate Wood for editing and

proofreading this book. Her attention to detail is much appreciated.

Another Kate I want to thank is Kate Munro, my fellow 2023 debut author. She is always willing to let me bounce ideas off her, and it's been so nice to have someone right there with me as we both try to figure out how to do this whole 'being an author' thing.

Next, a big thank you to my newsletter subscribers who bravely volunteered to appear in the fan forums, even though all I told them was that they'd have cameos posting comments about paranormal porn stars. Vanessa, Kristen, Natacha, Jovi, SNik, Toni, Elizabeth, Jovan, Pinar, and Felix, thank you! I hope you liked your comments!

And finally, thank you, dear reader! This is only my second book, and I'm grateful that you were willing to give it a try. I hope you enjoyed reading it as much as I enjoyed writing it, and I look forward to sharing more stories with you in the future.

If you could spare a moment to leave a review of *Mate-Hub: Legend* on Amazon or a site such as Goodreads or BookBub, it would mean the world to me. Reviews help indie authors gain visibility and reach more readers, and I appreciate each one, no matter how long or short.

Please feel free to reach out to me on any of the social media sites listed on my About the Author page. I'd love to hear from you.

Thank you again, and happy reading!

ABOUT THE AUTHOR

Marie Reynard is an American in Japan, teaching English by day and writing M/M paranormal romance by night. Her steamy, snarky stories will take you from first kiss to forever with a few Fs in between—including found family, flirty banter, fake dating, and a fair amount of fu...n. Check out her website for more information on her books, and join her mailing list to get a free story or two and be the first to know about upcoming releases!

Website - https://www.mariereynard.com/
Newsletter - http://subscribepage.io/gO6BOu
Facebook Group - https://facebook.com/groups/
mariereynardsden/

 facebook.com/authormariereynard

tiktok.com/@marie_reynard

x.com/marie_reynard

instagram.com/marie_reynard

amazon.com/author/mariereynard

goodreads.com/mariereynard

bookbub.com/profile/marie-reynard